Writers' France

A REGIONAL PANORAMA

HAMISH HAMILTON

Writers' France

A REGIONAL PANORAMA

John Ardagh

PHOTOGRAPHS BY

Mayotte Magnus

By the same author

The New French Revolution (The New France)
A Tale of Five Cities
France in the 1980s
Rural France
The South of France
Germany and the Germans

HAMISH HAMILTON LTD
Published by the Penguin Group
27 Wrights Lane, London w8 5tz, England
Viking Penguin Inc., 40 West 23rd Street, New York, New York 10010, U.S.A.
Penguin Books Australia Ltd, Ringwood, Victoria, Australia
Penguin Books Canada Ltd, 2801 John Street, Markham, Ontario, Canada l3r 1b4
Penguin Books (N.Z.) Ltd, 182–190 Wairau Road, Auckland 10, New Zealand

Penguin Books Ltd, Registered Offices: Harmondsworth, Middlesex, England

First published in Great Britain 1989 by
Hamish Hamilton Ltd
Text copyright © John Ardagh 1989
Photographs copyright © Mayotte Magnus 1989
1 3 5 7 9 10 8 6 4 2

Designed by Cinamon and Kitzinger
Maps drawn by Hanni Bailey
Typeset in Linotron 202 Aldus by
Wyvern Typesetting Ltd, Bristol
Colour origination by Technik Litho Plates Ltd
Printed and bound by L.E.G.O Vicenza, Italy

A CIP catalogue record for this book is available from the British Library
Library of Congress number 89–85021

ISBN. 0 241 12351-8

To my wife
KATINKA
and to my son
NICHOLAS

Contents

1 : Introduction

The immense regional diversity of France, so attractive to the visitor, is richly reflected in its literature. Balzac's Touraine, Giono's Provence, Mauriac's Bordeaux country – the list is endless. Nature and landscape may less frequently play a strong emotive role than they do in English literature: but the *genius loci* is often present, the sense of local history or tradition, the flavour of local character, or the feeling for a real precise place re-experienced through the filter of memory, as with Proust's jangling bell on the garden gate at Illiers-Combray.

This book of words and photographs has been a true labour of love, both for myself and for Mayotte Magnus – the harvest of our many recent excursions to explore the former homes of writers, the places they have described in their books and that have provided some of their inspiration. I myself have never enjoyed any project so much, neither the research nor the slogging at a typewriter. It has greatly enriched my understanding of France.

Our book covers all mainland France except for Paris, which seems to me a separate subject. It has been covered on its own in other books of this kind, while the literature of the provinces has been given less attention. Our chapters follow a regional pattern, and within each chapter the writers are arranged in an order that is part geographical, part chrono-logical and part related to subject-matter, so there is inevitably much criss-crossing. We include writers of all epochs, not only French ones but foreign visitors too, from Smollett and Goethe to Scott Fitzgerald. The text consists of extracts from the authors' works interspersed with my own accounts of their links with the area; and here I have given precise topographical indications of where each writer lived and where many of the novels are located. I hope that in this way our book will not only provide enjoyable armchair reading but will also serve as a practical guidebook and vade-mecum.

Our selection is a personal one, and experts will easily be able to come up with some significant books or authors that we have omitted. But the subject is so vast that we cannot be comprehensive. If we have played down or disregarded some major figures, it is simply because they are not writers of the kind who describe places or have any special local association. On the other hand, we have featured quite prominently a number of interesting regional writers – Maurice Genevoix, Julien Gracq and Barbey d'Aurévilly amongst others – who have been unjustly neglected outside France. A few post-war authors are included, for example Jean Genet and Jean Carrière, and I would gladly have had more, were it not that so few of them write about identifiable places. We have included not only novels but also some memoirs and works of philosophy or social history (for example, Emmanuel Le Roy Ladurie's *Montaillou*). But poetry features much less prominently than I think it would in an equivalent book about Britain (and indeed *has*, in Margaret Drabble's excellent *A Writer's Britain*, for which Jorge Lewinski took the photographs). The reason for this? I can only give my own view that the French poetic heritage is a good deal less rich than the British. They have produced more great novelists, but fewer great poets.

The so-called 'regional' novel can either be purely a chronicle of local life, or it can also contain more universal themes and implications, as in the work of Thomas Hardy. In France it has become a flourishing literary genre in both these forms. But only in the mid-19th century did it begin to produce novelists whose works are deeply rooted in their own native area. Before that, they had often come from outside – as Balzac, who in the 1820s had embarked on his great series that ranges widely across France. He himself had some roots in Touraine, which is the setting of one of his best novels, *Le Lys dans la vallée*: but for others he went elsewhere to do his research, often staying for longish periods with friends, as he did in Angoulême for *Les Illusions perdues* and in Fougères for *Les Chouans*. Closely following him was Victor Hugo, who set parts of *Les Misérables* in Provence, the north, and the Ile-de-France; and other writers, such as Pierre Loti who came from the Charente but located in Brittany and the Basque country his two best-known books about France. Emile Zola in particular, Italian/Provençal by birth but a Parisian, would sally forth into the provinces and utilise his masterly journalistic skills to collect details of a local way of life and a social problem, as he did in the coalmines of the Nord for *Germinal* and in the Beauce for *La Terre*.

Novels of this kind may be excellent literature, but they are not indigenous: they are studies made by outsiders. The true regional novel is emotive in a different way from Balzac or Zola: it is usually more personal, and in varying degrees of love or love-hate it expresses a reaction to a particular background known in childhood and youth. It could be said that Rabelais in his own satiric style was an early forerunner, for some of the most vivid scenes in *Gargantua* are set very precisely in his homeland, near Chinon; and so in a different literary form were poets with strong local roots such as Ronsard (northern Touraine) and Lamartine (the Mâconnais). But the regional novel in its authentic glory emerged around 1845–60, first with Georges Sand, extolling her love for the landscapes and simple country people of the Berry, where she was brought up, and then with Flaubert, giving a sharply sceptical view of the bourgeoisie of his native Rouen and its region. His friend and disciple Guy de Maupassant depicted his part of eastern Normandy with a somewhat lighter touch, but several of his novels and stories do give a penetrating portrait of the wily and stubborn Norman peasantry – a counter-balance, maybe, to the naive idealism of Sand. Regional fiction was by now truly concerning itself with local character, generally more so than with landscape.

Ever since Sand's time, regional writers have been popping up all over France, some of them spending all their lives in their homeland, others moving to Paris and writing about it from there. Some, such as Sand herself and Barbey d'Aurévilly (western Normandy), have sought to give a voice to often inarticulate country folk and to put on record their customs and traditions, seen as menaced by modern change; in a similar vein, some writers have even appointed themselves the champions of a regional revival, like the epic poet Frédéric Mistral, writing in Provençal. Some, such as Maurice Barrès in Lorraine have integrated their local patriotism into a wider French nationalism. And others have been influenced by the society and landscapes of their youth, or by family memories, to produce novels that essentially are about spiritual struggles: this is true of the Catholic novelists Mauriac and Bernanos, and in a different manner of André Gide, in Normandy.

A number of provinces have thrown up writers who may not be great literary figures but are essentially 'regionalist' in their preoccupation with local life, its joys and struggles, and are closely identified with their area – among them Emile Erckmann in Alsace, Eugène Le Roy in Périgord, and in this century André Chamson in the Cévennes, Henri Queffélec in Brittany, Henri Vincenot in Burgundy. Until quite recently, writers of this kind were frequently dismissed as parochial and uninteresting by France's literary establishment, generally Paris-based and Paris-focussed (and also so often parochial in its way). But today, with the post-war regional revival in France and the renewed interest in country life, books of this kind have come into vogue and are now much more highly respected: witness Pierre-Jakez Hélias' non-fictional study of his rural Breton world, *Le Cheval d'orgueil* (1975), which has sold over two million copies, most of them outside Brittany.

Some regional novels have expressed the opposition between Paris and the provinces, or the problems of ambitious young provincials who try to win success in the capital. This was a favourite theme of Balzac's (e.g. *Les Illusions perdues*), and of course it dominates Stendhal's *Le Rouge et le noir*, as well as Barrès' *Les Déracinés*. But the protagonists of such books tended to come from small towns – and I have found it quite extraordinary how very few of the better-known French regional novels are set in larger cities, as my choice of extracts will certainly indicate. Bordeaux is the setting for some chapters of Mauriac, but he describes the town and its life very little; Toulouse and Lille have little to offer; Marseille has Pagnol's *Marius* trilogy, but that is not a novel, nor is Stendhal's autobiographical *La Vie de Henri Brûlard* which so cleverly depicts

Grenoble. Even Lyon has inspired very few books of note. The larger Norman towns however fare a little better: Flaubert and Maupassant have some good passages on Rouen, and Le Havre perhaps surprisingly has been fertile in its inspiration, for Sartre, Queneau, Maupassant and others. But what else is there? Literary specialists will perhaps remind me that I have overlooked some names, such as José Cabanis in Toulouse, Bernard Clavel in Lyon, and Simenon the peripatetic Belgian all over the place. But how significant are these books? It was not until the present day that a number of French novelists have begun to write about life in Nice, Marseille, Strasbourg and elsewhere, and as yet this new trend has produced few books of much quality.

The main reason for this neglect would seem to be the obvious one of French centralism and the stranglehold that Paris at least till very recently has exerted over the provinces. Just as Stendhal's young Julien Sorel inevitably set his sights on the capital, and would hardly have been tempted by Lyon, so many an ambitious writer from some village or small town has made for Paris: Daudet, Maupassant, Mauriac and others may have been inspired by their own *pays* for much of their best work, but it was in Paris that they made their reputations and spent most of their adult lives. And, as compared with the life either of the dazzling capital or of some picturesque village community or graceful château, the middle-class daily round in, say, Nantes or Lille would seem to most writers to offer far less propitious material. It is also noticeable that there has been extremely little good indigenous writing about urban working-class life in the provinces: Zola's *Germinal*, as I have noted, is the reportage of an outsider – and where is the French *Sons and Lovers*?

Even novels of peasant life, in this most agricultural of countries, were slow to make their initial impact, though they have since proliferated. The dominance of the royal court and the Age of Enlightenment in the 17th and 18th centuries served to produce a sophisticated literary society with a refined culture, which was not so very interested in the stark realities of the peasant condition (this was true even of the utopia-minded Rousseau). And so they ignored it: La Bruyère described peasants as 'savage animals'. This attitude persisted even after the Revolution. The snobbish Balzac preferred to set his rural novels in the dignified château-owning milieu of his cultivated friends (e.g. *Le Lys dans la vallée*), and when in 1844 he did produce a novel called *Les Paysans*, set in the Morvan district of Burgundy, it gave a sombre account of them as wily and surly creatures. Of course his picture may have been somewhere near the truth – but it greatly angered the radical-minded Georges Sand, whose gently idealised portrait of the peasants of her native Berry, in *La Mare au diable* and other such novels, was in part at least a riposte to Balzac. Sand's aim was to rehabilitate the peasantry in the eyes of informed opinion, and to show her literary friends in Paris that the rural world was not what they thought. As in so many matters – and not only wearing trousers and smoking in public – Sand was an innovator as well as a rebel. Her country novels may be slight and simplistic, but they did help to establish a new genre.

Other books on the subject soon followed. Some novelists pursued a line not so different from Balzac's, notably Zola in *La Terre*, when he portrayed the small farmers of the Beauce as brutalised by their unending struggle to draw a living from the earth. But others followed a path closer to Sand's. Eugène Le Roy, for example, who also had Left-wing views, described the starving peasants of Périgord in the earlier 19th century, in heroic conflict with their oppressive feudal landlords. René Bazin, on the other hand, was a traditionalist of the Catholic Right, but like Sand he had a feeling for the simple country virtues, as well as for the older farmers' noble attachment to their soil and their way of life, and this he expressed in *La Terre qui meurt*, set in the Vendée in the 1890s. Since the 1914–18 war, novels of rural life have come even more to the forefront and some excellent writers have emerged. The most notable has been Jean Giono whose subject is not so much the milieu of farming as man in relation to nature.

Despite the potency of French rural traditions and the variety and splendour of the scenery, the feeling for nature and for landscape has possibly not been as strong in French as in English literature. The poet Pierre de Ronsard in the 16th century was one of the first to show a lyrical concern for natural beauties, and his joy in the Touraine countryside shines clearly through his work, even though it is draped in the classical conventions of the day, all naiads and Grecian fountains. In the 17th century both La Fontaine and Madame de Sévigné wrote of their love for trees, flowers and animals; but in general the Age of Enlightenment thought of nature as wild and barbaric – that is, until the arrival of Jean-Jacques Rousseau, the Swiss, who produced an entirely new and original vision of nature as the educator, the healer, the source of spiritual energy and truth. These ideas were to have a profound influence, and not only in France. They helped to fuel the Romantic movement, which in France began to flower first with Chateaubriand and then led to Lamartine, Hugo and Vigny. Lamartine in particular was philosophically and emotionally involved with landscape, though not as profoundly as Wordsworth or Eichendorff, and I would suggest that nature remained a less important influence on the French Romantics than on those of Britain or Germany.

In the golden age of the French novel, in the 19th century, writers were essentially concerned with social observation and psychological drama; nature, though often present, tended to play a background role, occasionally coming forward for a paragraph or two, to set the scene or to colour or counterpoint a mood – or to enable the writer to show off his descriptive powers. Sometimes this role becomes important, as in the opening scenes of *Le Lys dans la vallée*, or in Fromentin's *Dominique* or Barbey d'Aurévilly's *L'Ensorcelée*, and in later books such as Maupas-

sant's *Une vie* or Loti's *Ramuntcho*; in all of these the landscape,
lyrically lovely or elegiacally mournful, or even threatening, helps to
mould the characters' feelings and to set the tone for the story. But rarely
is there much Hardyesque sense of nature as a positive agent in the drama
– save perhaps in *La Terre* where the book's true heroine has the title role,
as a mysterious fecundating force that shapes the lives of those who
depend on her. But this was the somewhat intellectual concept of Zola the
city-dweller, and I doubt that he felt it in the blood. It has often been
suggested – and it may seem a paradox – that Frenchmen of the educated
classes tend to be townsmen at heart, detached from the peasantry despite
the peasant roots of so many of them, and even when living in the
country they traditionally have seemed less likely than the English to
have the instinctive countryman's approach.

Of course there were some 19th-century exceptions to this. And, since
the early part of our own century, French writers' perception of nature
has been evolving down new and subtle paths. Proust, like Rousseau and
Sand before him, was a great innovator, in his own manner. He was
hardly a true countryman: but (*pace* Wordsworth) he looked on nature
as in the hour of thoughtless youth *and* heard in it the music of his own
humanity; his was a highly original and poetic sensitivity to the physical
world, so that in his pages the shifting colours of the sea at Cabourg, or
the flowers and trees by the river at Illiers, stand out in a brilliant sharp
focus and with a new intensity of feeling. From Proust also – as well as
from Alain-Fournier, and in a sense from the strange Gérard de Nerval
(*Sylvie*) back in the 1850s – there stems the genre of poetic, dreamlike
evocations of a remembered country childhood, a genre in which the
French so excel.

Since the 1914–18 war there has also emerged a new kind of French
rustic novel, that looks very closely at the impact of landscape upon
human character and at man's day-to-day involvement with nature.
François Mauriac's educated well-to-do landed families, especially
Thérèse Desqueyroux herself, are seen as intimately influenced by the
brooding pine-forests of the Landes or the storm-prone vineyard country
of the Garonne. But it is the uneducated peasants of Maurice Genevoix
and Jean Giono that are more central to this new kind of writing. The
Sologne poacher of Genevoix' magnificent *Raboliot* lives so close to
nature, knowing the cry of every bird, the shape of every leaf, that he
comes to identify himself with the wild animals he is hunting. Jean
Giono, with a touch more poetry and philosophic allegory, moves his
Provençal upland farmers even closer to the cosmic mysteries of nature;
his characters may sometimes seem too idealised to be fully realistic, but
his feeling for landscape and wild rural life has made him into one of the
greatest of recent French novelists. With him and Genevoix, the novel
has come a very long way from the use of landscape as mere décor.

It is worth stressing, too, that Genevoix and Giono, and also Colette,
are among the relatively few French authors who have written with

sympathetic sensitivity about the life of animals (the French attitude is generally so much more practical and less emotional than the British: one Paris publisher, turning down the chance to buy Gavin Maxwell's *Ring of Bright Water*, explained: 'Sorry, it won't sell: so few French people own otters'). Giono also was supremely concerned with ecology and environmental protection, as few writers had been till then except for Ronsard and Rousseau (to this day, the French with their wide open spaces have far fewer Greens than the tight-packed urbanised Germans). Lastly, the development in the past fifty years of what might be called the metaphysical novel has led a number of writers to allegorise on man's solitary communion with cosmic nature on the empty upland heights: this theme occurs in Giono, and even more forcefully in Julien Gracq's *Un Balcon en forêt*, set in the Ardennes, as well as in *L'Epervier de Maheux*, Jean Carrière's study of the Cévennes.

In order to research *Writers' France* I have visited almost all the places associated with the writers and featured in this book, and have noted the changes between their time and now. I suppose the biggest change is that the farming people are infinitely more prosperous and comfortable than even forty years ago. The country areas have become much less isolated, and although a certain picturesqueness may have been lost, local identity has been preserved. Has the countryside been spoilt by new building? In some cases, yes, for in the 1950s and 1960s a good deal of ugly concrete development went unchecked. But today the French have become much more concerned to preserve and protect their heritage, scenery and architecture alike – this, much more than the fight against pollution, is the direction that their environmental enthusiasm takes.

One aspect of this new care for *le patrimoine* is that an increasing number of former homes of writers are now being restored and turned into museums. Some of these are sizeable châteaux, some are much more modest – and, if a number of the 19th-century residences seemed to me to be drearily fusty and gloomily furnished (notably the Proust house at Illiers), I suppose this is an aspect of their authenticity. Among the more interesting of these literary museums, I would cite Zola's house near Paris, Rostand's sumptuous villa in the Basque country, Pierre Loti's oriental extravaganza at Rochefort, and Mistral's Provençal folk collection at Arles.

My field research also led me into a good deal of detective work, in an effort to find out exactly where certain novels are located, for many writers have had a habit of jumbling up their geography while pretending to be very precise – after all, they were writing fiction, not guidebooks. Bernanos and Mauriac, for instance, take real names of local villages but shift them to some miles distant. So I found it fascinating, text and map in hand, to try to follow in the exact traces of Thérèse Desqueyroux, or Jean de Florette, or to work out whether the village of Ry was really Flaubert's model for Emma Bovary's Yonville – and above all to discover how Alain-Fournier merged two distinct areas, the Sologne and the Berry, each with its own mysterious manor-house, to create a landscape at once vividly autobiographical and quite imaginary.

We include foreign writers too in this book, starting with Petrarch in Avignon and going up to Graham Greene in Antibes in 1980, fulminating against the Nice mafia in *J'Accuse*. Goethe, like Petrarch, lost his heart to a girl in France – over in Alsace. Ezra Pound came to Périgord in search of troubadours, Stevenson to the Cévennes in search of solitude and Huguenots, and Gertrude Stein to a village near Annecy to escape the German occupation of Paris. Of British writers, the heaviest concentration has of course been on the Côte d'Azur: but many have come also to the Nord/Pas-de-Calais – either to fight in the trenches of the Somme and Artois, or simply passing through via the Channel ports, as Smollett did with such ill grace. He, as well as Arthur Young and Henry James, wrote detailed journals of their travels round France, as did Flaubert, Hugo, Stendhal and some other major French authors. Apart from one choice piece of Hugo, I have not quoted from the French travel literature: but I have given some space to Smollett, Young and James, who are all extremely revealing of the attitudes of early Anglo-American tourists in France.

Smollett went there for his health, and in most respects he hated the place. Like a parody of today's bigoted francophobe, in his journal he complains endlessly of the cooking, the plumbing, the transport and the auberges, and is continually having rows with innkeepers and believing that he is being robbed or cheated. The only town that he really seems to like is Montpellier. Arthur Young, a gentleman farmer and agronomist, was much more balanced, sensible and liberal, though also very critical on some points. His travels in 1787–90, which happened to coincide with the Revolution, left him profoundly shocked at the poverty and the desperate state of agriculture (as compared with prosperous and well-ordered England at that time), and he put it all down – with much justification – to the evils of absentee landlordism and the dreadful governmental system of the *ancien régime*. His enthralling little book, *Travels in France*, has been out of print in Britain for much too long, and is better known today in France than in his own country. The edition that I managed to track down in the London Library, dated 1890, contains a remarkable introduction by a lady named M. Betham-Edwards who had just made exactly the same journey as Young, a hundred years later. She noted that in every region farming had improved out of recognition, and she claimed – but Zola would certainly have disagreed with her – that the peasants of the 1880s were now civilised, prosperous and contented. One typical passage:

Great is the change that awaits the traveller in sunny, light-hearted, dance-loving Anjou. . . Many and many a time, the labours in the field over, the merry supper taken out of doors ended, have I been invited to join the peasant folk in the joyous round. Accompanied only by the sound of their own voices, and needing no other stimulus, for ball-room a stretch of sward, for illumination the stars, young and old forget the long day's toil and the cares of life in these innocent Bacchanalia.

But of course Anjou is a wine-producing area, and therefore its peasants are different from the more sombre Bretons, Normans and Beaucerons noted by Young, Zola and others.

A hundred years further on from Miss Betham-Edwards, and the provincial French remain marvellously hospitable, so far removed from the false image (usually based on Parisians) that still persists in Britain. Many people all across France helped us with the book, giving freely of their time and often of their social generosity, and my list of acknowledgments is on page 312. The bibliography on pages 309–11 also records my debt to the many English translators I have used for the extracts quoted. Some of the prose translations into English are my own, but more of them are by others more skilled than I, and in many cases their books are available in the Penguin Classics series. The poetry I have left in French, with my own literal translations underneath. So now to Brittany.

2: Brittany

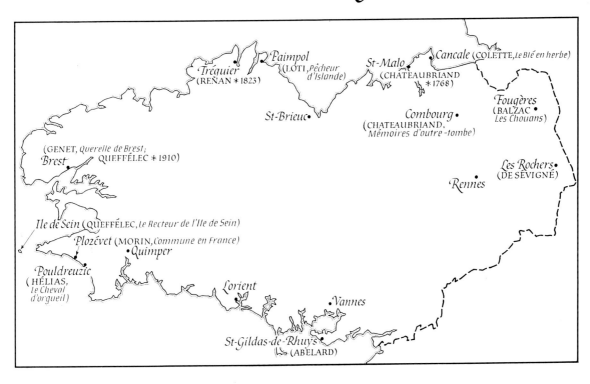

The Breton coast:
where Hélias saw the dawn
of a new era.

Unlike their fellow Celts in Ireland, the Bretons have not been prolific in producing great writers or an important national literature. This may seem strange, for a people of such individuality and poetic eloquence. One explanation could be that the language has remained more an oral than a written vehicle, for the French authorities for many decades would not allow it to be taught in schools or universities and made efforts to prevent it being used publicly. Some Breton nationalists reacted by refusing, unlike the Irish, to write literature in the language of their colonisers: some have produced books in Breton, but even today relatively few of these have been translated into French, and they are not widely known even among Bretons. The few important native authors, such as Chateaubriand and the biblical scholar Ernest Renan, have had little to say about their homeland and turned their main attention elsewhere. And Brittany has no Yeats or Joyce – indeed no Mistral.

The Breton cultural revival since the 1950s has now changed this picture a little. On the one hand, the old rural life-style and traditions have been submerged by the inrush of economic change and modernism; on the other, many Bretons are today reacting to this by attempting to rescue what they can of these traditions and to re-affirm the Breton personality in a new context. These conflicting but complementary trends have produced one very remarkable and famous book, written in Breton but then translated into French by its author: Pierre-Jakez HÉLIAS' 600-page autobiographical study of his own peasant culture, *Le Cheval d'orgueil* (1975). This is the best and most detailed portrait of 20th-century rural Brittany that exists, and certainly the most important book to have come out of Brittany since the war.

Hélias, now a genial sage in his mid-seventies, had interesting origins. As he describes in his book, he was born in 1914 into a very poor family of farm labourers in the village of Pouldreuzic, out near the coast beyond Quimper in the far south-west of Brittany: this is the Pays Bigouden, an ancient ethnic unit of its own, with a strong sense of its own identity. Hélias spoke only Breton till he went to school, but was clever enough to progress via *lycée* to Rennes university and later became a journalist and teacher. He would go round the villages with a tape-recorder, collecting details of old tales and customs, and these formed the raw material for *Le Cheval d'orgueil*. It has since sold 2.2 million copies (only 750 of them in Breton) and has been translated into 16 other languages including Welsh and Chinese; Claude Chabrol made a film of it, but a disappointingly lifeless one. The book tells first of the world of Hélias' childhood and of the endless struggles against the scourge of poverty, which the peasants saw as a devouring wolf-like being, oddly named '*la Chienne du Monde*', the bitch of the world:

In the Pays Bigouden, poverty was still the lot of many people at the beginning of the century. It was a calamity like any other, against which one couldn't do much. The least blow of fate was enough to push into it those who were at the devil's mercy. . . . Shipwreck, ill-health, an illness striking the family or livestock, fire in the hayloft, a bad harvest, a too harsh employer or simply the usual daily mishaps, would cast you for a while onto the street, obliging you to go begging at doorways, a prayer between your teeth and your eyes closed against your own humiliation. Sometimes, the men chose to hang themselves and there was always in the outhouse a rope waiting just for that. The women preferred drowning and there was always a well to hand in their courtyard or a washing-place at the end of the field. Such was the obsession with poverty that you expected to meet it at a bend in the road, in the form of a gaunt and bristly she-dog, her chops pulled back from her yellow teeth: the Bitch of the World. Silent and cunning, she jumped upon you unawares – that was the worst of it.

But in Hélias' world there are happier times, too – the wedding parties with their 'milk soup' ceremonies, the religious '*pardons*' with everyone in local costume, the winter '*veillées*' when old folk-tales are told round the fire, and the many special food rituals such as the killing of a pig, one of the most valued of a peasant's possessions:

You must kill a pig as you would pick certain fruits: with a thousand precautions and a preliminary prayer. Otherwise the pigs take vengeance by offending your eyes, nose and tongue, and your reputation too. . . . Yann ar Vinell [the master pig-killer] composes recipes according to the temperament of each animal. And it's he, of course,

Loti's Pêcheur d'Islande: *images of hilltop crosses that mourn drowned sailors.*

who chooses the best day for the sacrifice of the plump prince. Don't think that it's easy! You must take account of the season and especially of the moon. I can't quite remember whether a waxing or a waning moon is the more favourable, but I know that you must avoid salting the meat during the 'wolfs' sun', that is, the full moon, or else the pickling won't succeed... The day of glory has arrived! – hardly have I reached the threshold of my house than I hear behind me the indignant howls of the pig in its death-agony. Yann ar Vinell's great knife has performed its office in the courtyard. The entire village knows already that the fresh meat is about to be placed in the larder of the house of a happy mortal who is none other than myself.

For the Bigouden villagers in those pre-war years, France is an alien world; and, when Per-Jakez and his friends are sent to school at Quimper and forced to learn French, they feel totally uprooted: 'We are immigrants despite ourselves in a civilisation that is not our own.' Those caught talking Breton in school are punished by their teachers (such was France's *mission civilisatrice* of those days). Later, however, modern influences begin to unfurl with such force upon the Pays Bigouden that its own way of life is forced to change radically. Hélias wittily describes the arrival of the first tourists in the 1930s – how the peasants at first watch with incredulity as they bathe in the sea, something they had never dreamed of doing themselves, and then cautiously start to imitate them:

Little by little, on summer Sundays, we would see families of peasants coming to sit by the sea, first on the grassy clifftops, to watch the half-naked holiday-makers frolicking down below in their one-piece bathing costumes. Then in their turn they would go timidly down to the shore, first to wash their hardened feet, the men first, the women behind... And one day, mark my words, while two or three of us youngsters were drying our skins on the shingle, a girl wearing a tall Bigouden *coiffe*, dressed all in black velvet bordered with glass beads, arrives by the jetty in a car. She gets out, looks around her at the unusually calm sea, gets back into her carriage. When a moment later she gets out again, we remain stunned with amazement. She is wearing a black bathing-costume, but she has kept her *coiffe* on her head. What else could she do? She runs to the sea, plunges into it and begins to swim... She swims on her back, half sitting up. And it's an astonishing sight to watch the girl's *coiffe* sailing lightly on the bright swelling sea. We could hardly believe our eyes. I don't know why, but it was that day that there rose before me, in face of the bay of Audierne, at the spot called Penhors, the dawn of a new era.

Those tall elegant lace *coiffes* take so long to fix and unfix on the hair that the poor girl had little choice: but today they are seldom worn except by a few older women at weddings or festivals. Modern progress has spread its ravages. But happily it has also slain *la Chienne du Monde* in the process, and in his final chapter Hélias describes brilliantly how the Bigoudens are today finally seeking to restore some of the old traditions, in a new way. In the 1950s and '60s, in the full flush of change and modernism, they had at first deliberately rejected everything that reminded them of their old hated poverty, turning from the *biniou* (Breton bagpipes) to pop and rock, building modern villas, and selling off their lovely old carved rustic furniture, or storing it away in the crumbling barns that had till now been their cottage homes. Since about the early 1970s, however, their battle won to enter the modern world, they have been turning back to tradition, maybe somewhat contrivedly. 'Cercles celtiques' and costumed Breton musical and folk-dancing groups are now all the rage, especially among students and young intellectuals in search of the 'Breton personality'; Breton wrestling has won a new vogue; and many young couples send their children to Breton-speaking nursery schools. The old farm accoutrements are now used for modish decoration, as 'the stable lantern lords it in the sitting-room' and wagon-wheels embellish the garden. For Hélias, one of the most potent symbols of his childhood world is the traditional Breton box-bed (*lit clos*), a two-tier cupboard where several of the family would sleep together: he was born in one such bed, and he remembers happy rough-and-tumbles at night with his uncles, amid laughter, jokes and the noise of rustling straw, as 'the great chest creaked all over whenever someone turned over'. But today, what has happened to those beds?

Ah, those *lits clos*, what a good buy! I have found some that have been converted into a coat-cupboard in the hall, a library in the study, a buffet or drinks cupboard in the living-room, a music-box combining pick-up, radio and television. I have even seen one that functions as a toilet, to the great satisfaction of its users.... Finally, the one that has received the highest honour has become the frame for a canvas by a great

The coast near Cancale, where Colette's adolescents awoke to their sexuality.

Then Yann Gaos, the young fisherman who toils all summer in far Icelandic waters, finally weds his beloved Gaud, and the wedding party go to visit an old seaside chapel outside the hamlet where he lives:

They continued their walk beyond the hamlet of Pors-Even and the home of the Gaoses, in order that they might repair, in accordance with the traditional custom of newly-married couples in the district of Ploubazlanec, to the Chapel of the Trinity, which is as it were on the edge of the Breton world. At the foot of the last farthermost cliff, it stands on a ledge of low rocks, quite near the water, and seems to belong already to the sea. To reach it you have to follow a goat's path among blocks of granite. And the wedding party spread itself over the slope of this isolated cape, amid the rocks, their words of merriment and words of love quite lost in the noise of the wind and the waves.

But this happiness is overcast by a more sombre mood:

At the crossways the old Christs, which kept guard over the countryside, spread out their dark arms on the calvaries, like real men crucified, and in the distance the Channel stood out clearly as a great yellow mirror under a sky which was already obscured in its lower part, already tenebrous towards the horizon. And in this country even this calm, even this fine weather was melancholy; there remained, in spite of all, a sense of disquiet brooding over things; an anxiety borne in from the sea, to which so many existences had been entrusted, and of which the eternal menace was only slumbering.

*La Chapelle des Péris,
'the chapel of the perished',
in Loti's fishing-hamlet
of Pors-Even.*

Indeed the book ends in great sadness for, when the fishing-fleet sails back to Iceland, Yann's boat never returns, and each day his bride waits and watches with fading hope:

She had now made it a habit to go in the morning to the furthermost point of the land, along the high cliffs of Pors-Even. She went alone to the extreme edge of this district of Ploubazlanec, which stretches out like a reindeer's horn into the Channel, and sat there all day long at the foot of a solitary cross which dominates the immense distances of the water. . . these granite crosses rise up everywhere on the advanced cliffs of this mariners' land, as if beseeching mercy; as if seeking to appease the great moving, mysterious thing, which lures men and does not give them back, keeping by preference the most valiant, the most beautiful. . . One could see, outlined into the far distance, one beyond the other, all the indentations of the coast; the land of Brittany ended in denticulated points which stretched out into the tranquil emptiness of the waters. In the foreground rocks riddled its surface; but beyond, nothing disturbed its mirror-like polish; it gave out a scarcely perceptible caressing noise, soft and immense, which ascended from the depth of all the bays. And the distances were so calm, the depths so still! The great blue emptiness, the tomb of the Gaoses, preserved its impenetrable mystery. . .

Today the Chapelle de la Trinité is still there, outside Pors-Even, facing the rocky islets strewn across the bay. And in the hamlet of Pors-Even, north-east of Paimpol, at 95 rue Pierre-Loti you can still see the blue-shuttered cottage where the writer lodged with the fisherman who served as his model for the noble-hearted Yann. It is called 'Ti-Yann'. But today there is no more deep-sea fishing based on Paimpol, which instead has grown nicely prosperous on oyster-breeding, market gardening and, of course, tourism. If tragedy still sometimes strikes at sea, today it is due less to the mysterious malignant ocean itself than to the fallibility of those who work on the car-ferries and giant oil-rigs – *n'est-ce pas?*

No sailor could conceivably be more different from Yann Gaos than Georges Querelle, seductive promiscuous homosexual and cunning mass-murderer, whose exploits in Brittany's largest naval port are admiringly chronicled by Jean GENET in his novel *Querelle de Brest* (1953). Brest was one of several European towns where Genet in the 1930s had earned his keep as tramp, pickpocket and male prostitute, and he poetically describes the low-life of its dockside brothels, the joyous bouts of buggery in the swirling fog, and the sailors' turds littering the grassy banks below the ramparts. Almost every page is a litany of Genetic obscenities: but through the forest of swirling genitalia the reader can also pick out, here and there, some good descriptions of the town itself:

The further you go down towards the port, the denser the fog appears to grow. So thick is it at Recouvrance, after crossing the Penfeld bridge, that the houses – walls, chimney-stacks, roof and all – look as if they are floating in the mist. There is a sense of desolation in the narrow alleys that lead down to the quayside. The disconsolate rays of a wan sun, haloed with the buttery gleam to be observed at the half-open door of a dairy, occasionally filter through. On you go through the vapourish twilight till you are at last confronted once more by the semi-opaque yet ever-enticing wall of fog, a protection now fraught with dangers: a drunken sailor reeling home on a heavy pair of legs, a docker stooping over his girl, a lurking tough armed, perhaps, with a swiftsure knife. . .

Today, after much wartime bombing, the areas of the ramparts and Recouvrance have been rebuilt and much tidied up, and the naval vessels are fewer. But you can still catch echoes of the kind of ambience that set the young poet's manhood quivering:

It rains sometimes in Brest in September. Wet weather makes the light linen clothes – open shirts and blue jeans – stick skin-tight to the muscular bodies of the men working in the port and arsenal. It happens of course that the weather is fine on certain evenings when the groups of masons, carpenters and mechanics surge out from the shipyards. They are dog-tired. . . Slow and ponderous, they move across the bows of the lighter, more rapid, hither-and-thither roving matelots out on the razzle, who are from that time on the chief adornment of the town. Brest will scintillate till daybreak with their dazzling antics, their incandescent gusts of laughter, their songs, their fun and skylarking, with their cat-calls and insults and wolf-whistles shouted at the girls, their kisses. . .

Another and again very different picture of love and desire in North Brittany is conveyed by a third non-Breton visitor to the region, COLETTE, who spent some time in a seaside villa at La Gaimorais, between Cancale and St-Malo, and there wrote *Le Blé en herbe* in 1923. This charming study of adolescents on holiday, discovering their sexuality, is coloured by a sensitive mood-portrait of this wild and lovely coast:

*The grotto associated
with Pierre Abélard,
at Clisson
near his birthplace.*

All that could be seen through the window was the westerly weather of August, bringing rain in its wake. The earth came to an abrupt end out there, on the brink of the links. One more squall, one more upheaval of the great grey field furrowed with parallel ridges of foam, and the house must surely float away like the ark. But Phil and Vinca knew the August seas of old and their monotonous thunder, as well as the September seas and their crested white horses. They knew that this corner of a sandy field would remain impassable, and all through their childhood they had scoffed at the frothy foam-scuds that danced powerlessly up to the fretted edge of man's dominion. . .

Vinca's smooth brown legs, crossed under the hem of her white frock, gleamed in the rays of the September sun. Far below them, a harmless ground-swell, soothed and smoothed by the passing of the heavy fog patch, was beginning to dance and by degrees be decked out in its clear weather finery. Gulls cried overhead, and a string of fishing-smacks hove into sight, sail following sail from behind the shadow of the Meinga to gain the open sea. . .

After seven years of harassment by the Czech authorities, the novelist Milan Kundera finally left his native Prague in 1975 and chose exile in France: he came to live in Rennes, where for some years he taught at the university, and here he wrote *The Book of Laughter and Forgetting*. More than eight centuries previously an even more celebrated fugitive from official persecution, much more severely hounded for his critical views, had also sought asylum in Brittany: Pierre ABELARD. He was born in 1079 into the minor nobility of the Nantes area, just beyond the southern edge of Brittany. He then settled in Paris, but after his radical doctrines had provoked charges of heresy, and after his love-affair with Héloise had led to his castration, he was forced to flee from one provincial monastery to another. Finally he agreed to become abbot of the remote abbey of St-Gildas-de-Rhuys, on the Morbihan coast (the church still exists, but much rebuilt). This, he hoped, 'would bring me some respite from the plots against me': but, as he tells in the famous letter written later to a friend, *Historia calamitatum*, it turned out otherwise:

The country was wild and the language unknown to me [he was brought up speaking Latin and French, not Breton], the natives were brutal and barbarous, the monks were beyond control and led a dissolute life which was well known to all. . . In addition, the abbey had long been subject to a certain powerful lord in the country who had taken advantage of the disorder in the monastery to appropriate all its adjoining lands for his own use, and was exacting heavier taxes from the monks than he would have done from Jews subject to tribute. . . Each one of them provided for himself, his concubine and his sons and daughters from his own purse. They took delight in distressing me over this. . . The entire savage population of the area was similarly lawless and out of control; there was no one I could turn to for help since I disapproved equally of the morals of them all.

Earlier he had written to Héloise from St-Gildas: 'I wish you could see my house, you'd never take it for an abbey: the doors are decorated only with the feet of hinds, wolves, bears and boars, and the hideous hides of owls.' When he found that the monks were trying to poison him, he took flight, and later ended his days in Burgundy.

Pages 30–31: *Masked by trees, Chateaubriand's high-turreted feudal castle –*
'The song of the bird in the Combourg woods
told me of a happiness which I hoped to achieve . . .'

Madame de Sévigné adored her château and park of Les Rochers – 'Oh, how I love solitude!'

Five centuries later, Brittany was very much kinder than this to another immigrant, the Marquise DE SÉVIGNÉ. The celebrated letter-writer was born in Paris in 1626, then married a Breton nobleman who died in a duel when she was only 25, bequeathing her his château of Les Rochers, south-east of Vitré on the eastern confines of Brittany. There she stayed for several long periods, partly for financial reasons as it was cheaper than her home in Paris; from 1678 she was at Les Rochers almost continuously, though it was at her daughter's home in Provence that she died (see p. 293). As she recounts in her sprightly letters to that daughter, she hated the social life of the local nobility which as a *châtelaine* she was obliged to undergo: she had simple tastes, and was something of a puritan, and she found it all provincial, coarse and greedy. 'I have to dine with Monsieur de Rennes, these feasts never stop,' she writes; 'the largest supper, and always the same thing: noise, trumpets, violins.' She was shocked by society weddings where 1,200 chickens were consumed at a sitting, and by official banquets where 'there was far too much to eat, roasts were taken back again as though untouched' and 400 bottles of wine were downed – 'As much wine flows into the body of a Breton as water under the bridges.' But she loved Les Rochers and its park, where she felt:

. . . free in my avenue of trees to do what I please. And what I please means to walk up and down there in the evening until eight o'clock. Oh, how I love solitude! . . . I go out walking every day and am making a sort of new park round those wide open spaces at the end of the mall, and am planting avenues with four rows of trees all round. It will look very fine.

Today new trees have been planted; but the same avenues are there, bearing the names that the marquise gave them, 'la Solitaire, 'l'Infini', 'l'Humeur de ma fille', etc. The château, set in lovely wooded country, is 14th-century, rebuilt in the 17th. It is inhabited, and only two or three rooms can be visited – the small baroque chapel that was built for the marquise, and her bedroom with some portraits and other souvenirs. It is rather dull and fusty, not at all evocative of the daily routine that she describes:

We lead such a regular life that it is hardly possible to be ill. We get up at eight, very often I go out and enjoy the fresh air of the woods until the bell for Mass at nine. After Mass, we dress, pass the time of day with each other, go back and pick orange blossom, then have dinner. Until five o'clock work or reading, and since my son is no longer with us, I read to save his wife's weak chest. At five I leave her and go off to these lovely groves. A manservant follows me, I have books, I change destinations and vary the routes of my walks. A religious book and one on history, turn and turn about for the sake of a change. . . Finally at about eight I hear a bell; it is for supper. Sometimes I am at some distance, and I pick up the marquise amid her nice flower-beds. We are company for each other. We have supper at dusk and the servants do the same. . . Isn't this solitude very suitable for a person who has to think about herself and who is or wants to be a Christian?

So the marquise fully enjoyed her introspective old age in Brittany. However, some ninety years later, another aristocrat spent a distinctly miserable childhood in another château, not far to the north-west. François-René de CHATEAUBRIAND (1768–1848) is the best known of all Breton writers, but probably less for his *oeuvre* than for his life and personality: he has been called 'the first of the great French romantics', and like Byron he lived the part, constantly travelling and having wild love-affairs. The early chapters of his best-known book, the *Mémoires d'outre-tombe*, balefully chronicle his childhood: he was born at St-Malo, the youngest child of an impecunious and eccentric Breton count, but soon the family moved to their high-turreted feudal castle at Combourg, north of Rennes. Here, life with his sister, mother and sternly unsociable father was anything but fun:

All through the year, not a visitor presented himself at the castle, save a few gentlemen, the marquis de Montlouet, the comte de Guyon-Beaufort, who begged a night's lodging on their way to plead their suits before the Parliament. They used to arrive in winter, on horseback, with pistols in their saddle-bows, hunting-knives at their sides, and followed by a servant, also on horseback, with a livery trunk behind him. My father, always very ceremonious, received them bare-headed on the steps, in the midst of the wind and rain. . . During the bad weather, entire months would pass and not a single human being knock at the gate of our fortress. The sadness was great that hung over the moors of Combourg, but greater still at the castle. . . The

The steps of Combourg castle, where Chateaubriand's taciturn father would shoot at brown owls.

gloomy stillness was increased by my father's taciturn and unsocial humour. Instead of drawing his family and his retainers closer to him, he had dispersed them to all the wings of the building.

Chateaubriand details the family routine. His father would rise at four a.m., winter and summer alike, and later would go fishing, while his pious mother would retire to the gloomy chapel and spend some hours in prayer. On summer evenings after dinner, the family would sit outside on the steps and his father would shoot at the brown owls which emerged from the battlements at nightfall. In winter, mother and children would gather round the fireplace, but father would pace up and down till bedtime, his half-bald head covered in a big white cap, and would permit no conversation. Young François-René's bedroom was 'a sort of isolated cell' at the top of a side turret. And the whole place was haunted:

I called the waiting-woman and escorted my mother and sister to their rooms. Before I went, they made me look under the beds, up the chimneys, behind the doors, and inspect the surrounding stairs, passages and corridors. All the traditions of the castle concerning robbers and ghosts returned to their memory. The servants were persuaded that a certain comte de Combourg, with a wooden leg, who had been dead three centuries, appeared at certain intervals, and that he had been seen in the great staircase of the turret; sometimes also his wooden leg walked alone, accompanied by a black cat. [There is another story, told elsewhere, of a cat that had been walled up alive in the towers.] . . . The window of my donjon opened upon the inner courtyard; by day I had a view of the battlements of the curtain opposite, where hart's-tongues grew and a wild plum-tree. Some martins, which in summer buried themselves, screeching, in the holes in the walls, were my sole companions. At night I could see only a small strip of sky and a few stars. When the moon shone and sank in the east, I knew it by the beams which struck my bed across the lozenged window-panes. Owls, flitting from one tower to another, passed and passed again between the moon and me, outlining the mobile shadow of their wings upon my curtains. Banished to the loneliest part, at the opening of the galleries, I lost not a murmur of the darkness. Sometimes the wind seemed to trip with light steps; sometimes it uttered wailings, suddenly my door was violently shaken, groans issued from the basement, and then

Chateaubriand loved the park: but he hated the haunted and windswept castle, and the ennui of life there with his gloomy parents.

these sounds would die away, only to commence anew. At four o'clock in the morning, the voice of the master of the castle, calling the footmen at the entrance to the venerable vaults, made itself heard like the voice of the last phantom of the night.

At the age of eighteen Chateaubriand left Combourg for Paris, and then the castle was devastated in the Revolution. It has since been restored, with heavy Victorian furnishings, and still belongs to the family: but, with its winding stone stairs, its parapets and 11th-century donjon, it still seems forbidding, even lugubrious. In the salon, a portrait of one of Chateaubriand's sisters, guillotined at the age of twenty-three, adds to the general air of haunted gloom. But the park outside is now neatly landscaped, whereas in Chateaubriand's time it was wild heath and oakwood. Here he roamed as a boy. These walks, he wrote later, were the strongest formative influence on his brooding and self-indulgent character:

The song of the bird in the Combourg woods told me of a happiness which I hoped to achieve... It is in the woods of Combourg that I became what I am, that I began to feel the first attacks of the weariness which I have dragged with me through life, of the sadness which has been my torment and my felicity... I beheld with ineffable pleasure the return of the season of storms, the passing of the swans and the ring-doves, the muster of the crows on the pond-field, and their perching at nightfall on the tallest oaks in the Great Mall. When the evening raised a bluish vapour in the cross-roads of the forest, and the plaintive lays of the wind moaned in the withered moss, I entered into full possession of the sympathies of my nature.

Alienated from his parents, it was only with his beloved sister Lucile that he was able to share these moods:

The life which my sister and I led at Combourg heightened the exaltation natural to our age and character. Our chief pastime was to walk side by side in the Great Mall, in spring on a carpet of primroses, in autumn on a bed of dead leaves, in winter on a sheet of snow edged by the footprints of birds, squirrels and weazels. We were young as the primroses, sad as the dead leaves, pure as the newly-fallen snow: our recreations were in harmony with ourselves.

He seems to have had few other pleasures at Combourg – save for the occasional annual fair or party which his father as *seigneur* was obliged to offer his dependants:

The Angevin Fair was held in the meadow by the pond on the 4th of September each year, my birthday. The vassals had to take up arms and come to the castle to raise the liege lord's banner; thence they went to the fair to establish order and enforce the collecion of a toll due to the counts of Combourg on each head of cattle, a sort of royalty. During that time my father kept open house. We danced for three days: the gentry in the great hall, to the scraping of a fiddle; the vassals in the Cour Verte, to the squealing of a bag-pipe. We sang, cheered, fired off arquebuses. These noises mingled with the lowing of the droves at the fair; the crowd wandered through the woods and gardens, and at least once in the year one saw at Combourg something akin to merriment.

By coincidence, the English traveller Arthur YOUNG visited the little town of Combourg in 1788, just two years after Chateaubriand had left for Paris. His visit was on September 1, just before the fair started: but he seems to have found little prospect of merriment:

My entry into Bretagne gives me an idea of its being a miserable province. . . To Combourg, the country has a savage aspect. . . the people almost as wild as their country, and their town of Combourg one of the most brutal filthy places that can be seen; mud houses, no windows, and a pavement so broken, as to impede all passengers, but ease none – yet here is a château, and inhabited; who is this Monsieur de Chateaubriant [sic], the owner, that has nerves strung for such a residence amidst such filth and poverty?

The worldly and well-connected Mr Young, normally assiduous in obtaining introductions to all the best French country houses, seems not to have called on this one. Maybe he was wise. So he goes on further into Brittany, where his liberal conscience continues to be appalled:

The poor people seem poor indeed; the children terribly ragged, if possible worse clad than with no cloaths [sic] at all, as to shoes and stockings they are luxuries. A beautiful girl of six or seven years playing with a stick, and smiling under such a bundle of rags as made my heart ache to see her: they did not beg, and when I gave them any thing seemed more surprised than obliged. One third of what I have seen of this province seems uncultivated, and nearly all of it is in misery. What have kings, and ministers, and parliaments, and states, to answer for their prejudices, seeing millions of hands that would be industrious, idle and starving, through the execrable maxims of despotism, or the equally detestable prejudices of a feudal nobility?

The answer to his question came a bare ten months later, at the Bastille in Paris (and yet, ironically, in the mid-1790s it was those same Breton peasants who rallied to the Royalist rebellion *against* the Revolution). Later, Young visits a fair in north-west Brittany:

The men dress in great trowsers [sic] like breeches, many with naked legs, and most with wooden shoes, strong marked features like the Welch [sic], with countenances a mixture of half energy half laziness; their persons stout, broad and square. The women furrowed without age by labour, to the utter extinction of all softness of sex. The eye discovers them at first glance to be a people absolutely distinct from the French.

Young was not the only visitor to have been distressed by the Brittany of that time. Just as Abelard earlier had found the natives of mediaeval Morbihan so 'brutal and barbarous', so Honoré de BALZAC, coming to the Combourg/Fougères area not much later than Young, has this remarkable passage about Brittany near the start of *Les Chouans* (1829):

The inhabitants are incredibly ferocious and brutishly stubborn, but their sworn word is to be trusted absolutely. They do not recognise our law, manners, dress, our new money or our language, but live with patriarchal simplicity and practise the heroic virtues. That paints the portrait of a people more intellectually backward and less subtle even than the Mohicans and redskins of North America, but just as noble, as full of guile, and just as tough. . . Some public-spirited individuals, as well as the Government, have made attempts to win this lovely corner of France, with its wealth of little-known treasures, for social integration and prosperity; but they all founder against the obdurate immovability of a population dedicated to doing what it has

The ramparts of Fougères castle, with the upper town in the background.
Balzac set the final scenes of Les Chouans *here.*

L'Île Verte, where Ronsard the nature-lover
wished to be buried.

3: The Loire

(Pays de la Loire and Centre regions)

The gentle country of the Loire valley, where the broad river flows past fertile meadows and a suite of royal châteaux, has long been thought of as a heartland of true French tradition and history. 'Normandy is Normandy, Burgundy is Burgundy, Provence is Provence; but Touraine is essentially France,' wrote Henry James in *A Little Tour of France*. 'It is the land of Rabelais, of Descartes, of Balzac, of good books and good company, as well as good dinners and good houses. Georges Sand somewhere has a charming passage about the mildness, the convenient quality, of the physical conditions of central France – "*son climat souple et chaud, ses pluies abondantes et courtes*".'

James could have added Ronsard's name, too. And further afield, though still within the borders of the modern region so poetically named 'Centre', lie lands that have nurtured or inspired other writers as central to the French tradition as Proust and Alain-Fournier. But the heart of this heartland is Touraine itself, where the spoken French is the purest and most accent-free in France. Its serenity and confidence have seemingly been propitious to literary genius just as its climate and rich soil bring

*La Devinière, Rabelais'
family hunting-lodge,
which he transformed into
Gargantua's mighty
fortified city.*

*Opposite: The ford of Vède,
where Gargantua's
mare drowned
an army with her piss.*

forth its strawberries and melons, asparagus and sparkling wines. It was
in fact Rabelais himself who first called this province 'the garden of
France' ('*Je suis né et ay este nourry jeune au jardin de France, c'est
Touraine*,' says Panurge in *Pantagruel*): and the tag has stuck ever since,
cheerfully exploited by the tourist brochures.

François RABELAIS, the rebellious humanist and life-lover, scourge of
clerics and herald of the Renaissance in France, was a product of the jovial
douceur de vivre of his native Touraine, just as his own writings in turn
have since served to enhance that local tradition. His father, a wealthy
lawyer at Chinon, had a country residence in the lush valley to the south-
west, La Devinière, which he used also as hunting lodge and farm-centre.
It was probably here (but records are scant) that young François was
born, around 1494. This trim little stone manor-house on a low hillside,
nicely restored, is today inevitably a Rabelais museum, with some

souvenirs and period furniture. But its main interest is the view that it affords over the villages and châteaux in the valley that Rabelais evokes in *Gargantua* and *Pantagruel*. For although this pair of hyper-satiric novels range widely over France and the world, parts are set with vivid geographical precision in his own homeland – and to visit this placid

valley today, nearly half a millenium later, with Rabelais' books as guide, is to receive a strange insight into the workings of his rumbustious imagination. Half right, the ivy-covered stump of a stone tower in a ploughed field is all that is left of the abbey of Seuilly where Rabelais began his education, and which in the novel is the home of the monk, Frère Jean, courageous ally of the gentle giant Gargantua. Straight ahead, the meadow of La Saulaie is where Gargamelle gives birth to Gargantua through her left ear, in the best Rabelaisian manner, after eating too much putrid tripe:

The tripes were plentiful, as you will understand, and so appetising that everyone licked his fingers. But the devil and all of it was that they could not possibly be kept any longer, for they were tainted, which seemed most improper. So it was resolved that they should be consumed without more ado. For this purpose there were invited all the citizens of Cinais, of Seuilly, of La Roche-Clermault, and of Vaugaudry, not to

forget those of Le Coudray-Montpensier and the Gué de Vède and other neighbours: all strong drinkers, jovial companions, and good skittle-players. . . After dinner they all rushed headlong to the Willow-grove; and there on the luxuriant grass they danced to the gay sound of the flutes and the sweet music of the bagpipes, so skittishly that it was a heavenly sport to see them thus frolicking.

Later, after Gargantua has become adult, this valley is the scene of the famous episode of the Picrocholean War, when the giant's father, the lord Grandgousier, is attacked by the dastardly King Picrochole ('bitter bile' in Greek), of the nearby village of Lerne. This violent mega-conflict was the comical projection of a real but peaceful quarrel between Rabelais' father's clients and the hateful Gaucher de Sainte-Marthe, of Lerne, over fishing and water rights in the Loire; moreover there was always in reality a rivalry between Lerne, *bourg* of artisans, and Seuilly, hamlet of peasants (hence the incident at the start of the war, when the cake-bakers of Lerne bash up the shepherds of Seuilly). But Rabelais enjoys inflating these villages to the size of mighty fortified cities: La Devinière at Seuilly becomes the castle of Grandgousier with its garrison of 30,000 men and 8,000 horse, assaulted by Picrochole's 51,000 men-at-arms. At first the war goes Picrochole's way, and he manages to capture the castle of La Roche-Clermault (today a handsome but tumble-down farmhouse just across the railway, dwarfed by the huge silos of the local Coopérative Agricole). But, after Gargantua arrives from Paris (where he has drowned 260,418 Parisians by pissing on them from the tower of Nôtre Dame), he swings into action, combing the cannon-balls out of his hair like grape-pips. He gets help from Frère Jean and from others too:

Meanwhile his mare pissed to relieve her belly, but so abundantly that she made a flood twenty-one miles wide, and all her piss drained down to the Ford of Vède [just by the D759, south-east of Cinais], so swelling the stream along its course that the whole of that enemy band was hideously drowned, except for some who had taken the road towards the slopes on the left.

Picrochole is defeated, and Gargantua rewards his lieutenants by distributing properties to them. To the faithful Gymnase he gives the château of Coudray-Montpensier (built in 1481, and still in perfect condition, this is the imposing pepperpot-towered edifice on the hill just south of the modern commuter villas of Lerne; the writer Maurice Maeterlinck used to live here, and now it is a private medical centre). And on the Loire, near Ussé, Gargantua founds the wonderful Abbey of Thélème, where monks and nuns live freely together, bound by only one rule, '*Fay ce que vouldras*' (do what you please). Thélème, alas, is entirely fictitious, though Rabelais may have vaguely had in mind the nearby Abbey of Fontevraud (today a State cultural centre), which was inhabited by both sexes and run by nuns.

Rabelais writes little about Chinon itself, even though his father's town house was there (now long destroyed, it was in the rue de la Lamproie, running up from the river), and even though its castle was already famous as an English and French royal fortress, where Joan of

Pages 46–7: *Fishermen near the Loire,
in the Rabelais country.*

To the faithful Gymnase, Gargantua gave the château of Coundray-Montpensier (today a medical centre).

Arc met the Dauphin (*'petite ville grand renom'*, comments Rabelais). But the people of the town and its area ('la Rabelaisie') today remain immensely proud of their local genius, and they endeavour to keep up his convivial tradition, helped by quantities of their esteemed local wine. In fact, the local bacchic brotherhood, Les Bons Entonneurs Rabelaisiens (*entonner* means *both* to sing *and* to cask wine), is the leading wine *confrérie* in France after the Chevaliers du Tastevin in Burgundy, and its 5,000 red-robed members include such luminaries as Elizabeth Taylor, Gérard Depardieu and Paul Bocuse. They hold banquets four times a year in the 'Caves Painctes', huge formerly-frescoed caverns in the rock, under the castle: these were known to Rabelais (*j'y ai bu maints veres de vins frais'*) and were the inspiration for his temple of the Divine Bottle where Pantagruel and Panurge come to seek truth. An invitation to one of these jollities reads: *'Nous y partagerons notre pantagruelique repas quand Monsieur l'Appétit nous viendra... Venez-vous esbaudir avec nous et échanger propos inspirés de Maistre François Rabelais, notre Père spirituel.'* New initiates swear on oath to live up to the Rabelaisian spirit of courage, tolerance and joie-de-vivre.

*The château of Ussé, by the Loire north of Chinon, which Charles Perrault
is thought to have taken as his model for the castle in* The Sleeping Beauty.

fountain. He did, and his stone paving survives. But today it is a peasant *lavoir* beside messy undergrowth, down a track. No signpost, no plaque, no effort whatsoever to tidy up the spot that inspired one of the greatest of French sonnets. However, the local authorities should not perhaps be blamed too much, for in Ronsard's day, too, these springs may have been nothing much to look at. Steeped in Graeco-Roman poeticism, he peopled all his local woods with Naiads, and made every Loirland trickle into a lyrically lovely Fons Bandusiae.

Ronsard's close friend and fellow lyric poet, Joachim DU BELLAY (1522–60), a more austere character, came from western Anjou over in the Loire valley where his father, a *seigneur*, owned a château outside the village of Liré, across the river from Ancenis. Here Du Bellay passed a rather lonely and unhappy childhood. But he always loved the gentle Anjou countryside; and it was when he later spent four years in Rome, 1553–7, as assistant to his brother Jean, a cardinal, that he so nostalgically wrote his poems about 'mon Anjou' and the 'Loire fameux'. For example,

Joachim du Bellay, a more austere character than his friend Ronsard.

> Faucheurs, coupeurs, vendangeurs, louez doncques
> Le pré, le champ, le vignoble Angevin:
> Granges, greniers, celliers on ne vid oncques
> Si pleins de fein, de fourment et de vin.

(Reapers, cutters, grape-harvesters, therefore praise / the meadow, the field, the vineyard of Anjou: / Barns, granaries, cellars one never sees / so full of hay, ferment and wine.)

In his famous sonnet beginning, 'Heureux qui, comme Ulysse, a fait un beau voyage', he imagines returning to 'mon petit village', which he compares with the Rome of his self-imposed exile:

> Plus me plait le séjour qu'ont bâti mes aïeux,
> Que des palais romains le front audacieux,
> Plus que le marbre dur me plait l'ardoise fine,
> Plus mon Loire gaulois que le Tibre latin,
> Plus mon petit Liré que le mont Palatin,
> Et plus que l'air marin la douceur angevine.

(The abode that my forefathers built for me pleases me more / than bold-fronted Roman palaces, / fine slates please me more than hard marble, / my Gallic Loire more than the Latin Tiber, / my little Liré more than the Palatine Hill, / and more than the sea air the sweetness of Anjou).

Du Bellay's feeling for this *douceur angevine* was very real, even if his poetry shows a less impassioned and dedicated concern for nature than Ronsard's. His boyhood home of La Turmelière, a mile or so west of Liré, was devastated in the Terror of the 1790s: but today its ivy-clad ruins including one gaunt tower are still visible, on a hillside behind a big ugly 19th-century mansion that is now a school. In the village, a smaller Renaissance house that also belonged to his family is now a Du Bellay museum, adorned with old prints of his dignified, mournful face and photos of modern Anjou folk-festivals. I asked the young lady curator

The hilltop château at Saumur, towering above the house
where Eugénie Grandet lived her life of sacrifice.

The salon in the château of Saché,
where Balzac would read his day's work to his admiring hosts.

*The château of Saché,
where Balzac fell in love
with the leisured life-style
of the Touraine rural
aristocracy.*

*Opposite: The Pont-de-
Ruan on the Indre south
of Tours, heartland of
Balzac's favourite corner
of France – 'Infinite
Love. . . I found expressed
by this long ribbon of
water streaming in the sun. . .'*

After Félix, the book's young hero, has first met Henriette at a ball in
Tours and impulsively kissed her naked shoulders, he then travels on foot
to stay with friends at the château of Frapesle (taking the same route that
Balzac used to take when walking to Saché), and there he meets Henriette
again, for she lives in the château of Clochegourde, just across the Indre,
by the village of Pont-de-Ruan. As his love for her grows, so in his heart
it becomes blended with his joy in the beauty of the valley: Henriette for
him *is* 'the lily in this valley' – one of the many flower-images that fill the
book. Balzac's ninety-odd novels and stories are seldom noted for their
lyrical rhapsodising over nature, but the pages describing Félix' first
arrival in the valley are a shining exception:

Infinitive love. . . I found expressed by this long ribbon of water streaming in the
sun between two green banks, by these lines of poplars guarding this vale of love with

their quivering tracery, by the oakwoods rising up between the vines on hillsides bordered by the winding river, and by these horizons full of contrasts. If you want to see nature lovely and virgin like a girl betrothed, go there on a day in spring. . . At this moment, the mills by the waterfalls of the Indre gave a voice to this trembling valley, the poplars swayed smilingly, not a cloud was in the sky, the birds sang, the cicadas cried out, all there was sweet melancholy. Ask me no more why I love Touraine; I love it not as one loves one's birthplace, nor as one loves an oasis in the desert; I love it as an artist loves art. . . without Touraine, perhaps I could not longer live. . . Soon I

saw a village that the poetry flowing up within me made me find without equal. Imagine to yourself three mills set among islands gracefully divided and crowned with clusters of trees amid a water-meadow. . . Amaryllis, nenuphar, waterlilies, rushes and phlox decorate the banks with their splendid tapestries. A quivering bridge made of rotting planks, its supports covered with flowers and its railings planted with evergreen grass and velvety moss, all of it leaning out over the river yet not falling; some rickety little boats, fishermen's nets, the monotonous chant of a shepherd, ducks gliding between the islands or preening themselves on the gravelly sand. . . Imagine, beyond the bridge, two or three farms, a dovecot, turtle-doves, thirty or so tumbledown cottages separated by gardens and by hedges of honeysuckle, jasmin and clematis; fresh manure in front of every doorway, and cocks and hens in the pathways. Thus is the village of Pont-de-Ruan, a pretty village overlooked by an old characterful church, a church from the time of the crusades, of the kind that painters seek for their pictures. Then frame all this with very old nut-trees and young poplars their leaves a pale gold; put graceful ornamentations in the midst of the long meadows where the view fades beneath a warm and misty sky – and you will have an idea of one of the thousand panoramas of this lovely spot. I followed the Saché road on the left bank of the river. . . Often my eyes were drawn to the horizon by the beautiful gilded blade of the Loire where, on the rippling surface, the sails borne by the wind carved fantastic shapes. Climbing a hill-top, I admired for the first time the château of Azay, a facetted diamond set in the Indre and mounted on flower-covered piles. Then I saw in a hollow the romantic hulk of the château of Saché, a melancholy dwelling full of harmonies too sober for superficial people but dear to poets whose soul is sad.

This valley today is still lovely in fine weather, but probably less so than in Balzac's day, for it is now partly engulfed by the Tours commuter-belt and by mass tourism. The Montsaufs' château de Cloche-gourde is purely fictitious, but the château de Fraspesle is believed to have been based on that of Valesne, still standing near the river. Pont-de-Ruan still has its broad millrace and its old church, and the château de Saché is still there just as it was. It is to Saché that Félix retires broken-hearted at the end of the book, to nurse his grief after Henriette's death. And it was to Saché that Balzac himself went often for long periods, when it belonged to landed-gentry friends of his mother's, the Margonnes. This handsome 16th-century manor, in a pastoral setting where cows graze, is now a neat Balzac museum full of memorabilia. He came here whenever he wanted an escape from his hectic life in Paris and his angry creditors, and here he wrote several novels including *Le Père Goriot*. Visitors today must follow the guided tour, for since the theft of a Rodin bust of Balzac in 1982 they may no longer roam at will. They see the salons where in the evenings Balzac read his day's work to his admiring hosts; upstairs is the museum with its portraits of some of Balzac's many mistresses and of the great man himself, corpulent and bulbous-eyed. Most fascinating are the copies of page-proofs with those massive, intricate, semi-legible correc-tions that drove his printers so mad that they demanded double pay for coping with them. His bedroom is just as it was, with his ink-well, quill pen and coffee-pot. His routine here was to rise very early, maybe at 2 a.m., then work intensively for twelve or fourteen hours, surviving on strong black coffee alone. Often he would write in bed, like Proust. His bed is amazingly short, in the fashion of those days, when people would sleep not lying flat but half sitting up, on pillows – possibly because they all had digestive problems.

Georges Sand also slept up, though to judge by the intensity of her love-life you might think her more familiar position was that of *une grande horizontale*. Her little bed can be inspected in her family château at Nohant, in the Berry, 90 miles south-east of Tours. This was her dearly-loved *pays*. Though she was born in Paris (in 1804), she was marked above all by the wild Rousseauesque adolescence she spent among local country folk in the Berry. Then she married a baron, moved back to Paris, had love-affairs with Chopin, Musset and others, smoked and wore trousers, espoused Left-wing views, wrote novels under her masculine

The Moulin de Chenet in the Georges Sand country.

*Old houses by the water
at La Châtre, still much
as Georges Sand
must have known them.*

pen-name (her real name was Lucile-Aurore Dudevant, *née* Dupin), and
then finally settled back at Nohant as *châtelaine*, where she played
hostess to the cultural great of the day – including Balzac. Here, most
passion spent, she devoted her later years to good works, much revered
locally and known as 'la bonne dame de Nohant'.

The château, an unpretentious stone manor, is entrancingly set in a
very rustic old hamlet north of La Châtre, opposite a tiny 11th-century
romanesque church and cottage gardens which in spring are a mass of
cherry-blossom. No cars are allowed. The house, open to the public and
preserved as it was in Sand's day, has an authentic mid-19th-century
fustiness. In the dining-room, the table is laid under a fine pink-and-blue
chandelier, with place-names for Flaubert, Turgenev, Delacroix, etc.
(they *were* all guests here, though not all at the same time). In the salon is

At Nohant, where Georges Sand lived, loved and died: the little church and (below) her grave in the family cemetery.

the table where Chopin and Liszt composed, and on one wall the famous portrait of Sand – a shock of black hair, an imperial nose, mysteriously deep dark eyes and a look of arrogant disdain. The most interesting room is the tiny theatre, with its charming *trompe-l'oeil* backdrop, where Sand and the villagers would rehearse her new plays before they were staged professionally in Paris (where usually they flopped). Today her theatrical tradition is kept alive, in a touristy way, with an outdoor 'romantic festival' each June and a 'folklore festival' in July, when a Berry folk troupe act a dramatised version of *La Petite Fadette* in the château grounds. Here Sand lies buried under a yew-tree in the little cemetery.

She had a strange duality in her nature. A true Paris bohemian and globe-trotting amorist, she also remained deeply involved with the country folk of this southern corner of Berry, which she called '*la vallée noire*' because in summer its woodlands were so thick as to be almost black in some lights. Her father was a *seigneur*, but her mother's father was a local bird-seller – and Sand the romantic Leftist was proud of these humble origins. Indeed her most enduring novels are not the worldly romances of European high-life such as *Consuelo*, but the very simple idealised tales of the Berry peasantry such as *La Petite Fadette*.

The *vallée noire* is the valley of the Indre and its tributary, the Vauvre, just west of Nohant. It is an area far more off the beaten track than

In Georges Sand's pastoral Vallée Noire country, where castles are legion: the reddish Château de Sarzay (opposite) and the Château de Montreuil (below).

of the peasantry, however misjudged artistically, was also intended politically as a polemic against public contempt and indifference. Above all, Sand had deep roots in one particular area, and her provincial writing stems from this; in a sense she was the creator of a genre of rural regional fiction that was to flower later in the work of Genevoix, Giono and others. The critic Pierre de Boisdeffre has written: 'We find in her descriptions of the Vallée Noire, of its hollowed roads or the clearings in the forest of Châteauroux, a kind of first draft of *Le Grand Meaulnes.*'

ALAIN-FOURNIER's poignant vision of the *pays* of his childhood may be very different from Sand's, but the setting is much the same: it is again the rolling country of southern Berry, in this case around his home village of Epineuil-le-Fleuriel, thirty miles east of Nohant. His marvellous book may have its dream-fantasy elements but it is also realistically anchored in the rural world that he knew, and as such it is one of the most authentic of French regional novels. But what of its bewildering topography? Usually it is the Sologne, 60 miles to the north of Epineuil and well outside Berry, that is identified as *'le pays du Grand Meaulnes'*, but unfairly: the book's main setting is Epineuil. The confusion, and the rivalry, have risen because the author chose to jumble the two areas – and unscrambling them makes for intriguing detective-work.

Henri Fournier (his real name), son of a village schoolmaster, was born in 1886 at La Chapelle-d'Angillon, north of Bourges, on the edge of the melancholy forests and lagoons of the Sologne, where his mother's family lived. At five he moved with his parents to the primary school at Epineuil and remained there until he was twelve. He would return to La Chapelle for the holidays, but it was Epineuil he always loved best. In his strange story of children playing at being grown-ups, written in his mid-twenties, he mixed his real childhood memories with his childhood dreams and yearnings, all within the framework of a somewhat convoluted adventure-story. But the autobiographical element is clear. The school and village scenes are very precisely Epineuil, which Alain-

The modest schoolhouse at Epineuil, setting for Alain-Fournier's nostalgic vision of his boyhood in Le Grand Meaulnes.

*The Abbaye de Loroy,
near La Chapelle: along
with Cornançay,
one of the originals for
Meaulnes' enchanted manor.*

Fournier names Ste-Agathe (there is also a real village called Meaulne nearby). But the mysterious forest where Augustin Meaulnes finds his enchanted manor is definitely a Sologne landscape: he takes the road to Vierzon, then gets lost somewhere near 'Vieux-Nançay' (Fournier had relatives in the Sologne village of Nançay):

> The spot where he found himself was one of the most desolate of the Sologne. All morning he saw no one but one shepherdess, on the horizon, leading her flock. . . Not even the cry of a curlew in the reeds of the marshes.

Then above the pinewoods Meaulnes glimpses a slim grey tower! This is the manor, *le Domaine sans nom*, certainly an amalgam of several châteaux that the imaginative Henri saw as a child. One of them was Loroy, a whitish steep-roofed building hidden in the Sologne woodlands three miles south of La Chapelle. Another was the château de Cornancay, a stately red-brick 18th-century manor set in its own park amid open *bocage* country three miles west of Epineuil – and the role that Cornancay is believed to have played in the imaginative conception of the book is totally fascinating. In the 1890s it was the home of the Vicomte de Fadate, a wealthy but benevolent landowner who possessed eleven farms in the area, providing a living for many of the local artisans and peasants.

murmured; 'I love it for its beauty which fills my eyes, for the soft curves of its banks, for the shining strands which tremble in the sun, the purple strands in the shadows of the water willows, the strands blue under the moonlight, for the lively freshness of the currents dancing on the reddish pebbles, for the glaucous mystery of the river-pools and the silvery river-fish that leap up by the wash-houses.'

Downstream from here is Orléans, where in 1792 the English poet Wordsworth stayed in a pension at the Coin Maugas and had a love-affair with Annette Vallon (she bore him a daughter, 'whom he abandoned', as the Hachette guide puts it, ever ready to produce new proof of Albion's perfidy). And north-west from Orléans, as far as Chartres, there stretches the great monotonous plain of the Beauce, which has been described by writers as different as Rabelais, Zola, Péguy and Proust. Today the Beauce is a rich wheat-growing area, but in mediaeval times it was covered with forest; and Rabelais in his account of Gargantua's first journey to Paris gives a typically comic explanation of this change:

So they passed joyfully along the highway in high spirits, till they came above Orléans, at which place there was a great forest a hundred and five miles long and fifty-one miles wide, or thereabouts. This forest was horribly abundant and copiously swarming with ox-flies and hornets, so that it was an absolute brigands' lair for the poor mares, asses and horses. But Gargantua's mare handsomely avenged all the outrages ever perpetuated there on the beasts of her kind, by a trick of which they had not the slightest inkling beforehand. As soon as they had entered this forest and the hornets had opened their attack she threw out her tail, and at her first skirmish swatted them so completely that she swept down the whole wood. Crossways and lengthways, here and there, this way and that, to front and to side, over and under, she swept down the trees as a mower does the grass, so that since that time there has been neither wood nor hornets, and the whole country has been reduced to a plain.

At the sight of this Gargantua felt very great delight. But the only boast he made was to say to his people: 'I find this fine' (*Je trouve beau ce*); from which saying the country has ever afterwards been called La Beauce.

Three and a half centuries later, Emile ZOLA also found the Beauce *beau* – but not its peasant inhabitants whom in *La Terre* (1887) he describes as mostly brutal and brutish, malicious and suspicious. Born in Provence, Zola was of Venetian origin on his father's side: but his mother came of Beauce country stock, and as a boy he had listened eagerly to his father's talk about the area. So, when he decided to include a novel about the peasantry in his mammoth Rougon-Macquart cycle (see also *Germinal*, p. 169, *La Débâcle*, p. 173), it was natural that he should choose the Beauce for its location. He did his field research in the area south of Châteaudun, setting *La Terre* in the small village of Romilly-sur-Aigre, which he calls 'Rognes', just east of the market town of Cloyes which he allows to keep that name. Here he sets the scene:

... beneath the late October sky, vast and overcast, the rich yellow farmland, bare at this time of year, extended for a score of miles and more, its broad stretches of arable alternating with green expanses of clover and lucerne, with no sign of a hillock or a tree as far as the eye could see; everything merged and fell away over the far

Set on the wide plain of the Beauce, Zola's novel La Terre *has only one true heroine:* La Terre *itself.*

The Pré Catelan, which became Swann's garden – at the heart of Proust's imaginative world.

Opposite: *The upper Loir at Illiers/Combray, which Proust called the river Vivonne: 'Here and there, floated blushing like a strawberry, the scarlet heart of a lily set in a ring of white petals'.*

mornings at Combray (because on those mornings I did not go out before mass), when I went to say good morning to her in her bedroom, my aunt Léonie used to give me, dipping it first in her own cup of tea or tisane...

And as soon as I had recognised the taste of the piece of madeleine soaked in her decoction of lime-blossom which my aunt used to give me (although I did not yet know and must long postpone the discovery of why this memory made me so happy) immediately the old grey house upon the street, where her room was, rose up like a stage set to attach itself to the little pavilion opening onto the garden which had been built out behind it for my parents (the isolated segment which until that moment had been all that I could see); and with the house the town from morning to night and in all weathers, the square where I used to be sent before lunch, the streets along which I used to run errands, the country roads we took when it was fine... so in that moment all the flowers in our garden and in M. Swann's park, and the water-lilies on the Vivonne and the good folk of the village and their little dwellings and the parish church and the whole of Combray and its surroundings, taking shape and solidity, sprang into being, town and gardens alike, from my cup of tea.

Of those country walks that the Proust/Amiot family would take
when fine, there were two main ones. The one led west towards the
village of Mèréglise. The family would leave the house by the back gate
and go down the rue des Trois-Maries and the rue des Lavoirs, past the

two ruined towers on the right (still there today) which had special
meaning for the young Proust; they would cross a small footbridge over
the river Loir (the very same Loir that Ronsard loved, but some way
upstream) and would visit the Pré Catelan, a pleasant landscaped garden
belonging to Uncle Jules (today municipally owned), with pools, dove-
cotes, holly bushes and a variety of trees; then they would climb the steep
hawthorn path onto the broad fields of the Beauce. For the other walk,
towards the village of St-Eman to the north-west, the family left by the
front door and walked through the meadows by the Loir.

These two walks acquired a gigantic, almost metaphysical significance
for Proust and they play a central part in the novel. The one he renamed
'the Méséglise way' for euphony, but he also called it 'Swann's way', for
in his book the Pré Catelan became the park of Swann's house; and the
St-Eman walk he named 'Guermantes way', for in the book it leads to the

château of the Duchesse de Guermantes. These two 'ways' become a kind of metaphor for the search for Time itself, for Marcel as a child is never able to reach their destinations and he believes that they lead in opposite directions, whereas it is only at the book's end that he finds that really they are quite close together and 'reconcilable'. One of the greatest and most directly autobiographical passages in the book reveals what these walks meant to Proust:

So the 'Méséglise way' and the 'Guermantes way' remain for me linked with many of the little incidents of the life which, of all the various lives we led concurrently, is the most episodic, the most full of vicissitudes; I mean the life of the mind. . . The flowers which played then among the grass, the water which rippled past in the sunshine, the whole landscape which surrounded their apparition still lingers around the memory of them with its unconscious or unheeding countenance. . . The scent of hawthorn which flits along the hedge from which, in a little while, the dog-roses will have banished it, a sound of echoless footsteps on a gravel path, a bubble formed against the side of a water-plant by the current of the stream and instantaneously bursting – all these my exaltation of mind has borne along with it and kept alive through the succession of the years, while around them the paths have vanished and those who trod them, and even the memory of those who trod them are dead.

. . . It is pre-eminently as the deepest layer of my mental soil, as the firm ground on which I stand, that I regard the Méséglise and Guermantes ways. It is because I believed in things and in people while I walked along those paths that the things and the people they made known to me are the only ones that I still take seriously and that still bring me joy. . . The Méséglise way with its lilacs, its hawthorns, its cornflowers, its poppies, its apple-trees, the Guermantes way with its river full of tadpoles, its water-lilies and its buttercups, constituted for me for all time the image of the landscape in which I should like to live, in which my principal requirements are that I may go fishing, drift idly in a boat, see the ruins of gothic fortifications, and find among the cornfields – like St-André-des-Champs – an old church, monumental, rustic, and golden as a haystack; and the cornflowers, the hawthorns, the apple-trees which I may still happen, when I travel, to encounter in the fields, because they are situated at the same depth, on the level of my past life, at once establish contact with my heart. . .

. . . What I want to see again is the Guermantes way as I knew it, with the farm that stood a little apart from the two neighbouring farms, huddled side by side, at the entrance to the oak avenue; those meadows in which, when they are burnished by the sun to the luminescence of a pond, the leaves of the apple-trees are reflected; the whole landscape whose individuality grips me sometimes at night, in my dreams, with a power that is almost uncanny, but of which I can discover no trace when I wake. . . The Méséglise and Guermantes way left me exposed, in later life, to much disillusionment and even to many mistakes. For often I have wished to see a person again without realising that it was simply because that person recalled to me a hedge of hawthorns in blossom, and I have been led to believe, and to make someone else believe, in a renewal of affection. . . When, on a summer evening, the melodious sky growls like a tawny lion, and everyone is complaining of the storm, it is the memory of the Méséglise way that makes me stand alone in ecstasy, inhaling through the noise of the falling rain, the lingering scent of invisible lilacs.

So for the visitor today to walk up that narrow hawthorn path, past the municipal garden, is indeed to tread on holy ground. It was here on the Méséglise walk that Proust would turn back to look at the tall slim steeple

The steep hawthorn path, beside his uncle's garden, that Proust transmuted into the poetic metaphor of the Méséglise way (Swann's Way): 'It is the memory of the Méséglise way that makes me stand alone in ecstasy. . .'

of Illiers church that also plays such a part in the book ('It was the steeple of St-Hilaire that shaped and crowned and consecrated every occupation, every hour of the day, every view in the town'). And from higher up, across the plain, he could see other village spires on the horizon – Méséglise, Vieuvicq, Saint-Eman, Marcheville – that shifted perspective as he walked and thus inspired the beautiful passage about the moving spires seen from Dr Percepied's carriage.

The St-Eman walk led towards the source of the Loir, the subject also of a poem by Ronsard. Proust calls the river the Vivonne; towards the end of the book, Marcel finally penetrates to its source but is disappointed: 'I imagined [it] as something as extra-terrestrial as the gates of hell, and which was merely a sort of rectangular basin in which bubbles rose to the surface.' Today it is a *lavoir* in the small village of St-Eman, very neat and non-bubbly; and next to it is the tiny romanesque church that Proust calls 'St-André-des-Champs'. Down the road towards Illiers, there stands beside a pond the old stone manor house of Mirougrain that plays a curious role in the book, for in part it inspired the passage about sad Mlle Vinteuil, whose sadistic and lesbian practices are observed by Marcel as he hides in the bushes. This homosexuality was another of Proust's transfers from Paris to Combray, and he further confuses the issue by renaming the manor 'Monjouvain' which in fact is a variation on the name of a real millhouse (Monjouvain) beside the river Thironne on the south side of Illiers. This is near the handsome manor of Tansonville which gave its name, but no more, to Swann's house.

The new Paris–Brittany motorway today cuts within a few yards of Monjouvin and Tansonville. But modernism, strangely enough, seems to have little affected Illiers itself which remains a rather dreary and ugly little town. Many years ago it got its name officially changed to Illiers-Combray, and is the only French town thus honoured apart from Ferney-Voltaire. But today it does remarkably little to attract tourists – mercifully, you could say. Proust is caviare to the general, and there are no charabancs à la Stratford or Colombey, no Grand Hôtel Marcel Proust, no souvenir shops displaying Swann ashtrays or Vinteuil 'moi-j'aime-les-filles' T-shirts, just a few discreet Tante Léonie madeleines on sale. The people seem sullen and uninterested, backward, typically Beauceron. In the market-place, the handsome high-vaulted 15th-century church of St-Jacques (Proust called it St-Hilaire) still has the rose window that he adored, but it lost most of its other stained-glass in the war. Outside, in the square, Proust's grandparents' former grocery at no. 11 is now a household electrical shop; at no. 6 is the flat where his widowed grandmother lived; and no. 14, once Jules Amiot's drapery store, is now again a clothes shop, in other hands. It is all very prosaic.

The Amiot town house where Proust stayed is just round the corner at no. 4 rue du Docteur-Proust and is remarkably ill-signposted although it is now a Proust museum. It was sold in 1919, but in 1950 the Amiots' grand-daughter Germaine managed to buy it back and she had it refurbished in the original 1870s style: most of its present furniture she acquired specially, but the wood panelling is the same that Proust knew, and so are the lozenged stained-glass windows which, to Marcel's delight, would cast shifting sunlit patterns on the floor. To our modern taste, the house appears poky, fusty, gloomy, if not downright hideous, in the true late-Victorian manner: but it is full of Proustian ghosts and fascinating souvenirs – the tiny kitchen where the servant Ernestine ('Françoise') did her work, many family photos including one of Céleste, Proust's faithful housekeeper in his later Paris days, and a copy of Vermeer's *View of Delft* that he called 'the most beautiful painting in the world'. In the summer-house are photographs by Nadar of many of the great society figures on whom Proust based some of his Paris characters. And upstairs, down Marcel's 'long corridor', is his bedroom, suitably decked out with copies of that famous magic lantern and of Sand's *François le Champi* that his mother would read him at bedtime. It is all a little contrived, but as authentic as can be achieved. Proust's ugly childhood environment did not stunt his artistic powers but nourished them – and on this let Painter have the last word: 'The contents of his bedroom at Illiers had a quality more precious to him than beauty: they were raw material for his imagination. In the 1890s he was to go through a period of "good taste"; afterwards, however, to the end of his life, he filled his rooms with hideous but sacred objects which spoke to him of his dead parents, his childhood, time lost. He had come into the world not to collect beauty ready made but to create it.' And so now to Normandy – to Balbec and Albertine!

4: Normandy

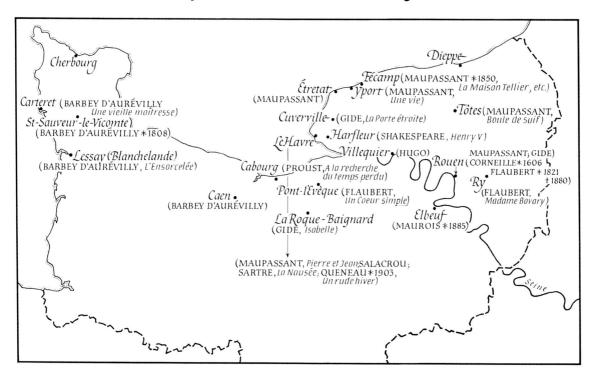

Cherbourg

Carteret (BARBEY D'AURÉVILLY
Une vieille maîtresse)
St-Sauveur-le-Vicomte)
(BARBEY D'AURÉVILLY *1808)

Lessay (_Blanchelande_)
(BARBEY D'AURÉVILLY, _L'Ensorcelée_)

Caen •
(BARBEY D'AURÉVILLY)

Dieppe

Fécamp (MAUPASSANT *1850,
La Maison Tellier, etc.)
Étretat   • Yport (MAUPASSANT,
(MAUPASSANT)   _Une vie_)
Cuverville • (GIDE, _La Porte étroite_)   • Tôtes (MAUPASSANT,
Boule de suif)
Le Havre   • Harfleur (SHAKESPEARE, _Henry V_)
Villequier • (HUGO)   MAUPASSANT, GIDE)
Cabourg (PROUST, _A la recherche_   Rouen (CORNEILLE *1606
du temps perdu)   • FLAUBERT *1821
† 1880)
Pont-l'Évêque (FLAUBERT,   Ry •
Un Coeur simple)   (FLAUBERT,
Madame Bovary)
La Roque-Baignard   Elbeuf
(GIDE, _Isabelle_)   (MAUROIS *1885)

(MAUPASSANT, _Pierre et Jean_; SALACROU;
SARTRE, _La Nausée_; QUENEAU *1903,
Un rude hiver)

Seine

Proust's 'immense and wonderful aquarium': the dining-room of the Grand Hôtel at Cabourg ('Balbec'), still much unchanged today.

A great white wedding-cake of a turn-of-the-century hotel, handsome with its red awnings and manicured lawns in front, stands beside the casino, backing onto the Promenade Marcel-Proust and one of the finest broad sandy beaches of Normandy's Côte Fleurie. This Grand Hôtel, today managed by the Pullman group, serves all its guests an obligatory madeleine for breakfast, its luxury restaurant is 'le Balbec' and its beach-club 'L'Aquarium', while a bust of the great man stands on the reception desk and its bar will serve you a sea-green 'cocktail Proust' made up of gin, cointreau, grand marnier and blue curaçao. The casino's bar, the 'Du Côté de Chez Swann', could be the right starting-point for the evening's amusements – maybe a Belle Epoque costumed ball. In short, if sleepy provincial Illiers largely ignores its great heritage, assertively touristy Cabourg certainly does not.

Of course the hotel is no longer a major pleasure-haunt of aristocrats and parvenus as PROUST knew it; but Cabourg remains, after Deauville, perhaps the most stylish resort along this coast. It was created from almost nothing in the 1860s and was laid out in a spiral pattern, with

and wonderful creatures, or whether the obscure folk who watch them hungrily out of the night will not break in some day to gather them from their aquarium and devour them).

Cabourg, however, even if today it has moved somewhat down-market, remains a place of quiet traditional villas, many of them the homes of the commuting Caen bourgeoisie or the secondary residences of well-to-do Parisians who arrive by the *autoroute* and no longer on Proust's 'beautiful, generous' 1.22 pm train from the Gare St-Lazare; and visually, even though its tramway has now gone, it has not changed so very much since the days when those villas were brand new and the narrator Marcel went to visit the painter Elstir, habitué of the Verdurin salon, in his studio:

Elstir lived at some distance from the front, in one of the newest of Balbec's avenues. The heat of the day obliged me to take the tramway which passed along the rue de la Plage, and I endeavoured, in order to persuade myself that I was in the ancient realm of the Cimmerians, in the country, perhaps of King Mark, or on the site of the Forest of Brocéliande, not to look at the gimcrack splendour of the buildings that extended on either hand, among which Elstir's villa was perhaps the most sumptuously hideous...

Proust enjoyed also the gimcrack splendour of his fellow hotel guests, 'these unspeakable people', alike the assorted society Parisians and the

The exterior of the 'aquarium', its windows today less of a divisive social barrier than in Proust's time.

local nouveaux riches who did not know how to behave in a smart hotel. Nor are the staff spared his barbs – as in this scene of Marcel's first arrival:

> . . . We had finally landed in the hall of the Grand Hôtel at Balbec, and I stood there in front of the monumental staircase of imitation marble, while my grandmother, regardless of the growing hostility and contempt of the strangers among whom we were about to live, discussed 'terms' with the manager, a pot-bellied figure with a face and a voice alike covered with scars (left by the excision of countless pustules from the one, and from the other of the divers accents acquired from an alien ancestry and a cosmopolitan upbringing), a smart dinner-jacket, and the air of a psychologist who, whenever the 'omnibus' discharged a fresh load, invariably took the grandees for haggling skinflints and the flashy crooks for grandees! . . . Social position was the one thing by which the manager was impressed – social position, or rather the signs which seemed to him to imply that it was exalted, such as not taking one's hat off when one came into the hall, wearing knickerbockers or an overcoat with a waist, and taking a cigar with a band of purple and gold out of a crushed morocco case – to none of which advantages could I, alas, lay claim.

Today's manager presides over a very different social scene. The likes of the Marquise de Villeparisis, insofar as her society still exists in France, are now more likely to holiday in Cannes or the Caribbean; the casino stages not only the Belle Epoque balls but 'soirées minijupes'. Most people seem happily prosperous and lower-middle-class, and the 'obscure folk' watching 'hungrily out of the night' today have no desire to break into the 'aquarium' and swallow its rich fishes, for they can easily dine there themselves if they wish. The Grand itself now survives mainly on business seminars, out of season. But it has been intelligently restored: in the vast foyer, the same chandeliers and pseudo-marble pillars as in Proust's day; elegant pale-green Art Nouveau mouldings around the high ceiling of the 'aquarium'; and a newly-opened 'chambre Marcel Proust' whose Belle Epoque furnishings include a big brass bedstead and old-fashioned bath-taps (but, oddly, a very modern white telephone). When, a few years back, the newly-named Promenade Marcel Proust was ceremonially inaugurated, the mayor of Cabourg committed the gaffe of proclaiming, 'What a shining example Proust sets to the young men of today!', which caused the journalists to titter and the Prefect to choke with embarrassment.

The topography of the Cabourg area has changed little since Proust's time. His beloved 'Little Train', that bore him to nearby resorts and villages where he had so many friends, now follows a different route, for the branch line to Mezidon ('Doncières') has closed, and the train follows the coast via Deauville in order to reach the main line to Paris at Lisieux. Not that his own location of 'Balbec' itself was at all precise, any more than that of Combray: in fact, he did not set it on this Côte Fleurie at all, but seemingly much further west, on some rocky coast that seems more like the Cotentin. For Balbec in the novel is a symbol as well as a reality. In part its portrait is a very autobiographical souvenir of people and incidents: but Balbec is also a territory of the mind, a focus for the narrator's yearnings and for his sense of loss and of some other, deeper reality just beyond his grasp. Thus, the narrator Marcel has heard a great deal about Balbec before his first visit (Swann has even told him, 'It's exquisite; as beautiful as Siena!'), but when he arrives he finds nearly everything disappointing – the 13th-century half-romanesque church 'Persian in its inspiration', the hotel, the 'torment' of his bedroom, even the view of the sea from the hills above – and he fears that by visiting the real Balbec he has shattered the spell of his dreams of it: 'No sooner had I set foot in it than it was as though I had broken open a name which ought to have been kept hermeticaly closed.' It is the theme of disillusion with reality that runs through the book. However, Marcel does later find some fulfilment in Balbec, especially when, after much timid eyeing of elusive girls glimpsed from horse-carriages or in the ballroom, he finally meets the love of his life. He sees her first among the 'little band' of lively young girls 'which progresses along the esplanade like a luminous comet'. She is:

> a girl with brilliant, laughing eyes and plump, matt cheeks, a black polo-cap crammed on her head, who was pushing a bicycle with such an uninhibited swing of the hips, and using slang terms so typically of the gutter and shouted so loud when I passed her (although among her expressions I caught that tiresome phrase 'living one's own life') that, abandoning the hypothesis which her friend's hooded cape had prompted me to formulate, I concluded instead that all these girls belonged to the population which frequents the racing-tracks, and must be the very juvenile mistresses of professional cyclists.

This is Albertine, the unique and unforgettable, a homosexual writer's sublime tribute to heterosexual love. Later in the book, as Marcel's love intensifies, he comes to equate her in his mind with Balbec ('. . . it was not only the sea at the close of day that existed for me in Albertine, but at times the drowsy murmur of the sea upon the shore on moonlit nights'), especially in that marvellous moment, perhaps the most evocative in the entire book, when he watches her asleep in the flat in Paris where he is virtually holding her prisoner:

> Her sleep . . . . was to me a whole landscape. Her sleep brought within my reach something as serene, as sensually delicious as those nights of full moon on the bay of Balbec, calm as a lake over which the branches barely stir, where, stretched out upon the sand, one could listen for hours on end to the surf breaking and receding.

I can thing of few sentences more profoundly erotic. And yet, disillusionment returns, for not only does Marcel's affair with Albertine end tragically, but even before that, on later return visits to Balbec, he finds himself disenchanted with 'the corrupting effect' of the countryside round it, 'in this too social valley' where he has made too many boring acquaintances who have come to mean too little to him. Just as in the case of Combray, a visit several years later fails to recapture the magic of an earlier one:

> . . . What a difference there was between the two pictures of Balbec, on my first visit and on my second, pictures composed of the same villas from which the same

*Back in Illiers-Combray,
the staircase in
Tante Léonie's house.*

girls emerged by the same sea! In Albertine's friends at the time of my second visit, whom I knew so well, whose good and bad qualities were so clearly engraved on their features, how could I recapture those fresh, mysterious strangers who once could not thrust open the doors of their chalets without a screech over the sand or brush past the quivering tamarisks without making my heart throb? Their huge eyes had sunk into their faces since then, doubtless because they had ceased to be children, but also because those ravishing strangers, those ravishing actresses of that first romantic year, about whom I had gone ceaselessly in quest of information, no longer held any mystery for me. They had become for me, obedient to my whims, a mere grove of budding girls [*jeunes filles en fleur*], from among whom I was not a little proud of having plucked, and hidden away from the rest of the world, the fairest rose.

Is this not the same elegiac lament for lost youthful magic that echoed on the banks of the Cher after Meaulnes' sad wedding-picnic, a book written at almost exactly the same time? And yet, at the end Marcel does

The manor by the Seine at Villequier,
where Victor Hugo knew personal tragedy.

find a kind of resolution, even before he hears again within him the jangling bell of the Combray gate. It could well be said that the dominant theme of Proust's great novel is not its portrait of a brilliant, decadent society, nor even the nature of time and of memory, but above all the quest for love and the loss of love; and in this context it is Balbec and Albertine, more than the madeleine, more than the jangling bell, that are at the very core of the book's meaning:

> . . . I should not have known Albertine had I not read in an archaeological treatise a description of the church at Balbec, had not Swann, by telling me that this church was almost Persian, directed my taste to the Byzantine Norman, had not a financial syndicate, by erecting at Balbec a hygienic and comfortable hotel, made my parents decide to grant my wish and send me to Balbec. To be sure, in that Balbec so long desired, I had not found the Persian church of my dreams, nor the eternal mists. Even the famous 1.22 train had not corresponded to my mental picture of it. But in exchange for what our imagination leads us to expect and we give ourselves so much futile trouble trying to find, life gives us something which we were very far from imagining. Who would have told me at Combray, when I lay waiting for my mother's good-night with so heavy a heart, that those anxieties would be healed and would then break out again one day, not for my mother, but for a girl who would first be no more, against the horizon of the sea, than a flower upon which my eyes would daily be invited to gaze, but a thinking flower in whose mind I was so childishly anxious to occupy a prominent place that I was distressed by her not being aware that I knew Mme de Villeparisis? Yes, it was for the good-night kiss of such an unknown girl that, in years to come, I was to suffer as intensely as I had suffered as a child when my mother did not come up to my room. And yet if Swann had not spoken to me of Balbec, I should never have known this Albertine who had become so necessary, of love for whom my soul was now almost exclusively composed.

The neat triangle of land between Rouen, Le Havre and Dieppe – the Pays de Caux, between the looping Seine and the coastal cliffs – has more literary connections than almost any area of France of that size. This is the *pays* of those eminently Norman writers, Flaubert and Maupassant, also of Corneille and Queneau, Salacrou and Maurois, even of André Gide. Others, such as Sartre, came to the area from outside. As did Victor Hugo, whose association became one of personal tragedy. He had grown friendly with a family of wealthy Le Havre shipowners, the Vacquerie, who owned a handsome manor house beside the Seine at Villequier, near Caudebec; and in 1843 his elder daughter Léopoldine married Charles Vacquerie. Six months later the young couple were both drowned in the river when their sailing-boat capsized in a storm. Hugo was shattered, for he had idolised Léopoldine, then only nineteen; and for some years his life and work were much affected. Finally, on a return visit to the tragic spot, he wrote about his feelings in a well-known poem, *A Villequier*, which forms part of the *Contemplations*. It contains the lines:

> Maintenant que je puis, assis au bord des ondes,
> Emu par ce superbe et tranquille horizon,
> Examiner en moi les vérités profondes
> Et regarder les fleurs qui sont dans le gazon;

miles from Rouen, between the Abbeville and the Beauvais roads, at the
end of a valley watered by the [fictitious] Rieulé, a little stream which
works three water-mills before flowing into the [real] Andelle. . . Here
you are on the borders of Normandy, Picardy and the Ile de France, a
bastard region whose speech is without accentuation as its scenery is
without character. It is here that they make the worst Neufchâtel cheese
in the whole district. . .' This geographical specification well fits the
market and spa town of Forges-les-Eaux: but a strong rival claim to have
been the 'real' Yonville comes from the village of Ry (pop. 544) which is
much nearer to Rouen, just north of the N31 to Beauvais, in the pretty
valley of the Crevon. And this claim is based on the curous saga of the
tragic Delamare family, which lends a piquant detective-story mystery to
the question of just what inspired Flaubert to write *Madame Bovary*. It is
known that a Dr Eugène Delamare, a youngish widower and former pupil
of Flaubert's father, settled in Ry in the 1840s and married a farmer's
daughter, Delphine Couturier, from the nearby village of Blainville; and
there are municipal records to prove that she died in 1848, aged only
twenty-seven, and he a year later. According to some accounts he hanged
himself, though his tomb is today in the village churchyard, close to the
lovely Renaissance porch of the church, and it is not quite clear how the

*The church at Ry, where
Dr Delamare lies buried
– did Flaubert base the
Bovarys' tragedy on that
of the Delamares?*

Flaubert's squat little pavilion at Croisset,
where Julian Barnes might, or might not, authenticate the parrot.

Some of his best-known stories are set in and around Rouen. *Boule de Suif* begins with the Prussian occupation of the city; then the jaunty prostitute and her bemused companions take thirteen hours to make the nineteen-mile coachride northwards to Tôtes, where the drama unfolds in the Hôtel du Commerce (Maupassant had in mind the Hôtel du Cygne, which is still there, in the village centre). As for that other famous tale of *filles de joie*, *La maison Tellier*, its First Communion outing was to the village of Bois-Guillaume, now engulfed in the Rouen suburbs. But the Tellier brothel itself was in Fécamp – 'a homely-looking house, quite small, with yellow walls, standing at the corner of a street behind the church of St-Etienne; and the windows looked out onto the dock, full of ships unloading, the great salt marsh known as La Retenue, and, in the background, the Virgin's hill with its old grey chapel.' There was indeed a *maison de passe* in that spot in those days, but the area round the church has since been rebuilt and no trace survives; and the dock today has few ships unloading, for Fécamp's great days are over as a major deep-sea fishing-port, and the old grey chapel now looks down on a rather gloomy

The château of Miromesnil, near Dieppe, where Maupassant spent part of his infancy.

The sad heroine of Maupassant's Une Vie *lived close to the fishing-village of Yport.*

and depressed little town where unemployment might be too high for Tellier-type trade to have much chance of flourishing so joyously.

Less ironical than his better-known short stories, Maupassant's novel *Une Vie* is a touching if slightly sentimental portrait of an unhappy marriage and a woman's wasted life, and it is set in the gentle countryside just inland from Yport. The life of the local rural gentry is sensitively depicted; and the landscapes changing with the seasons reflect the shifting modes of his sad heroine, Jeanne, who sometimes goes to brood alone on a clifftop by the sea, or with her father visits the fishing-village of Yport, near Fécamp:

The empty silent streets kept an odour of the sea, of fish and seaweed. The huge tanned nets were continually being dried, hung up in front of doorways or stretched out on the shingle. The grey cold sea with its endlessly seething foam began to ebb, leaving bare the greenish rocks at the foot of the cliffs towards Fécamp. And along the beach the big fishing-smacks aground on their sides looked like huge dead fish. As evening fell the fishermen moved in groups to the harbour wall, walking heavily with their great sea-boots, their necks wrapped up in woollens, a litre of brandy in one hand, a ship's lantern in the other. . . And the hefty sailors' wives, their heavy frames bursting out of their thin dresses, remained till the last fisherman had departed and then returned to the drowsing village, disturbing with their shrill voices the heavy sleep of the dark streets.

Maupassant knew intimately the harbours, chines and towering chalky cliffs along this coast, which also inspired so many of the paintings of Claude Monet. In his novel *Pierre et Jean*, about a middle-class family in Le Havre, Jean and his sweetheart go for a ramble down a coomb at St-Jouin, south-west of Etretat, with the idea of catching prawns amid the rocks:

> When they reached the bottom of the coomb, on the very edge of the precipice, they spotted a little path going down the face of the cliff, and beneath them, between the sea and the foot of the precipice, about half-way, an amazing jumble of huge rocks that had fallen and were piled one upon another into a sort of grassy, uneven expanse formed by an ancient landslide running southwards as far as the eye could see. On this long shelf of brushwood and grass shaken up, so to speak, by volcanic action, the fallen rocks looked like the ruins of a great vanished city which formerly overlooked the ocean and was itself overlooked by the endless white walls of cliffs.

This book also gives a remarkable picture of the bustling prosperity and self-confidence of the mighty port of Le Havre in the 1880s, during the great days of sea travel and sea commerce. Pierre goes to the harbour:

> He struck a match to read the list of ships reported in the roadstead and due to come in on the next tide. Liners were expected from Brazil, the River Plate, Chile and Japan, also two Danish brigs, a Norwegian schooner and Turkish steamer . . . A few steps further on he stopped to look out at the roadstead. To his right, above Sainte-Adresse, the two electric beacons on Cap de la Hève, like two gigantic twin Cyclopes, threw their long powerful beams across the sea. . . Then two other lights on the two jetties, children of these giants, marked the harbour entrance, and far off across the Seine yet others could be seen, lots of others, fixed or winking, with either blinding flashes or darkness, opening and shutting like eyes, the eyes of the seaports, yellow, red, green, watching the dark sea covered with ships, the living eyes of the welcoming land saying, just by the mechanical, invariable, regular movement of their lids: 'It's me, I'm Trouville, I'm Honfleur, I'm the river of Pont-Audemer.' And dominating all the others, so high in the sky that from such a distance it could be taken for a planet, the aerial light of Etouville showed the way to Rouen through the sandbanks of the estuary of the great river.

And from the Place de la Bourse Pierre's father surveys at close quarters the commercial harbour (near the present P&O car ferry terminal):

> . . . full of shipping which overflowed into other basins, in which the huge hulls, belly to belly, were touching each other four or five deep. All the numberless masts along several kilometres of quays, with their yards, mastheads and cordage, made this open space in the middle of the town look like a great dead forest.

Le Havre has changed utterly since that time, and even the descriptions of it written in the 1930s by Sartre, Queneau and Salacrou are today largely unrecognisable. First, world shipping is no longer the same: there are few passenger liners any more, and most of the heavy commercial traffic now

Maupassant knew intimately these chalky cliffs around Yport and Etretat, which also inspired the painter Monet.

consists of the huge roll-on-roll-off container vessels that can unload and load in a few hours and then depart again. So there is far less lively bustle of sailors and dockers on shore. Some of Maupassant's beacons are still winking, but most of the nighttime dazzle of lights now comes from the giant oil refineries up the estuary where the great tankers unload. Secondly, the port and downtown areas were blasted to bits in the war, and after 1945 the city was hurriedly rebuilt on a spacious but graceless grid pattern, with monotonous grey concrete façades: the hideous blocks of workers' flats along the broad avenue Foch remind one of the Stalinallee in East Berlin. But even men of the Left sometimes lament the changes. The playwright Armand SALACROU, who spent his youth in Le Havre and still lives there, wrote in *L'Humanité* in 1977, 'What has become of all those handsome sailors in blue who sang for the girls in the streets of St-François?' In 1935 he had written:

> Great city of Le Havre. . . one must know you well to love you well, but then what a love! One must love the wind and the rain, one must love to walk out in a nor'west wind on a winter's night by the sea boulevard where the spindrift dies on the stones of the houses. . .

Few other big French towns have inspired so much good writing. Maybe this in part has been a response to the seething picaresqueness of the old port area, and to the sharp contrasts between the life of the pre-war working-class slums and that of the *beaux quartiers*, aloof on their hillside above the sea at Sainte-Adresse and the Côte Félix-Faure. Paris-born Jean-Paul SARTRE spent five years in Le Havre in the 1930s, teaching philosophy at the Lycée François-Premier (this still exists today); and his love-hate relationship with the town is nicely pictured by Annie Cohen-Solal in a fine descriptive passage in her book *Sartre: a Life*. Sartre chose to live in the 'dirty, seedy, sinister' Hôtel Printania, near the station and port. On his free days he would go to Rouen to be with Simone de Beauvoir who was teaching at a lycée there: but many of his spare evenings he spent exploring the low-life cafés, bars and bistrots of the port area, especially in the red-light St-François district that is now so neat, dull and antiseptic. 'Here in this city of Le Havre,' writes Cohen-Solal, 'Sartre acquired daily habits he would never relinquish: he became involved with public places, and turned his patronage of cafés and hotels into a moral necessity.' Sartre was then just turning thirty, and these were highly formative years when he was also preparing his first novel, *La Nausée*. This transmutes the city into the imaginary 'Bouville' and changes the street-names; but the setting remains indisputably Le Havre, with its noisy trams (now no more), garish cafés, workers' marches and Sunday promenades along the jetty. The book seems to compound Sartre's fascinated love of low life with his horror of modern industrial ugliness and human wretchedness, and also with the central metaphysical theme of the main character's revulsion against all tangible matter. The scene is clearly set:

> From my window I can see the red and white flame of the Rendez-vous des Cheminots at the corner of the boulevard Victor-Noir. The Paris train has just come in. . . And here comes tram no. 7, *Abattoirs – Grands Bassins*. It arrives with a great clanking noise. It moves off again. Now, loaded with suitcases and sleeping children, it's heading towards the Grands Bassins, towards the factories in the black east. . . On the right-hand pavement, a gaseous mass, grey with streaks of fire, is making a noise like rattling shells: this is the old station. Its presence has fertilised the first hundred yards of the boulevard Noir – from the boulevard de la Redoute to the rue Paradis – has spawned a dozen street-lamps there and, side by side, four cafés, the Rendez-Vous

Le Havre has been bombed and much rebuilt since Sartre's horrified pre-war portrait of it in La Nausée: *but it still remains grimly industrial.*

des Cheminots and three others, which languish all day long but light up in the evening and cast luminous rectangles on the roadway.

And then the workers' rally:

It's Sunday. Behind the docks, along the coast, near the goods station, all around the town there are empty warehouses and machines standing motionless in the darkness. In all the houses, men are shaving behind their windows: their heads are thrown back, they stare alternately at their mirror and at the cold sky to see whether it is going to be a fine day. The brothels are opening their doors to their first customers, peasants and soldiers. In the churches, in the light of the candles, a man is drinking wine in front of kneeling women. In all the suburbs, between the interminable walls of the factories, long black processions have set off, they are slowly advancing on the centre of the town. To receive them, the streets have assumed the appearance they have when there is rioting: all the shops, except for those in the rue Tournebride, have lowered their iron shutters. Soon, in complete silence, the black columns are going to invade these streets which are shamming death: the first to arrive will be the railway workers from Tourville and their wives who work in the Saint-Symphorin soap factories. . .

Gradually, as the nightmare intensifies in Roquentin's mind, Bouville itself assumes the nature of a character in the drama:

The vegetation is besieging Bouville on only three sides. On the fourth side, there is a big hole full of black water which moves all by itself. The wind whistles between the houses. . . [And then, as finally he leaves for Paris.] The town is abandoning me first. I haven't left Bouville and already I am no longer here. Bouville is silent. I find it strange that I have to stay another two hours in this town which, without bothering about me any more, has put away its furniture and covered it with dust-sheets so as to be able to uncover it in all its freshness for new arrivals, this evening or tomorrow. I feel more forgotten than ever.

Raymond QUENEAU (1903–76), author of *Zazie dans le Métro*, was born and brought up in Le Havre and later wrote several poems about it and one novel, *Un rude hiver*, set during the 1914–18 war. This book, less full of surrealistic puns and cheeky neologisms than much of Queneau's work, has something of the same desolate quality as *La Nausée*, as the main character, a bourgeois widower with highly reactionary views, roams disgustedly around the town, a little in the manner of Sartre's Roquentin:

A tram took him to the Eure, from where he came back by the quays and the working-class districts, a long walk through a world of work and horror. Everywhere machines and slaves were in movement, the activity seemed inordinate, abominable. . . Lehameau gorged himself with contempt and horror and his soul leapt in exultation. Delightedly he indulged his absolute and fanatical revulsion for the plebs of the port and factories, for the peak-capped riff-raff, the proletarians who tormented their own children, were insolent towards decent people, drunken, brutal, seditious and dirty. Some parts of the town with their slums bedecked with linen and crawling with urchins, with their brothels and bars, represented for him the closest earthly image of hell, supposing that such a place existed.

This seems to tie in with Sartre's marching workers – and to exemplify writers' reactions to Le Havre's sharp social contrasts of those days. Lehameau later goes to visit the graves of his family, in their resting-place on the bourgeois hilltop:

After lunch he took the tramway to the cemetery. He stopped in front of the tombs of the English, noting the names of the regiments, interested in their origins. Further on the tombstones were engraved with Arab characters. He walked slowly, taking it all in. The wind blew continually, it was a hard winter, the trees were bare, the only flowers were the artificial ones hanging from the crucifixes.

Today this cemetery beside the ruined fort of Tourneville still contains the graves of local well-to-do families; also of many British soldiers of 1916–18, mostly those wounded at the front and then brought to hospitals in Le Havre where they died. But these were not the first English to have perished on active service here: in the eastern suburbs of the city is the old seaport of Harfleur, now a tangle of refineries, factories and high-rise council flats, and it was here in 1415 – according to an English playwright who, as far as we know, never visited France – that young King Hal, just before the battle where he captured Harfleur, summoned his dear friends once more unto the breach – 'or close the wall up with our English dead!'*

While on the subject of graves and death: André GIDE (1869–1951) and his wife Madeleine lie buried in the tiny village churchyard at Cuverville, north-east of Le Havre and a few miles inland from Etretat. His former home at Cuverville provides the setting for the most beautiful and perfect of his novels, *La Porte étroite* (1909). Gide on his father's side was of Protestant stock from Uzès in the south (see p. 000), but his mother came from a wealthy factory-owning Rouen family (his great-grandfather had been mayor in 1789) and he spent part of his childhood in that city. There too he met and fell in love with his first cousin Madeleine, whose parents owned the stately white-fronted manor house on a low hilltop about a kilometre south of Cuverville; there the Gides were married in 1895, just before the house became their property by inheritance. For all Gide's free-thinking, free-roaming, bisexual nature, the marriage was in some ways a happy one and so should not be taken too closely as the original for the tender but tragic relationship in *La Porte étroite*, where Alissa retreats into religious fanaticism because she cannot bear to face her own love for her cousin Jérôme. However, there were some details in common – and the physical setting at least is accurately autobiographical: 'a white two-storeyed building' where 'a score of large windows look east onto the front of the garden' which is 'rectangular and enclosed by a wall':

Behind the house on the west side the garden spreads more spaciously. A walk, gay with flowers, runs along the south espalier wall and is protected from the sea winds by a thick screen of Portugal laurel and a few trees. Another walk running along the north wall disappears under a mass of branches. My cousins used to call it the 'dark walk' and would not venture along it after twilight. These two paths led to the kitchen garden, which continues to a flower-garden on a lower level, and which you reach by a small flight of steps. Then, at the bottom of the kitchen garden, a little gate with a secret fastening leads, on the other side of the wall, to a coppice in which the beech avenue terminates right and left. As one stands on the doorstep of the west front one can look over the top of this clump of trees to the plateau beyond with its admirable clothing of crops. On the horizon, at no great distance, can be seen the church of a little village and, when the air is still, the smoke rising from half a dozen houses.

Every fine summer after dinner we used to go down to the 'lower garden'. We went out by the little secret gate and walked as far as a bench in the avenue from which there was a view over the country; . . . before us the little valley filled with mist, and over the distant woods we watched the sky turn golden. . .

*Much later, another English writer was much more directly inspired by Le Havre. In the summer of 1855 the young William Morris, then an undergraduate at Oxford, went on a walking tour of northern France with his close friend Edward Burne-Jones. Their visit to the city was the occasion of a decisive moment in their lives, as Burne-Jones later related: 'It was while walking on the quay at Le Havre at night that we resolved definitely that we would begin a life of art, and put off our decision no longer – he should be an architect and I a painter. . . That was the most memorable night of my life.' In the event, Morris' talents turned less to architecture than to writing and to crafts, and to decisively influencing British design.

Here the young couple walk in the garden, or sometimes slip out through the 'secret gate' to read Swinburne aloud on a bench in the beech-copse:

> The summer sped so pure, so smooth, that of its swift-slipping days scarce anything remains in my memory. Its only events were talks and readings... She [Alissa] was at the bottom of the orchards, picking the first chrysanthemums at the foot of a low wall. The smell of the flowers mingled with that of the dead leaves in the beech copse and the air was saturated with autumn...

But, as the years go by, Alissa retreats into her own spiritual world, rejecting the young man she adores and seeking 'something better than love'. On a last desperate visit to her, Jérôme comes again to Cuverville, entering by the *porte étroite* which by now has assumed a symbolic significance not only religious (the reference is to the biblical, 'Strait is the gate, and narrow the way, which leadeth unto life, and few there be that find it') but also sexual:

> We had again reached the small garden door through which she had come out to me a little before. 'Good-bye!' said she. 'No, don't come any further. Good-bye, my beloved friend. Now... the better thing ... is going to begin.' One moment she looked at me, at once holding me fast and keeping me at arm's length, her hands on her shoulders, her eyes with unspeakable love. As soon as the door was shut, as soon as I heard the bolt drawn behind her, I fell against the door, a prey to the extremest despair, and stayed for a long time weeping and sobbing in the night. But to have kept her, to have forced the door, to have entered by any means whatever into the house, which yet would not have been shut against me – no, not even today, when I look back to the past and live it over again – no, it was not possible to me...

Only at the end of this short but almost unbearably moving novel does Jérôme realise, on reading her diary after her premature death, that, with just a little less diffidence on his part, he could so easily have won her. The story could be construed as Gide's most heartfelt attack on a certain kind of repressive spirituality. Today the Cuverville house and garden are in other private hands and are not open to visits: but when I drove up the place seemed to be unoccupied and I was able to poke around the garden discreetly. It was all somewhat run-down and untidy, but otherwise just as Gide describes it – the lawns, the coppice, the beech avenue by the road, the view of a distant steeple. A big white farm dog barked at me amiably. The famous little gate at the back looked worn and shabby, and it carried a 'keep out' notice with a picture of a dog saying, '*Je garde ces lieux: vous y entrez à votre péril.*' That seemed suitably Gidean. But I felt that a garden full of such delicate literary ghosts deserved better upkeep.

Gide's mother's family, besides living in Rouen, also possessed a fine moated country property in the pretty Pays d'Auge, at La Roque-Baignard north-west of Lisieux. The house and its park may have inspired the setting for his novella, *Isabelle*, a somewhat *Rebecca*-like melodrama about a Norman château brought into melancholy and decay by the heroine's tragic love-life. But Gide's own memories of La Roque

*Gide's former home at Cuverville: the narrow garden gate that lent its name
to his* La Porte étroite – *a symbolism both religious and sexual.*

itself were happy ones: he adored his visits to it, and even became mayor of the village at the age of 27. In his autobiography, *Si le grain ne meurt*, he writes, 'Flocks of swallows whirled incessantly round the house. . . When I think of La Roque, I first of all hear the swallows' cries.'

Over in the far west of Normandy, the Cotentin peninsula south of Cherbourg was the homeland of one of the most bizarre figures in French 19th-century literature: Jules-Amédée BARBEY D'AURÉVILLY (1808–89), ardent Royalist, arrogant dandy, and lover of the macabre. He was born into the local gentry in the big village of St-Sauveur-le-Vicomte, where a tiny museum is now devoted to him, and his bust by Rodin stands beside the old castle. As a student in Caen he got to know Beau Brummell, then well past his prime and working there as British consul; later, in Paris, Barbey took Brummell and Byron as his models and managed to establish himself as a flamboyant leader of fashion and haughty but respected critic. Despite all this Parisian dazzle, he also

Opposite: *St-Sauveur-le-Vicomte castle, where Barbey d'Aurevilly lies buried: he wanted to be 'the Walter Scott' of the Contentin, giving a voice to its people and their traditions.*

The heathland of western Contentin, now less wild and sinister than in Barbey's day.

remained closely attached to the country people of the Cotentin and their traditions, and most of his best work deals with that area. For all his oddity, he is thus a genuine regional writer.

The Cotentin is more wild and rugged, rather more like Brittany, than the rest of gentle orchardy Normandy. The houses are of austere granite, not quaintly half-timbered, and until recently the region has been very poor. Traces of a feudal spirit survive even today; and in Barbey's time the country areas were given over to superstition, witchcraft and strange legends. His stated aim was to become 'the Walter Scott' of this region, and to provide a voice for the local people and their traditions. He sympathised with the Royalist 'Chouans' who had rebelled against the revolution in the years before his birth; and he wanted, as he saw it, to put their record straight before history, as Scott had done for the Scots after Culloden. But, for all his literary gifts, he was no Walter Scott.

Few of his novels or stories have been translated into English. Many of them tell of morbid passions leading to strange crimes, and they contain a

Gothic element of terror and mystery; but the heightened style has a certain poetic resonance too, and the feeling for the lonely Cotentin countryside is genuine and moving. *Le Chevalier des Touches* was written in part as an attempt to justify the Chouans' revolt; *Les Diaboliques* (translated as *Weird Women*) is a set of stories about the power of evil. Another weird woman plays the title role in *Une vieille maîtresse*, a novel about a young man whose happy marriage is destroyed when his Spanish ex-mistress turns up and starts writing him letters in her own blood. The setting is the little port of Carteret on the west coast, opposite Jersey, now a popular summer resort: here, just beyond the lighthouse on the headland, above a superb stretch of beach, you can still see the caves in the cliff where husband Ryno made love with his *femme fatale*, and the ruined Roman lookout-post where they held their first fatal tryst:

> The tower of the lookout-post was set on a jutting piece of cliff high above the sea. It was two in the afternoon and the weather, misty in the morning, had developed the purity and clarity of crystal under a fresh north-east breeze. The sun that had risen behind Barneville, and was now behind St-Georges, fell obliquely on the platform where a scene had just occurred very foreign to the calm habits of these shores. This passionate scene, enacted between sky, earth and water, had no other witnesses, it seemed, than God and the seagulls that had passed over the heads of Ryno and Vellini. . .

A more powerful and extraordinary novel than this is *L'Ensorcelée* (1854), a ghoulish yarn steeped in witchcraft, murder and blasphemy. Barbey sets it on the heathlands of western Cotentin: he had in mind the Lande de Rainville at St-Sauveur which today is still rough and wild, but he transposes the action to the larger Lande de Lessay further south, today neatly cultivated but in those days more sinister:

> Set between La Haie-du-Puits and Coutances, this Norman desert, where you would encounter neither trees, nor houses, nor hedges, nor traces of man or beast save those of the odd passer-by or of the morning flock in the dust, if it was dry, or in the footpath's sodden clay, if it had rained, displayed a grandeur of solitude and desolate sadness that was hard to forget. . .

To this blasted heath there comes the dread Abbé de la Croix-Jurgan, immensely tall and proud, his face hideously scarred by tortures suffered during the Chouan wars:

> Never perhaps, since Niobe, had the sun lit up so poignant an image of despair. The most horrible of the sufferings of life had encrusted on his face its last anguish. Handsome, but marked with a fatal stamp, the visage of the stranger seemed sculpted in green marble, so pale was it! And this ravaged and greenish pallor emerged harshly beneath the headband round his temples, for on his head he wore a knotted scarf like all the humans who slept in the open air. . . Couched half on his side, like a brave stricken wolf, this lonely man in the dust of this ditch had an incomparable grandeur, the grandeur of the supreme moment. Towards the evening sun, which like a compassionate hangman seemed to be sadly offering him a few last moments of life, he turned a slow and arrogant gaze. . .

*On this coast north of Carteret, Barbey's hero Ryno
made love with his Spanish* vieille maîtresse.

Croix-Jurgan inhabits the mysterious Abbey of Blanchelande (three miles north-east of La Haye-du-Puits), half ruined in the Revolution; at the manor of Hautmesnil, to the north, he had spent a wild orgiastic youth in earlier days. A local squire's wife, Jeanne, falls in love with this charismatic monster. But later, as the plot thickens, she is found drowned in a *lavoir*, having been bewitched either by the abbé or, more probably, by a trio of nomadic shepherds possessed of evil magic powers (Barbey has no illusions about the local peasantry, whom he regards as sly, malicious and self-interested, full of *Schadenfreude*). A horde of villagers then attack a crony of the abbé's, an old hag with the odd name of La Clotte; they lynch her, and cart her body across the Lande:

> They entered the heath, the heath, the terrain of mysteries, the property of spirits, the heath ever trodden by prowling shepherds and sorcerers! They no longer dared

Blanchelande abbey, the setting for Barbey's L'Ensorcelée: fears, cruelties and myths in a time of turbulence.

look at this corpse drenched in blood and mud that spattered their heels. They left it and fled. . . Silence covered the land. . . The belltower of Blanchelande, whose noisy ringing had stopped after twenty-four hours of continuous peals, was only a silent spire on which the shadows rose as the sun settled on the horizon. No sound came from the village. The frightful spectacle which had swept through it, like a vision of blood and wrath, had left a weight of dread upon these houses whose doors still seemed haunted by the morning's terror. The afternoon lengthened in a gloomy sadness; and when the evening of this day of fatal memory began to fall upon the land, in the bluish distance one heard neither the cheerfully melancholy chant of the cow-girls, nor the cries of children in the doorways, nor the sharp whipcracks of the millers returning to the mill, sitting astride their sacks, their feet slapping the flanks of their brisk mares. One would have thought Blanchelande dead at the end of its roadway. . .

Yet Barbey was no desk-bound concoctor of artificial horror-stories: he was steeped in his *pays*, and he felt himself to be truly recounting its fears, cruelties and myths in a time of turbulence soon after the Revolution. At the book's end, as the abbé is preparing to serve Easter Mass in Blanchelande church, he is shot dead at the altar by Jeanne's vengeful husband. And, ever after, travellers crossing the deserted heath at night can hear a mournful bell tolling from the derelict abbey; its windows are strangely lit, and within the abbé's ghost is celebrating a phantom Mass which he can never finish. . .

It remains to be said that today the beautiful abbey of Blanchelande, nicely rebuilt and set idyllically beside a lake in deep countryside, is inhabited by a youthful autonomous religious community who make a living by selling their own craftwork of pottery, textiles, woodwork and bread to locals and tourists. They assured me that they heard no midnight bells, saw no phantom priest. One girl with brilliant, laughing eyes and a black cap offered to sell me cakes and wicker baskets. She looked more bewitching than bewitched. Perhaps she was some latter-day Albertine. . .

5: Ile-de-France

(Ile-de-France region and southern part of Oise department)

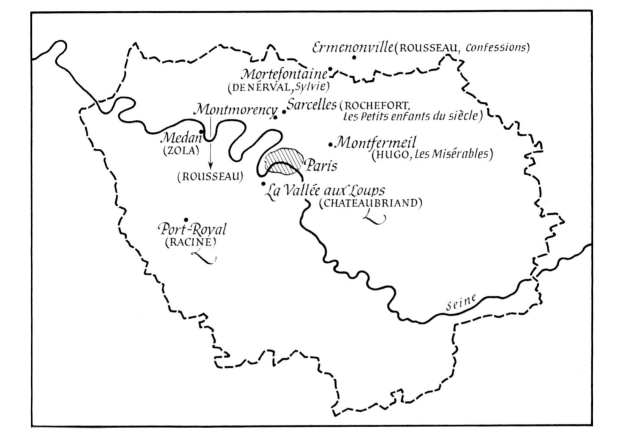

Ermenonville (ROUSSEAU, Confessions)

Mortefontaine (DE NÉRVAL, Sylvie)

Montmorency • Sarcelles (ROCHEFORT, Les Petits enfants du siècle)

Medan (ZOLA)

(ROUSSEAU)

•Montfermeil (HUGO, Les Misérables)

•Paris

La Vallée aux Loups (CHATEAUBRIAND)

Port-Royal (RACINE)

Seine

Jean-Jacques Rousseau's tombstone in the ornamental park at Ermenonville.

Many Parisian writers today have country homes in Provence, or some other sunny spot, where they spend part of each year. But in the 18th and 19th centuries, when transport was more difficult, they would be more likely to seek refuge from the hectic city in a place not too distant from it – maybe amid the woods and gentle valleys of the Ile-de-France, then much less built up than it is today. This was true of Chateaubriand, and of Zola – and also of that impecunious peripatetic paranoid but very great philosopher, Jean-Jacques ROUSSEAU. His intense feeling for nature, which is the basis of so much of his thought, was fostered principally by his native Switzerland, and then by the Chambéry district of Savoy (see p. 205): but it also found inspiration around the village of Montmorency and its adjacent forest, only ten miles north of central Paris and at that time still very rural. By 1756, aged then 44, Rousseau was growing weary of life in Paris where by now he was well known; he was

quarrelling with the other philosophers, and he hated the salon snobberies. So he was delighted when his well-to-do friend Madame d'Epinay
offered to lend him a small house on her country estate beside the Forest
of Montmorency. This brought him back close to nature – as he related
later in his memoirs, the *Confessions*:

> Violets and primroses already made their appearance, the trees began to bud, and
> the evening of my arrival was distinguished by the song of the nightingale, which was
> heard almost under my window, in a wood adjoining the house... The more I
> examined this charming retreat, the more I found it to my wishes. This solitary,
> rather than savage, spot transported me in idea to the end of the world. It had striking
> beauties which are but seldom found near cities, and never, if suddenly transported
> thither, could any person have imagined himself within four leagues of Paris...
> Although I had for several years past been frequently in the country, I seldom had
> enjoyed much of its pleasures; and these excursions, always made in company with
> people who considered themselves as persons of consequence, and rendered insipid by
> constraint, served to increase in me the natural desire I had for rustic pleasures. The
> want of these was the more sensible to me as I had the image of them immediately
> before my eyes. I was so tired of salons, *jets-d'eau*, groves, parterres, and of the more
> fatiguing persons by whom they were shown; so exhausted with pamphlets,
> harpsichords, trios, unravelling of plots, stupid *bon mots*, insipid affectations, pitiful
> story-tellers, and great suppers; that when I gave a side-glance at a poor simple
> hawthorn bush, a hedge, a barn or a meadow; when, in passing through a hamlet, I
> scented a good chervil omelette, and heard at a distance the burden of the rustic song
> of the Bisquières; I wished that all rouge, amber and baubles could go to the devil.

For a while all went well in this little house, l'Ermitage, and Rousseau
was writing with fecundity. But soon he found that Madame d'Epinay's
hospitality entailed its own social obligations; and in turn his own
neurotic behaviour and morbid sensitivity began to annoy her circle of
friends, especially when he fell wildly in love with her sister-in-law, the
Comtesse d'Houdetot. There was a quarrel, and by the end of 1757
Rousseau had moved off to a cottage called Mont-Louis at Montmorency
village. The Maréchal de Luxembourg, who became his next patron, also
lent him in the summers an elegant pavilion called the Petit Château in
the grounds of his own grand château:

> In this profound and delicious solitude, in the midst of woods, the singing of birds
> of every kind, and the perfume of orange flowers, I composed, in a continual ecstasy,
> the fifth book of *Emile*, the colouring of which I owed in a great measure to the lively
> impression I received from the place I inhabited. With what eagerness did I run every
> morning at sunrise to breathe the perfumed air in the peristyle! What excellent coffee
> I took there tête-à-tête with my Thérèse! My cat and dog were our company. This
> retinue alone would have been sufficient for me during my whole life, in which I
> should not have had one weary moment. I was there in a terrestrial paradise; I lived in
> innocence and tasted of happiness.

Most of his remaining time at Montmorency was spent by Rousseau at
Mont-Louis, which he had redecorated according to his own rustic taste;
with him was Thérèse Levasseur, the simple laundry-girl whom eventu-
ally he married. Today the Maréchal's château no longer exists, nor does

Rousseau's cottage at Mont Louis. He lived in the part to the right: to the left is the newer extension.

l'Ermitage: but Mont-Louis is still there, at 5 rue Jean-Jacques Rousseau. Here the philosopher's original cottage, plus a newer extension, together house a small museum: this contains some interesting portraits and other souvenirs, and some of his furniture including the table where he wrote *La Nouvelle Héloïse*. At the end of the small garden is the tiny pavilion ('mon donjon') where he would retire to work. Alas, the view that he knew down over the valley is now largely blotted out by the new suburban sprawl that surrounds Mont-Louis.

When *Emile* was published in 1762, this 'subversive' book so angered the Parliament that it decided on Rousseau's arrest, and he was forced to flee to Switzerland and later to England, not returning to France until 1767. But his six years at Montmorency had been the most fertile of his life, during which time he had completed three of his major works, *Emile*, *Du contrat social*, and *Julie ou la Nouvelle Héloïse*. The last, a long novel in epistolary form, became the most widely read of his works and made a huge moral impact on the France of the time. It was much more than simply the romantic story of Julie d'Etanges, her passionate love-affair with Saint-Preux, and her sublimation of this love when she marries the elderly Baron Wolmar and all three live together in utopian happiness on his estate: it is also a book that is infused with Rousseau's most deeply-held ideas about the need for man to live in close harmony with nature, thus restored to his original innocent and happy state, freed from the corruption of society. The countryside round Montmorency must certainly have influenced him as he wrote this, as did his love for Madame d'Houdetot, with whom he walked in the moonlight. His theme of an ideal prosperous countryside, contrasting with the real misery of peasant France at that time, emerges in the long passage where Saint-Preux is shown round Wolmar's model estate:

What then shall the man of taste do who lives for living, who knows how to make this enjoyment, who seeks true and simple pleasures, and who wants to create a promenade for himself at the gates of his house? He will make it so suitable and agreeable that he can please himself there all the hours of the day, and yet so simple and natural that he will seem to have done nothing. He will assemble water, greenery, shade and freshness, for nature also assembles all these things. He will make nothing symmetrical, for symmetry is the enemy of nature and variety...

Right at the end of his life, in 1778, the now very solitary Rousseau accepted the invitation of his friend and admirer the Marquis de Girardin to come and live in a pavilion on his estate at Ermenonville, over to the north-east of Montmorency, not far from Senlis: but he had been there only five weeks when he died suddenly of a stroke. Girardin was the author of an admired book on landscape gardening, much influenced by Rousseau's ideas and by English styles; his park at Ermenonville he had laid out in the 'English' manner and had adorned it with grottoes, cascades, a 'temple of philosophy' and other gentle follies, all scattered around a pretty lake. When Rousseau died he was buried there on a tiny island; later his body was transferred to the Panthéon, but the tombstone still stands, shaded by poplars. This pleasantly romantic park, largely unchanged, is today so much of a tourist attraction that most people tend to connect Rousseau with Ermenonville far more than with Montmorency. But of course this is incorrect.

Ermenonville appears quite often in the pages of Gérard De Nerval (1808–55), whose dream-like prose-poem *Sylvie* so beautifully evokes his childhood spent in this area. De Nerval was a very curious individual. He was born in Paris, but by the time he was two his mother was dead and his father away in the army, so he was brought up first by a nurse in the hamlet of Loisy, just west of Ermenonville, and then amid cousins at his great-uncle's house in the nearby village of Mortefontaine. Later he travelled widely, steeped himself in German romanticism, became a close friend of Théophile Gautier, drifted around, became steadily more manic-depressive, entered various mental hospitals, and finally killed himself. Not long before he died he wrote *Sylvie*, generally regarded as the masterpiece amongst his many poems and tales. Intermingling the real and imaginary, it expresses a vision of the lost world of childhood, love and innocence that had always been haunting him – and of course the parallel with Alain-Fournier is inescapable, though *Sylvie* is less

The grounds of Port Royal Monastery, beloved of Racine and Pascal.

The colonnaded entrance of Chateaubriand's mansion, La Vallée aux Loups,
and the lovely park where he planted trees.

This hope was never realised, for after Napoleon's defeat Chateaubriand was obliged to sell the house, and he returned to public duties. Today it is open to visitors: they can inspect, *inter alia*, the bedroom of Madame Récamier, who was the writer's closest consolation in the later part of his life. Personally I found La Vallée aux Loups much less interesting than the country house, over to the west of Paris, of another and greater 19th-century writer: Emile ZOLA. This big gabled Victorian villa, outwardly no beauty, is in the village of Medan, near Poissy, in a garden that slopes down to the main Paris–Rouen railway-line, with the Seine just beyond. Zola bought it in 1878, after *L'Assommoir* had made him rich and famous, and from then until his death in 1902 he spent about half of each year there. He gathered around him a circle of younger writers including Maupassant (they jointly published a collection of their stories, under the title of *Les Soirées de Medan*), and in summer he would take his guests for parties in the chalet that he constructed on the island in the river, just opposite. Today the house itself is an extremely well laid-out and fascinating museum, retaining the original décor that Zola chose – stained-glass windows, blue Delft tiles. One room is devoted to documents on the Dreyfus affair, another to family photos including some of Zola's beloved mistress, the laundry-girl Jeanne Rozerot, who bore his children. Upstairs is the big high-ceilinged study where he worked on the later Rougon-Macquart novels, facing out across the garden to the woods by the river.

I know few other museums in France that evoke so vividly the life and work of a writer, even if the surroundings are more built-over than when he knew them. The island chalet has made way for a public swimming-pool; hurtling electric trains at the foot of the garden have replaced the old chuff-chuffs, in one of which Zola travelled with the driver to do his research for *La Bête humaine*. On the lawn is a bust of him, scowling and bushy-bearded, looking suitably like his fellow Leftist who is buried in Highgate cemetery. Zola's widow bequeathed the property to the local Assistance Publique (welfare service for the needy) which still uses one side-pavilion as a medical training centre. It also runs the museum, but can afford to open it only at weekends, when local ladies of extreme erudition and enthusiasm show visitors round – a change from the usual kind of museum guide. On my visit in 1988 the museum's future seemed in doubt, for the Assistance Publique was due to end its subsidy, and the Ministry of Culture was still refusing to acquire the building as a State museum, claiming that its contents lacked artistic value.

Just before he bought the house at Medan, Zola made the acquaintance of a young American, Henry JAMES, then living in Paris. This Parisian period in his life later provided James with the material for *The Ambassadors* (1903), which is set mainly in the capital. But in one key scene the elderly Strether, in search of 'French ruralism', takes a train-ride out to some unspecified place beside a river west of Paris, which may well have been somewhere near Medan:

The view of the garden from Zola's house at Medan, with one of the stained-glass windows that he chose.

Zola's study at Medan, where he worked on the later Rougon-Macquart novels.

Towards six o'clock, he found himself amicably engaged with a stout white-capped deep-voiced woman at the door of the *auberge* of the biggest village, a village that affected him as a thing of whiteness, blueness and crookedness, set in coppery green, and that had the river flowing behind or before it – one couldn't say which; at the bottom, in particular, of the inn-garden. . . It may be mentioned without delay that Monsieur had the *agrément* of everything, and in particular, for the next twenty minutes, of a small and primitive pavilion that, at the garden's edge, almost overhung the water, testifying, in its somewhat battered state, to much fond frequentation. . . Strether sat there and, though hungry, felt at peace; the confidence that had so gathered for him deepened within the lap of the water, the ripple of the surface, the rustle of the reeds on the opposite bank, the faint diffuse coolness and the slight rock of a couple of small boats attached to a rough landing-place hard by. The valley on the further side was all copper-green level and glazed pearly sky, a sky hatched across with screens of trimmed trees, which looked flat, like espaliers; and though the rest of the village straggled away in the near quarter the view had an emptiness that made one of the boats suggestive. Such a river sets one afloat almost before one could take up oars. . . What he saw was exactly the right thing – a boat advancing round the bend and containing a man who held the paddles and a lady, at the stern, with a pink parasol. It was suddenly as if these figures, or something like them, had been wanted in the picture, had been wanted more or less all day, and had now drifted into sight. . .

Rousseau might have liked that scene. The couple in the boat could well have been Julie and Saint-Preux, on Wolmar's estate. But of course it is Chadwick Newsome and the Comtesse de Vionnet, their liaison at last revealed.

The flat plains of the Nord are criss-crossed by canals such as this one,
evoked in the writings of Van Der Meersch and others.

6: The North

(Nord-Pas-de-Calais, Picardy and Champagne-Ardennes regions)

The bare and windswept Nord-Pas-de-Calais, where the plains of Flanders, Artois and Hainaut lie studded with the neat war cemeteries of 1914–18 and the conical slagheaps of disused coal-mines, is a region whose literature has come mostly from outside, as a reflection of invasions, industry and tourism. Admittedly, it has produced some good indigenous writing, too, and can lay half-claim to Bernanos and Yourcenar among its natives: but above all it has served as a crossroads and halting place on the routes from Britain or the Low Countries to Paris and the south, and many writers have followed this itinerant tradition. Some came as soldiers in two world wars or earlier conflicts; others, notably Zola, arrived in the 19th century to investigate industrial poverty and exploitation; others again have depicted the area from a tourist standpoint – above all the British, who live so close at hand and yet so far. Except for the Riviera, no other provincial region of France has so often been described by British writers (and some Americans too).

The kind of francophobic culture-shock sometimes experienced by today's first-time day-trippers arriving at Calais or Boulogne was felt most acutely in 1763 by the supposedly sophisticated Tobias Smollett. Perhaps he should have known better, even though it can be said in his defence that not only was sea travel more hazardous then than now, but the French customs officials were infinitely more severe. At the start of his *Travels through France and Italy*, SMOLLETT with his usual truculence describes how, at the entrance to Boulogne harbour, he and his family were obliged to disembark from their packet boat and then shift from one small dinghy to another in the open sea: 'We were afterwards rowed a long league, in a rough sea, against wind and tide, before we reached the harbour, where we landed, benumbed with cold, and the women excessively sick: from our landing-place we were obliged to walk very near a mile to the inn. . .' As if this were not enough, Smollett then had his luggage searched minutely and had to pay customs dues on his bed and table linen and his silver, while his beloved stock of books was impounded and sent to Amiens for scrutiny (works judged prejudicial to State or Church were not allowed to enter France in those days – a habit since copied by other regimes). 'I know of no country in which strangers are worse treated, with respect to their essential concerns. If a foreigner dies in France, the king seizes all his effects.'

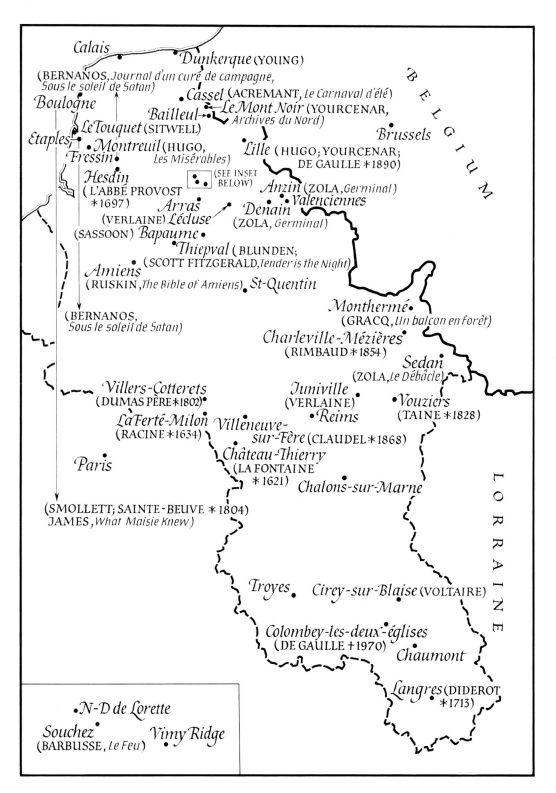

Calais
Dunkerque (YOUNG)
(BERNANOS, *Journal d'un curé de campagne,*
Sous le soleil de Satan)
Boulogne
Cassel (ACREMANT, *Le Carnaval d'été*)
Bailleul Le Mont Noir (YOURCENAR,
Archives du Nord)
Étaples Le Touquet (SITWELL)
Montreuil (HUGO,
Fressin *Les Misérables*)
Lille (HUGO; YOURCENAR;
DE GAULLE *1890)
Brussels
(SEE INSET
BELOW)
Hesdin
(L'ABBÉ PROVOST Anzin (ZOLA, *Germinal*)
*1697) Valenciennes
Arras Lécluse
(VERLAINE) Denain
(SASSOON) Bapaume (ZOLA, *Germinal*)
Thiepval (BLUNDEN;
(SCOTT FITZGERALD, *Tender is the Night*)
Amiens
(RUSKIN, *The Bible of Amiens*) St-Quentin
Monthermé
(GRACQ, *Un balcon en forêt*)
(BERNANOS,
Sous le soleil de Satan)
Charleville-Mézières
(RIMBAUD *1854)
Sedan
(ZOLA, *Le Débâcle*)
Villers-Cotterets Juniville
(DUMAS PÈRE *1802) (VERLAINE) Vouziers
Reims (TAINE *1828)
La Ferté-Milon Villeneuve-
(RACINE *1634) sur-Fère (CLAUDEL *1868)
Paris Château-Thierry
(LA FONTAINE
*1621) Chalons-sur-Marne
(SMOLLETT; SAINTE-BEUVE *1804
JAMES, *What Maisie Knew*)

BELGIUM

LORRAINE

Troyes Cirey-sur-Blaise (VOLTAIRE)

Colombey-les-deux-églises
(DE GAULLE +1970) Chaumont

Langres (DIDEROT
*1713)

N-D de Lorette
Souchez Vimy Ridge
(BARBUSSE, *Le Feu*)

The serene Boulonnais countryside contrasts with the starkness of Bernanos' novels set in the area.

The hypochondriacal Smollett found the climate of Boulogne as 'unhealthy' as its manners were unfriendly. After suffering 'a great discharge by expectoration' he decided to plunge into the sea – 'by this desperate remedy, I got a fresh cold in my head: but my stiches and fever vanished the very first day.' He goes on to complain, about the 'putrid vapours' from the marshes by the harbour:

This may be one cause of the scrofula and rickets, which are two prevailing disorders among the children in Boulogne. But I believe the former is more owing to the water used in the Lower Town, which is very hard and unwholesome. It curdles with soap, gives a red colour to the meat that is boiled in it, and, when drank by strangers, never fails to occasion pains in the stomach and bowels; nay, sometimes produces dysenteries.

Boulogne itself he found to be 'a large agreeable town, with broad open streets, excellently paved'. But in the small ramparted Upper Town he came across:

. . . . two or three convents of nuns; in one of which there are several English girls, sent hither for their education. The smallness of the expense encourages parents to send their children abroad to these seminaries, where they learn scarcely anything that is useful, but the French language; but they never fail to imbibe prejudices against the protestant religion, and generally return enthusiastic converts to the religion of Rome. This conversion always generates a contempt for, and often an aversion to, their own country.

As for the people of the area around Boulogne, he found them

very ferocious and much addicted to revenge. Many barbarous murders are committed, both in the town and country; and the peasants, from motives of envy and resentment, frequently set their neighbours' houses on fire. . . The peasants too are often rendered desperate and savage, by the misery they suffer from the oppression and tyranny of their landlords. In this neighbourhood the labouring people are ill lodged and wretchedly fed; and they have no idea of cleanliness.

However, the impressions of other 18th-century British visitors to these sea-ports have been far less harsh. Arthur YOUNG admired the neat houses with gardens built on the dunes near Dunkerque ('the magic of property turns sand to gold'), while the cheerful Lawrence STERNE in *A Sentimental Journey* (1768) derides Smollett under the name of 'Smelfungus' and gaily describes his own flirtation with a pretty lady met in Calais. Nearer to our own day, the young heroine of Henry JAMES' *What Maisie Knew* (1897) is delighted by the colourful life of the port at Boulogne, by the picturesque ramparts of the Upper Town and the walks along the cliffs. And Edith SITWELL in her long poem *Façade* (1923) offers a surreal glimpse of the smartest resort of the Opal Coast:

> For the lady and her friend from Le Touquet
> In the very shady trees upon the sand
> Were plucking a white satin bouquet
> Of foam, while the sand's brassy band
> Blared in the wind.

The art critic and philosopher John RUSKIN paid several visits in his youth to northern France, where his passion for the study of Gothic architecture drew him especially to Amiens' soaring cathedral, in Picardy. This 'fountain of rainbows by the Somme', as he called it, so

'A Madonna in decadence she is, though, for all, or rather by reason of all, her prettiness, and her gay soubrette's smile' – Ruskin on the south transept of Amiens cathedral.

delighted him that later he wrote a whole book about it, *The Bible of Amiens* (1880) which was translated into French by Marcel Proust. Ruskin considers this building 'in dignity inferior to Chartres, in sublimity to Beauvais, in decorative splendour to Rheims, and in loveliness of figure-sculpture to Bourges', and yet he agrees with Viollet le Duc in calling it 'the Parthenon of Gothic Architecture'. He then describes the ideal approach to it:

I *think* the best way is to walk from the Hôtel de France or the Place de Périgord, up the streets of Three Pebbles, towards the railway station – stopping a little as you go, so as to get into a cheerful temper, and buying some bonbons or tarts for the children in one of the charming patissiers' shops on the left. Just past them, ask for the theatre; and just past that, you will find, also on the left, three open arches, through which you can turn, passing the Palais de Justice, and go straight up to the south transept. . .

Today, after heavy destruction in two wars, those three arches are gone. But the Palais de Justice is still there, and so is the ornate Louis XVI façade of the former theatre, albeit now converted into a bank. More surprisingly, there is still a very chic and tempting patisserie in the rue des Trois-Cailloux. Ruskin then goes on to admire the south transept:

It is simple and severe at the bottom, and daintily traceried and pinnacled at the top, and yet seems all of a piece – though it isn't – and everybody *must* like the taper and transparent fretwork of the flèche above, which seems to bend to the west wind. . . And coming up quite to the porch, everybody must like the pretty French Madonna in the middle of it, with her head a little aside, and her nimbus switched a little aside too, like a becoming bonnet. A Madonna in decadence she is, though, for all, or rather by reason of all, her prettiness, and her gay soubrette's smile.

Inside the cathedral, Ruskin enthuses over the apse ('not only the best, but the very *first* thing done *perfectly* in its manner, by Northern Christendom') and especially the renowned flamboyant carvings of the 16th-century choirstalls:

Sweet and young-grained wood it is: oak, *trained* and chosen for such work, sound now as four hundred years since. Under the carver's hand it seems to cut like clay, to fold like silk, to grow like living branches, to leap like living flame. Canopy crowning canopy, pinnacle piercing pinnacle – it shoots and wreathes itself into an enchanted glade, inextricable, imperishable, fuller of leafage than any forest, and fuller of story than any book.

Even fuller of story, and tragically so, is the massive British war memorial on a hilltop at Thiépval, east of Amiens – a 150-foot red-brick arch, visible for miles across the wheat-plains of the Somme. Engraved on it are the names of 73,000 British troops who fell in the Somme battles of 1916 but have no known graves. Several British poets, the best being Wilfred Owen, were among those who fought in this sector between Albert and Bapaume, as well as further north in Artois and Flanders; and their verse reflects the changing mood of the troops, as the initial jaunty patriotism of 1914 gave way to the weary pessimism of the endless trench warfare. Siegfried S A S S O O N was the poet who became the most bitterly pacifist, and in *Blighters* he denounces the insensitive jingoism of the home front and its theatreland:

The stream near Thiepval's 'tragic hill', now so tranquil. Edmund Blunden was among the war poets who endured the Somme battles here, and later Scott Fitzgerald wrote a threnody.

> I'd like to see a Tank come down the stall,
> Lurching to rag-time tunes, of 'Home, sweet Home',
> And there'd be no more jokes in Music-halls
> To mock the riddled corpses round Bapaume.

In *The General* he criticises the cannon-fodder strategy of the general staff:

> Now the soldiers he smiles at are most of 'em dead,
> And we're cursing his staff for incompetent swine.
> 'He's a cheery old card', grunted Harry to Jack
> As they slogged up to Arras with rifle and pack.
> But he did for them all with his plan of attack.

And Edmund BLUNDEN describes *Thiépval Wood (September 1916)*:

> The tired air groans as the heavies swing over, the river-hollows boom:
> The shell-fountains leap from the swamps, and with wild-fire and fume
>   The shoulder of the chalk-down convulses.
> Then jabbering echoes stampede in the slatting wood,
> Ember-black the gibbet trees like bones or thorns protrude
>   From the poisonous smoke – past all impulses.

Today, like so many former battlefields, this area is a tourist venue. In the Newfoundland Regiment's memorial park at Beaumont-Hamel, near Thiépval, some of the original trenches have been preserved and are now neatly grassed over. But in the mid-1920s much of this sector was still a gaunt wasteland. Scott FITZGERALD visited it then, and in *Tender is the Night* Dick Diver drives there from Amiens, in 1925:

In front of him beneath a dingy sky was Beaumont-Hamel; to his left the tragic hill of Thiépval. Dick stared at them through his field glasses, his throat straining with sadness. 'This land here cost twenty lives a foot that summer,' he said to Rosemary... 'See that little stream – we could walk to it in two minutes. It took the British a month to walk to it – a whole empire walking very slowly, dying in front and pushing forward behind. And another empire walked very slowly backwards a few inches a day, leaving the dead like a million bloody rugs. No European will ever do that again in this generation. [?] All my beautiful lovely safe world blew itself up here with a great gust of high explosive,' Dick mourned persistently... After that they got in their car and started back towards Amiens. A thin warm rain was falling on the new scrubby woods and underbrush and they passed great funeral pyres of sorted duds, shells, bombs, grenades, and equipment, helmets, bayonets, gun stocks, and rotten leather, abandoned seven years in the ground.

Over to the north of Arras, in a gap in the woods on Vimy Ridge, two tall and elegant stelae of white stone point skywards like accusing fingers, towering above the industrial plain of the Lens coalfields. This is the magnificent Canadian memorial to those who died in the battles of Artois – and far more beautiful it is than the main French 1914–18 memorial in the area, the neo-byzantine basilica and ossuary of Nôtre-Dame-de-Lorette, high on an adjacent hill. Below it on the plain, the once-

The Canadian war memorial on Vimy Ridge.

destroyed villages such as Vimy, Souchez and Carency are now spruce and prosperous, with their little red-brick villas: apart from the hilltop memorials, the only reminders of the old nightmares are the well-kept war cemeteries and the old church of Ablain-St-Nazaire, whose toothy ruined stump has been kept as a poignant reminder, just like the Gedächtniskirche on West Berlin's Ku'Damm. But those people today who want a more detailed reminder of the horrors of those battles can visit the museum in the Nôtre-Dame-de-Lorette ossuary, with its photographs and newspaper cuttings. Or they can read the French literature about that war, most of which is in prose.

Some of the best is about Verdun (see p. 192). But the Artois battles are memorably evoked in Céline's lurid book *Voyage au bout de la nuit* (1932), and above all in Henri BARBUSSE's masterly *Le Feu* (1916). This is much the most powerful French novel about 1914–18 war. Barbusse, a man of the Left, had a Provençal father and, curiously, a Yorkshire mother. When the war came he was forty-one and a pacifist: but he volunteered and enlisted, fought in the trenches, and after he was wounded and hospitalised he turned his trench diaries into a novel which won the Prix Goncourt in 1917. It caused a furore, for its chillingly

The view from the memorial and ossuary of Nôtre-Dame-de-Lorette.

accurate picture of the horrors of the fighting did not endear its author to a Government and High Command that were trying to keep up morale and press for victory. Later Barbusse became an active Communist. One passage in *Le Feu* describes a night patrol:

> We have followed a road and have crossed the ruins of Ablain-Saint-Nazaire. . . We have paddled in swampy fields, lost ourselves in silent places where the mud seized us by the feet, we have dubiously regained our balance and our bearings again on another road, the one which leads from Carency to Souchez. The tall bordering poplars are shivered and their trunks mangled; in one place the road is an enormous colonnade of trees destroyed. . . Soon there is a sparkling of brilliant stars and a sudden jungle of fiery plumes on the hill; and a fairy mirage of blue and white hangs lightly before our eyes in the full gulf of night. . . Behind us we leave ruined Souchez, whose houses are only flat heaps of rubbish and her trees but humps of bramble-like slivers. We plunge into a hole on our left, the entrance to the communication trench. . . Buried in our holes up to the chin, our chests heaving against the solid bulk of the ground that protects us, we watch the dazzling and deepening drama develop. The bombardment is redoubled. The trees of light on the ridge have melted into hazy parachutes in the pallor of dawn, sickly heads of Medusae with points of fire; then, more sharply defined as the day expands, they become bunches of smoke-feathers, ostrich feathers white and grey, which come suddenly to life on the jumbled and melancholy soil of Hill 119, five or six hundred yards in front of us, and then slowly fade away. They are truly the pillar of fire and the pillar of cloud, circling as one and thundering together.

Barbusse achieves his effect through sustained poetic realism. In chapter after chapter of bold imagery, he details the horrors of exploding shells and rotting corpses, the stench of the trenches and the cries of the wounded, the agony of a bayonet charge under machine-gun fire. This is his picture of the big night attack on the German lines, across no man's land under heavy fire:

> The blast of one explosion so burns my hands that I let my rifle fall. I pick it up again, reeling, and set off in the tawny-gleaming tempest with lowered head, lashed by spurts of dust and soot in a crushing downpour like volcanic lava. The stridor of the bursting shells hurts your ears, beats you on the neck, goes through your temples, and you cannot endure it without a cry; your stomach turns and sickens with the stench of sulphur. The gusts of death drive us on, lift us up, rock us to and fro. . . We have to go through that whirlwind of fire and those fearful showers that vertically fall. We are passing through. We are through it, by chance. Here and there I have seen forms that spun round and were lifted up and laid down, illumined by a brief reflection over yonder. I have glimpsed strange faces that uttered some sort of cry – you could see them without hearing them in the roar of annihilation.

At another point, a *poilu* is describing the impact of German attacks:

> Besse got a bit of a shell that went clean through his belly and stomach. Barthélémy and Baubex got it in the head and neck. . . And little Godefroy – did you know him? – middle of his body blown away. . . And Mondain – that was the day after, yesterday in fact, in a dug-out that a shell smashed in. He was lying down and his chest was crushed. . . Vigile was with them too; his body wasn't touched, but they found him with his head completely flattened out, flat as a pancake, and huge – big as *that*. To see it spread out on the ground, black and distorted, it made you think of his shadow. . .

Later the squad enters a captured enemy trench, full of dead:

A German sergeant-major is seated. . There is a little hole under his eye; the thrust of a bayonet has nailed him to the planks through his face. In front of him, also sitting, with his elbows on his knees and his fists on his chin, there is a man who has all the top of his skull taken off like a boiled egg. Beside them – an awful watchman! – the half of a man is standing, a man sliced in two from scalp to pelvis, upright against the earthen wall. I do not know where the other half of this human post may be, whose eye hangs down above and whose bluish viscera curl spirally round his leg.

But in the final paragraph of the book, though it is still only 1916, Barbusse allows himself a glimmer of hope: 'And while we get ready to rejoin the others and begin war again, the dark and storm-choked sky slowly opens above our heads. Between two masses of gloomy cloud a tranquil gleam emerges; and that line of light, so black-edged and beset, brings even so its proof that the sun is there.'

In a clear light on a fine day, the view from the summit of Nôtre-Dame-de-Lorette is impressive, even sombrely beautiful, as the wind drives the distant banked clouds and the eye travels down to the slag-heaps and cooling-towers, and across to the plain of Flanders stretching northwards to the sea and into Belgium, its horizons jabbed by high redbrick belfry-towers. French Flanders, despite its flatness and its war memories, is not an area that I find depressing, for it has a strong and pleasing individu-ality. Its farms and villages are today well-tended, prosperous and picturesque, and its hard-workng people have always manifested a remarkable resilience. Among them it has produced a number of writers whose novels and poems depict the toil of textile factories and workshops, the boisterous Lenten carnivals and other local customs, and the misty melancholy landscape. Surprisingly, in view of the notorious language division in Belgium, much of the best poetry in French about Flanders has been written by Belgians: among them is that most charismatic of modern bards, the late Jacques Brel, born in Brussels, who has wistfully celebrated 'ce plat pays qui est le mien' (the title of one of his songs). Since Flanders is a single unity, I shall allow myself to overstep the territorial brief of my book by crossing the frontier to quote from another Belgian poet writing in French, Emile VERHAEREN (1855–1916), whose Le Moulin beautifully evokes this region:

> Le moulin tourne au fond du soir, très lentement,
> Sur un ciel de tristesse et de mélancholie,
> Il tourne et tourne, et sa voile, couleur de lie,
> Est triste et faible, et lourde, et lasse, infiniment.
>
> Depuis l'aube, ses bras, comme des bras de plainte,
> Se sont tendus et sont tombés; et les voici
> Qui retombent encore, là-bas, dans l'air noirci
> Et le silence entier de la nature éteinte.
>
> Un jour souffrant d'hiver parmi les loins s'endort,
> Les nuages sont las de leurs voyages sombres,

Et le long des taillis qui ramassent leurs ombres,
Les ornières s'en vont vers un horizon mort.

(The mill turns in the depths of evening, very slowly / against a sky of sadness and melancholy, / It turns and turns, and its sail, a purple-red, is sad and weak, and heavy, and infinitely weary. // Since dawn, its arms, like the arms of lament, / have become taut and have fallen; and there they are / falling again, over there, in the darkening air / and the whole silence of nature grows dim. // A suffering winter's day falls distantly asleep, / the clouds are weary of their sombre journeys, / and alongside the coppices with their gathering shadows, / the cart-tracks lead away to a dead horizon.)

On this plain between Lille and Dunkerque there has never been much sense of frontier, for the interchange has always been close between the Flemings on both sides, bound by their common culture; and especially is this so in today's Euro-age when teenagers flock over to each other's discos and a motorist crossing the border is seldom asked to stop his car. Only the customs officers, in their age-old battle with professional smugglers, have sought to preserve some reality of a frontier – a cat-and-mouse conflict that is well described in *La Maison dans la dune* (1932), a novel by Maxence VAN DER MEERSCH, set in the marshlands near the coast. His central character is a smuggler:

> He crossed the frontier without noticing it, in this flat and naked plain, as empty as the immense dome of sky that covered it. It was what is known here as the '*moers*', land that men have slowly won back from the sea and that in its desert-like nudity, in the monotony of its bare horizons, in its uniform stretches where the wind runs freely, still keeps something of the grandeur and melancholy of its maritime past. Pastures and fields of oats and rye divide this plain. And water, the enemy that has to be constantly contained, wells up everywhere, permeates the land, and can be detected immediately beneath the poor and sandy soil.

A more cheerful picture of Flemish life and landscape is given in the novels of another local writer, Germaine ACREMANT, born at St-Omer in 1889 and author of the slight but charming *Ces dames aux chapeaux verts*. Her book *Le carnaval d'été* is set in the tiny town of Cassel, perched atop one of the chain of isolated hump-shaped hills that punctuate the plain between St-Omer and Ypres:

> The Flemish plain is coloured like an oriental carpet with the ochre of the fields, the crimson of the tiled roofs, the green of the meadows, the mauve-grey of the towns, the pale yellow of the roads. On the horizon, the sea is lost in the firmament. The dunes form a silvery line... The skies of the terrace of Cassel are full of powerful emotion. The genius of Ruysdael seems to hover there. The great winds from the nearby sea unfurl fantastic cavalcades of clouds.

Above all, this part of Flanders was the *pays* of the historical novelist Marguerite YOURCENAR, the first and still the only woman ever to be elected to that bastion of male chauvinism, the Académie Française. She was born in Brussels in 1903 to a Belgian mother and a French Flemish father, Michel Cleenewerck de Crayencour (her pen-name Yourcenar is a near-anagram): then till the age of nine she spent the winters of her childhood in the family's town house in the old part of Lille, at 26 rue

The coastal dunes near the Belgian frontier, evoked by Maxence Van Der Meersch.

Jean-Moulin, near the Palais de Justice, and the summers in the family's château on the summit of Le Mont-Noir, so called because in those days it was covered with dark fir-trees. This is another in the chain of Flemish '*monts*', and it stands right on the frontier near Bailleul, north-west of Lille. It was here that Yourcenar was first imbued with that deep love of nature and of animals that was to mark her writing and that led her in later years to champion ecological causes from her home in Maine, USA. She has written in one book of memoirs, *Souvenirs Pieux*:

The strongest souvenirs are those of Mont-Noir because there I learned to love all that I love still; the grass and the wild flowers amid the grass; the orchards, the trees, the pinewoods, the horses and the cows in the wide meadows; my she-goat, whose horns my father had gilded; the she-ass Martine and the donkey-foal Printemps, my mounts, especially the she-ass whom early on I learned was sacred among all creatures because she bears on her back the trace of a cross for having served to carry Jesus on Palm Sunday; my sheep who loved to roll in the grass, the rabbits playing freely in the underwood whom I still love with a great love...

In 1912 the family moved to Paris and sold the château, which was then destroyed in the First World War. But the newer mansion in its grounds is today being converted into a literary and ecological centre in memory of Yourcenar, who died in Maine in 1987; you can stroll there and enjoy the view that inspired her, down through the trees to the tall graceful belfries of Bailleul and the distant industry of Artois. In the village of St-Jans-Cappel, just below, is a small Yourcenar museum. She returned several times to Le Mont-Noir in her closing years. Curiously, she set none of her novels in the area: but her fine book *Archives du Nord* traces the history of her own family in Flanders back to the Middle Ages ('In studying these ancestors of mine, I thought I could recognise in myself a little of what I call "the slow-burning Flemish ardour"' – *la lente fougue flamande*). This book in its opening pages also expresses an ecologist's horror at what man has done to nature and to landscape:

Towards Lille, Anzin and Lens, beneath the humus raked up by the exploitation of the mines, fossilised forests lie huddled, the geological residue of another and even more immemorial cycle of climates and seasons. From Malo-les-Bains to L'Ecluse, the undulating dunes built by the sea and the wind have in our time been defiled by coquette villas, lucrative casinos and little shops both luxurious and trashy, not to mention the military installations – cluttered rubbish that in ten thousand years to come will be indistinguishable from the organic and inorganic debris that the sea has slowly pulverised into sand.

The gently rolling and much less polluted country to the west, toward Boulogne and Le Touquet, was the birthland of two other important writers – l'Abbé Prevost, author of *Manon Lescaut*, born at Hesdin in 1697, and the critic Charles-Augustin Sainte-Beuve, born in Boulogne in 1804. Both soon moved elsewhere, and neither wrote much about the area. However, the devoutly Catholic writer Georges BERNANOS (1888–1948), though he was born and died in Paris, had some roots in the Boulonnais: he spent part of his adolescence in the village of Fressin, north of Hesdin, where his father had a villa. This *'vieille chère maison dans les arbres'* was destroyed by fire in 1940, but a plaque on its brick gateway today recalls Bernanos' stay; and it was during his wanderings in the neighbourhood that he met and talked with young country priests of the kind whom he later made the heroes of his two most famous novels, both set in this area – *Sous le soleil de Satan* (1926) and *Journal d'un curé de campagne* (1936). In these books Bernanos jumbles the topography, and many of his village names are fictitious: but 'Campagne' where the first novel is set and 'Ambricourt' in the second are both possibly modelled on Fressin, whose handsome church with its square slate-tiled tower may have been in his mind when describing the church at 'Lumbres' (*not* the real Lumbres near Calais) where the saintly Abbé Donissan of *Sous le soleil de Satan* later becomes curé:

The sanctuary light revealed little by little, in the night, the arches of the big triple-mullioned windows. The old tower, built between the choir and the vast nave, rose up with its timbered spire and heavy belfry. He [Donissan] no longer saw them. He was

Near Fressin in the Boulonnais, where Bernanos' young priests fought their lone spiritual struggles.

standing, facing the darkness, alone, as on the prow of a ship, the great wave of sombre darkness rolled around with a superhuman sound. From the four corners of the horizon the invisible fields and woods came rushing towards him . . . and behind the fields and woods other villages and other little towns, all the same, bursting with plenty, enemies of the poor, full of crouching misers, cold as shrouds. . .

There is a famous allegorical scene in this novel where the anguished Donissan endures a 'dark night of the soul' as he walks over the bare chalky hills towards Etaples, meets with Satan in the guise of a horse-dealer and receives his terrible kiss. (This same location was recently used by Maurice Pialat when shooting the film of the book; it won the Grand Prix at Cannes in 1987, and starred Gérard Depardieu and Sandrine Bonnaire.) Bernanos' young priests, locked in what so often they fear will be a losing struggle between good and evil for the soul of man, live and work in villages that in those days were desperately poor and backward, and the author searingly depicts a feudal peasant society, racked by the cancers of superstition, intolerance and social injustice. The *curé de campagne* describes at the start of his *Journal* his view of Ambricourt in the rain:

Suddenly I saw the village, so huddled up, so wretched beneath the hideous November sky. The water streamed down on it from all sides, and it seemed to be lying there, in the dripping grass, like a poor exhausted animal. How small it is, a village! And this one was my parish. It was my parish, but I could do nothing for it, sadly I looked at it plunging into the night and disappearing. In a few moments I would see it no more. Never had I felt so cruelly its solitude and my own. It made me think of the cattle that I heard coughing in the fog and that the little cowherd, on his way from school with his satchel under his arm, would soon be leading through the drenched pastures towards the warm, odorous stable. And the village itself, it seemed to be waiting too – without great hope – after so many other nights spent in the mud, for a master it could follow towards some improbable, unimaginable refuge.

Today, fifty or so years later, this gloomy picture has improved at least to the extent that the villages in this area are now strikingly prosperous, with their spruce white farmhouses, gleaming silos, and wheatgrowers driving new Citroëns and BMWs, and doing very nicely from EEC subsidies. But undoubtedly the villagers are less religious-minded than in former days and the influence of the curé has waned. Would Donissan, if he were alive, regard these changes as a victory for God or for Satan?

A view over the Nord-Pas-de-Calais coal basin that was the setting for Zola's Germinal.

Other chroniclers of the sufferings of the poor in the Nord-Pas-de-Calais have come from outside in a spirit of social enquiry and polemic – notably Hugo and Zola. The walled hilltop town of Montreuil, in the Bernanos country between Hesdin and Etaples, is doubly well-known to the British today. First, as the home of a stylish and very gastronomic hotel/ restaurant, the Château; and secondly as the scene of early chapters in a French classic novel whose rock musical adaptation has broken London box-office records. It is to Montreuil that HUGO's Valjean comes incognito in 1815 after stealing the bishop's candlesticks in Digne; here he turns over a new leaf, revives the town's jet-bead industry, is elected mayor, and helps the local peasantry by teaching them 'how to destroy corn-moth by spraying the barn and soaking the cracks in the floor with a solution of common salt, and how to get rid of boll-weevil by hanging bunches of orviot in blossom on the walls'. Curiously, Hugo's wordy saga contains no description of the town of Montreuil; nor is this where he sets his true *misérables*, apart from the hapless Fantine. However, he found others even more poor and wretched when in 1851 he went to Lille, and inspected slum cellars where families were living in appalling overcrowded conditions. In the *Lettres à Adèle* (his wife), he recounts a visit to one dark and airless cellar where a girl of six, feverish with measles, was lying almost naked on a pile of rotting straw: 'Beside her bed was a great pile of cinders that gave out a repulsive stench. It is peat-ash that these unhappy families collect and sell for living. If necessary the ash serves them as a bed.'

In much of his work Victor Hugo was at pains to shed light on the conditions of the poor in 19th-century France – and so even more passionately was Emile ZOLA, who was writing somewhat later, mostly in the 1870s and 1880s. When he decided to devote one novel in his

Rougon-Macquart series to the struggles of the Nord miners, in order to collect material he made a special visit in 1884 to Denain and Anzin in the Valenciennes coal-basin – and the result was *Germinal*, which many critics regard as his finest work. It is somewhat over-melodramatic in places, in the Zola manner, and maybe a touch exaggerated in its picture of the coarse brutishness of the underpaid mining families and their lives, and the horrors of their work below ground: but it is superbly vivid, exciting and impressive as well as compassionate, and as a social document it is of huge importance. Zola's ability on one short trip to have mastered so swiftly the technicalities of mining, as well as the complex social structure of miners and employers, and then to have described it all so cogently, remains an astonishing journalistic achievement. Near the start of the book, his hero Etienne Lantier (son of Gervaise Macquart of *L'Assommoir*) arrives on a hill above the mining town of Montsou (an amalgam of Denain and Anzin) and surveys the weary scene:

Could he not hear a cry of famine borne over this bleak country by the March wind? The gale had lashed itself into a fury and seemed to be blowing death to all labour and a great hunger that would finish off men by the hundred... Everything slid away into the dark unknown, and all he could see was distant furnaces and coke-ovens which, set in batteries of a hundred chimneys arranged obliquely, made sloping

lines of crimson flames; whilst further to the left the two blast-furnaces were burning
blue in the sky like monstrous torches. It was as depressing to watch as a building on
fire: as far as the threatening horizon the only stars which rose were the nocturnal
fires of the land of coal and iron.

Etienne then finds work in the mine of Le Voreux:

The pit gulped down men in mouthfuls of twenty or thirty and so easily that it did
not seem to notice them going down. The descent to work began at four; the men
came from the locker-room barefoot and lamp in hand, and stood about in little
groups until they were enough of them. Like some nocturnal beast the cage, with its
four decks each containing two tubs, leaped noiselessly out of the darkness and settled
itself on its keeps.

Girls from the age of ten are working long hours half-naked down this
mine, where the pitheads above are 'squat and evil-looking', the yards
around are 'like a lake of ink with heaps of coal for waves', and the slag-
heap is 'rising colossal like a giant's earthwork'. And as for the miners'
housing on this Nord plain:

The whole *département* is turning into a single industrial city. The little brick
houses, colour-washed to make up for the climate, some yellow, some blue, but

others black (perhaps so as to reach the ultimate black with the least delay), ran down the hill, twisting to right and left. Here and there the line of little huddled façades was broken by a large two-storeyed house, the home of some manager. A church, built of brick like everything else, looked like some new type of blast-furnace, with its square tower already black with coal-dust. But what stood out most of all among the sugar-refineries, rope-works and sawmills, was the immense number of dance-halls, bars, pubs – there were over five hundred of them to a thousand houses.

The miners find release from their toil in endless beer-drinking and drunken brawling, and other activities. Everywhere, on a fine day, Etienne finds couples coupling openly in the fields and factory yards:

The girls developed early in the coalfields... fourteen-year-olds already corrupted in the promiscuity of poverty... He was now at Requillart, where all the Montsou girls used to prowl around with their lovers in the ruins of the disused mine. This lonely, remote spot was the common meeting-place where haulage girls picked up their first baby when they did not dare to do so on the shed roof at home... It was as though round this dead machine, by this pit worn out with bringing forth coal, the life-force was taking its revenge in the untrammelled love which used the lash of instinct, and planted children in the wombs of those who were scarcely more than children themselves.

Later the miners go on strike in protest against a cut in their wages, and an angry mob of working families begins to attack the local bourgeoisie:

The women had come into sight, nearly a thousand of them, dishevelled after their tramp, in rags through which could be seen their naked flesh worn out with bearing children doomed and starved. Some of them had babies in their arms and raised them aloft and waved them like flags of grief and vengeance. Others, younger, with chests thrown out like warriors, were brandishing sticks, whilst the old crones made a horrible sight as they yelled so hard that the strings in their skinny necks looked ready to snap. The men brought up the rear: two thousand raving madmen, pit-boys, colliers, repairers in a solid phalanx moving in a single block, so closely packed together that neither their faded trousers nor their ragged jerseys could be picked out from the uniform earth-coloured mass. All that could be seen was their blazing eyes and the black holes of their mouths singing the *Marseillaise*... And indeed rage, hunger and two months of suffering and then this wild stampede through the pits, had lengthened the placid features of the Montsou miners into something resembling the jaws of wild beasts. The last rays of the setting sun bathed the plain in blood, and the road seemed like a river of blood as men and women, bespattered like butchers in a slaughterhouse, galloped on and on.

As Zola's lurid epic moves to its climax, fighting breaks out between the Army and the strikers; then a cynical Communist agent sabotages the pit, causing flooding and much loss of life, and finally the whole minehead collapses:

There was a volley of underground detonations, a monstrous cannonade in the bowels of the earth. On the surface the last buildings toppled over and crumpled up. First a sort of whirlwind blew away the ruins of the screening-shed and top landing. Then the boiler-house burst asunder and disappeared. Next the square tower containing the gasping-pump fell on its face like a man shot down. And then a terrifying thing: they saw the engine, torn from its bed, wrestling against death with dislocated limbs. It moved, stretching its crank, its gigantic knee, as though it meant

Little remains today of the now disused minehead at the Terril Bernard in Denain, where Zola researched Germinal.

to rise, but it fell back dead, smashed to smithereens, and was swallowed up. . . this was the end. The evil beast [Zola's frequent term for the mine] crouching in its hollow, sated with human flesh, had drawn its last long heavy breath. Le Voreux had sunk into the abyss, every bit of it. The crowd fled, screaming. Women ran alone holding their hands in front of their eyes. A wind of terror blew men along like a heap of dry leaves.

By now the long and bitter strike has ended, without results, and the miners are drifting back to work in other pits. Etienne leaves the area, disappointed: yet he feels that, although this particular struggle has failed, it will be the germinal force for others to come, for soon the miners will form unions and finally they will win their fight against exploitation. And on this note of hope *Germinal* ends:

The April sun was now well up in the sky, shedding its glorious warming rays on the teeming earth. Life was springing from her fertile womb, buds were bursting into leaf and fields were quickening with fresh green grass. . . On and on, ever more insistently, his comrades were tapping, as though they too were rising through the ground. On this youthful morning, in the fiery rays of the sun, the whole country was alive with this sound. Men were springing up, a black avenging host was slowly germinating in the furrows, thrusting upwards for the harvest of future ages. And very soon their germination would crack the earth asunder.

It was not hard for Zola to produce this prophetic touch, for although he set his story in the 1860s he did not write it till the 1880s, by which time the Second Empire had given place to the more socially progressive Third Republic and conditions in the mines had improved: female labour below ground had been made illegal in 1874, and the unions were by now fairly strong and active. Today, a century later, such coal-mining as still continues in France is of course fully modernised and the work is relatively comfortable and well paid: so the miners' old struggle is largely won. And yet, this industrial sector around Valenciennes remains poor and grim-looking by the standards of today's sleek and prosperous France, and the reason is somewhat ironic: whereas in the old days the greedy mines provided plenty of jobs but dismal pay, today the wages are good but work is hard to find in this area. There is still some mining to the west, between Douai and Béthune, but the Valenciennes seam is exhausted and its pits have closed, while the local steelmills too are in dire trouble; some replacement industries arrived in the booming 1960s, but their flow has now slowed and the dole-queues lengthen.

Anzin, in the northern suburbs of Valenciennes, and Denain to its west today both claim to be the original of Zola's Montsou, and probably both are right for he did his fieldwork in both; his book also refers frequently to the real village of Marchiennes, which he locates close to Montsou though in fact it is some way to the north-west. In the *coron* (settlement) of Beuvrages on the outskirts of Anzin, I saw rows of the same squat yellowbrick miners' cottages that Zola knew, standing beside disused slag-heaps on the edge of the polluted forest of St-Amand-Wallers (this is the forest of Vandame in *Germinal* where the miners held their prestrike rally). The roads in the *coron* were muddy and pot-holed, rubbish was everywhere, the houses looked very shabby and many seemed to be empty. Vermilion Communist Party posters adorned some walls. Three youths stood listlessly at a corner, and they told me they were all out of work. Zola would have found less sheer hunger than in his day, but also less teeming liveliness and working-class solidarity.

At Denain, the civic museum contains a photocopy of the letter authorising Zola to visit the local mining company's installation. Many of the pitheads' *terrils* (slag-heaps) have now been cleared away, but on the Douai road the great pyramid of the Terril Bernard, partly grassed over, has been carefully preserved: this mine was the scene of several violent strikes and conflicts in Zola's time and his Le Voreux is said to have been inspired by it. Nearby, the former Coron Jean-Bart was a model for the 'Coron 240' of *Germinal* with its 'four great blocks of little back-to-back houses' (it has now given place to the municipal music conservatory). So how does this area today regard Zola? For some years after the publication of *Germinal* the unions were furious at his unflattering portrait of the miners and their coarse ways, and anti-Zola songs were written and sung by the workers. But he is now forgiven: Communist-ruled Denain proudly has its Parc Emile Zola, while Anzin has its Collège Germinal. The miners' crusades as well as Zola's telling of them have become a major part of local history.

But, in sum, what a litany of woe and suffering, on so many levels, is the literature of this Nord-Pas-de-Calais region in modern times! – from Zola's exploited miners to the trench-warfare depicted by Barbusse, and then Bernanos with his tormented priests and destitute peasantry.

The drums of war literature beat scarcely less dolefully on the other side of the regional border, in the Ardennes – and here again we are in Zola country. When Jean Macquart, the hero of *La Terre* (see p. 84), joins up to fight the Prussians, he moves with his regiment to defend Sedan and thus takes part in *La Débâcle* of the French Army's monumental defeat in September 1870. In this novel, the fictional characters are mere lay figures in a vast historical semi-documentary, sweepingly panoramic and again brilliantly researched: Zola was not himself present at the battle of Sedan, but he interviewed scores of eye-witnesses and the result, *La Débâcle* (1892), gives a sharp and detailed picture (maybe a little exaggerated for dramatic effect) of the battle itself and its aftermath. Zola is derisively critical of the muddled incompetence of the French leadership, and this led him after the book's publication to be castigated by the Army and the Church for 'demoralising' the French nation: he always claimed however that he was not being anti-patriotic but was trying to show how the rank-and-file had been betrayed by its own generals. The book evokes the sheer chaos of war, the stench and the filth in the streets of Sedan, and the agony of the wounded – for example in this scene just outside the town at the end of the battle:

Gradually the tragic slaughtered forest was filled not only with the sobbing or dying trees but also with the shrieking pain of wounded men. At the foot of an oak tree, Maurice and Jean saw a Zouave, his belly torn open, howling continuously like a slaughtered animal. Further on, another was on fire: his blue sash had caught alight, the spreading flame was singeing his beard, and, unable to move because of his broken ribs, he was weeping bitterly. Then it was a captain, his left arm torn away, the whole right side of his body ripped open, who was dragging himself along on his elbows, imploring someone to put him out of his misery, in a shrill pleading voice.

In the days before film and TV cameras, this kind of reporting even when reconstructed later from eye-witnesses certainly made a much greater impact than it would today on a public sated with newsreel footage of Buchenwald or Vietnam. Some of Zola's best pages deal with the battle for Bazeilles, a village just south-east of Sedan, where civilians and soldiers together heroically contest the German advance house by house: 'The gutters ran with blood, the road was choked with corpses, the cross-roads were little more than charnel-houses, filled with the cries of the dying.' One of the main civilian characters, Weiss, tries to defend his own home; when the ammunition runs out, the Germans burst in and execute him in front of his wife. Zola certainly had in mind the famous episode at Bazeilles of the 'house of the last cartridge', when a group of French soldiers held out till they could fire no more. This Maison de la Dernière Cartouche is today a small museum filled with relics of the battle of Bazeilles; the elderly lady in charge of it seemed eager to give me details of the 'atrocities' committed by the Bavarian soldiers and their Prussian officers and of how 43 civilians were summarily shot without trial. Two world wars and a friendly peacetime later, anti-German feeling has today largely disappeared from France: but I still found it embedded in tribal memories in the Sedan area, where one youngish writer told me, *'Toujours on n'aime pas les Boches ici.'*

The Maison de la Dernière Cartouche at Bazeilles, near Sedan.

The beauty of the country round Sedan which, according to Zola,
so impressed Kaiser Wilhelm on his day of victory.

From the wooded hilltop just south of Sedan, by the village of Noyers, one can gain a clear impression of how the great battle developed, as the Prussian armies moved forward on either side of the Meuse to encircle the garrison of Sedan (today rebuilt in hideous style after more fighting in 1940) and to trap other French armies in the loop of the river to the north-west. It is on this same vantage-point of La Marfée that Kaiser Wilhelm stands, surveying his victory as the battle ends:

> The sun, slanting towards the woods, was about to set in an almost cloudless sky. It gilded the whole vast countryside, bathing it in a light so limpid that the smallest detail took on an extraordinary vividness. And beneath the sun's last rays, the monstrous blood-soaked battle, seen from above, was like some delicate painting: dead horsemen and disembowelled horses strewed the plain of Floing with patches of bright colour; on the right, towards Givonne, the fleeing men, in a final stampede, were no more than whirling black specks, scurrying hither and thither and tumbling to the ground; while on the peninsula of Igès, to the left, a Bavarian battery, its guns no bigger than matchsticks, looked for all the world like some well-mounted, theatrical spectacle, so clearly could one follow the clockwork regularity of its manoeuvres. This was victory unlooked for, overwhelming victory; and the King looked down upon it without any feeling of remorse, for these tiny corpses, these thousands of men, of no more account than the dust on the roads, this immense valley, the fires at Bazeilles, the massacre at Illy, the anguish of Sedan, could not alter the fact that, in this serene ending to a lovely day, impassive nature still remained beautiful.

This same theme of nature radiant and serene amid the tumult of war emerges with far greater poetic poignancy in a novel of an utterly different kind but also set in the Ardennes, near the Meuse. This is the remarkable *Un balcon en forêt* (1958) by Julien GRACQ, a reclusive and very private writer who deserves to be better known outside France. Set during the *'drôle de guerre'* (phoney war) of September 1939 to May 1940, *Un balcon en forêt* is about the inner feelings of a young subaltern who is sent to command a lonely blockhouse on the Maginot Line, beside the Belgian frontier on the high forested plateau above the Meuse north-east of Monthermé (Moriarmé in the book). As the war is still far away, the officer has little to do all day, and amid this splendid scenery with its wide vistas he has the exhilarating feeling of being on holiday. He goes on a night patrol with his corporal:

> They slipped out of the blockhouse on a night so calm that as they walked away down the road they heard eleven o'clock striking in a church far off in the valley, loud and heavy despite the distance, and then, much closer, the cracked chime of a Belgian belfry. . . To the right, he cast his eye over a long slope of forest descending towards the gullies leading into the Meuse; a wild moon drifted very high above the dark woods; the fumes of smoke from the charcoal-burners' fires, damped down by the cold night air, scattered the flat amphitheatre of the woods with large flakes of ash that turned and floated gently across the night. . . It seemed to him that he was casting his moorings; he was entering a world redeemed and washed clean of mankind, glued to its sky of stars with the swooning surge of empty oceans. 'There is no one in the world but me,' he said to himself in a mood of joyousness that overwhelmed him. . .

Then winter and snow come to this plateau of Le Toit (the roof of the world):

Never so much before as in this winter on the Toit did he feel that his life, all loose and mild, was freed from its attachments, isolated from its past and its future... A sky of violent blue burst upon the festive landscape. The air was acid and almost mild; at mid-day, as one walked down the forest ride, one heard rising from each side-path, in the shafts of sunlight that made the snow sparkle, the thick rumbling of the thaw, but as soon as the horizon of the Meuse grew pink in the short evening, the cold again cast a magic suspense upon the Toit: the sealed-up forest became a trap of silence, a winter garden whose closed gates yielded it up to the coming and going of phantoms. For the snow caught distant gleams of light, and at night the heights of the Meuse were all alive; behind the halo of the cement-works, very often now on a clear night the anti-aircraft searchlights swept the sky of the forest with their quadruple beams of light, on beyond the frontier...

Gracq himself was thirty in 1940, and his book with its aura of felt experience might appear to be autobiographical. But in fact he did his war service elsewhere and came later to the Ardennes, to imbue himself with the landscape. He went east of the Meuse to the plateaux around the hamlets of Les Hauts-Buttés and La Neuville-aux-Haies (the Falizes of his book) where the moorland clearings do indeed offer a roof-of-the-world view over the rolling forests. The wartime blockhouses in this area had by then been removed, but Gracq was able to find one further east, just inside France beside the D29 from Sedan to Sugny – a tiny ruined fort, today squalid and derelict – and this was his model for the 'home' of Lieutenant Grange. Gracq was a professor of geography, fascinated by ancient forests and by sandstone massifs like that through which the Meuse here so grandly winds. His work has a feeling for landscape and for nature that is poetic to the point of being surreal, even mystical, and this leads to the essential theme of *Un balcon en forêt*: Grange's growing alienation from daily reality as he feels himself liberated into a natural universe of his own. As spring arrives, and the German invasion across Belgium seems imminent, at first he has a sense of impending doom, aware that his woodland idyll will soon end:

Never so much as this evening did Grange have the feeling of inhabiting a forest that was lost: all the immensity of the Ardennes was breathing in this clearing full of ghosts, as the heart of a magic forest throbs around its fountain.

Then on May 10 Guderian attacks and the Allied troops and civilians are soon fleeing back across the frontier in panicky disorder, with the Panzers on their heels: but at first the Germans bypass and ignore the blockhouse, so that the calm of nature eerily returns as Grange and his three men are left isolated behind enemy lines. This induces in him a feeling of light-headedness:

It was a rather marvellous kind of fear, almost attractive, that came back to Grange from the depths of childhood and of fairy-tales: the fear of children lost in the forest at twilight, hearing in the distance the crunching of oak-trunks beneath the formidable heels of seven-league boots... The shellfire began to sound less loudly: there were

Julien Gracq's forest balcony above the Meuse:
his feeling for nature was poetic, even mystical.

now long periods of calm, during which they heard the crows again tapping in the oak-grove. 'Perhaps there is not a single Frenchman left east of the Meuse,' he thought as he walked along. . . 'Perhaps there is nothing any more?' The earth seemed to him beautiful and pure as after the flood; two magpies settled on the bank in front of him, like animals in a fable. . .

Finally the Germans do attack the blockhouse, two of his men are killed and the third escapes, and at the end of the book he is left alone, wounded:

Memories turned in his head, which were those of strange land without men – memories of long walks in the winter forest, of afternoons in the blockhouse when all he could see through the window, under the misty sun, were the mild drops of thaw swelling one by one on the tips of the branches. The war, strange and incongruous, was slipping away down there like a river torrent at night whose roar suddenly swells up as it flows to the horizon and subsides into the plain. Stretched out on the ground, the cold began to seize him, but an inexpressible sense of peace came over him.

The Meuse at Charleville, and the millhouse: did Rimbaud's boyhood games here with paper boats inspire Le Bateau ivre?

An imaginative landscape even more other-worldly informs the work of the Ardennes' greatest native writer, Arthur RIMBAUD (1854–91). This turbulent poet spent much of his short life roaming the world: but it was in the town of Charleville-Mézières on the Meuse, where he was born

7: Eastern France

(Lorraine, Alsace, Franche-comté and Burgundy regions)

De Gaulle's wartime emblem, that double cross of Lorraine, comes from a frontier province that has often regarded itself as the foremost citadel of French patriotism. So often invaded, so long disputed between France and Germany, Lorraine has inspired a literature that not surprisingly is strong on themes of wartime suffering and patriotic loyalty. Verdun is here, the subject of many harrowing books. And so is Domrémy, where a peasant girl's crusade to drive the English from France has prompted a great mass of writing, sceptical or otherwise, from Voltaire, Claudel, Anouilh and others – not forgetting Bernard SHAW. At the start of his play, the Maid makes a splendidly bossy stage entrance, in the castle of Vaucouleurs on the Meuse:

> Captain: you are to give me a horse and armour and some soldiers, and send me to the Dauphin. Those are your orders from my Lord.

No French writer of the past hundred years, Lorrain or other, has championed more fervently the old ideals of patriotism than Maurice BARRÈS (1862–1923). Auvergnat on his father's side, but Lorrain from his mother and by birth, he came from Charmes on the Moselle and was schooled in Nancy; most of his novels are set in this area. He espoused the belief that national patriotism must have strong local roots and that a man can best serve his country by staying deeply attached to his native soil: witness his novel *Les Déracinés* ('the uprooted ones', 1897), about a group of young Lorrains who go to Paris to seek success, but become adrift and disillusioned in the big city. Barrès entered politics on the extreme-Right, campaigned against Dreyfus, became an associate of Maurras and a supporter of Boulanger, two of the most reactionary figures of his day, and in the 1914–18 war was president of the Ligue des Patriotes. His semi-mystical nationalism may have served some purpose during that war: but in a peacetime context it appears sinister and fascistic. Today Barrès is thoroughly out of fashion and his books are little read. Even so, one has to admit that he was a powerful writer and fine stylist.

These qualities appear most notably in *La Colline inspirée*, probably his best novel and one of the least jingoistic. Its setting is the 'inspired hill' of Mount Sion which rises above the plain some 20 miles south of Nancy – a spot that for over 2,000 years had been endowed with sacred, magical attributes, first by Celtic pagans, then by early Christians. This fired the imagination of Barrès, a traditional Catholic with a mystical bent, and in the book's opening paragraph he impressively traces the list of those places in France 'where the spirit blows', places 'bathed in

In the distance, beyond the fields of corn, the Colline inspirée of Maurice Barrès.

mystery, elected for all eternity to the seat of religious emotion':
Lourdes; the 'melancholy beach' in the Camargue 'where the Saintes-
Maries direct us toward Sainte-Baume'; 'heroic Vézelay, in Burgundy';
'the caves of Les Eyzies, where the first traces of humanity are revered';
Carnac, in Brittany, with its lines of menhirs; 'the forest of Brocéliande,
where Merlin wails still in his fountain on stormy days'; 'Mont Saint-
Michel, rising up like a miracle from the shifting sands'; 'the black forest
of the Ardennes, all anxiety and mystery'; Domrémy; and some other
places too. Barrès calls them 'open-air temples'.

Lorraine possesses one of these inspired localities. It is the hill of Sion-Vaudrémont, a slight elevation on the most worn of French regions, a kind of altar laid out on a plateau that goes from the cliffs of Champagne to the range of the Vosges. . . a hill set on our vast plain like a table of our unwritten laws, like an appeal to Lorrain fidelity. . . In autumn, the hill is blue beneath a great slate-coloured sky, in an atmosphere penetrated by a soft light of apricot yellow. I love to climb up here on a golden September day, and on the summit to rejoice at the silence, the harmonious hours, the immense sky where clouds slip by and the unceasing wind that buffets us with its weight. A church, a monastery, an inn that has clients only on days of pilgrimage, occupy one of the corners of the crescent-shaped hill; at the other end, the poor village of Vaudrémont, with the two spires of its belfry and its tower, is dying amidst the Roman and feudal debris of its legendary past, a clearly-set and prodigiously isolated little spot in a great landscape of sky and earth. . .

Here Barrès recounts the story – based partly on fact – of the priest Léopold Baillard who in the mid-19th century builds a flourishing Christian community at Sion. For a while it is rich and famous throughout Europe: but gradually Baillard falls victim to his own pride and to the heresy of illuminism, believing in strange visions, symbols and spirits, and practising sacrilegious orgies. The wrath of the Church descends upon him, and finally he is outlawed and forced to retract. Barrès' attitude to the priest is interestingly equivocal. In many ways he sympathises with this charismatic leader, so inspired by the *genius loci*; but he also condemns his error in defying the Church and abusing the mystic forces that come from the hill:

Léopold loved it [the hill], with a love that seemed to come from the very depths of his animal nature. What power did it exercise upon this primitive soul? One thinks of that blue lake of the Vosges whose icy waters infatuated Charlemagne. . . When the clouds are low, on this moorland, there is mystery. Léopold took delight in it, discovering there again those great presentiments of a new order of the world. . .

But Baillard's visionary enthusiasm turns to a kind of madness – and on the final page Barrès pronounces that the eternal creative inspiration of this 'primitive place', valuable in itself, will turn to pagan destructiveness unless purified and guided by the Church. Barrès was the first to give the name 'Colline Inspirée' to this hill. But there had been a cult of the Virgin here since the 4th century, and from the time of the Crusades onwards people would come to Sion to pray for deliverance in time of war, or to give thanks. Just before Barrès' time, in September 1873, there had been a massive pilgrimage, to mourn for the German annexation of Alsace and northern Lorraine, and to offer thanks to God that the southern part of the province, including Nancy and Sion, had been spared this fate. Barrès describes this scene:

On a rostrum set in front of the porch, a cardinal and seven bishops blessed thirty thousand pilgrims who filed past to the chant of canticles and the noise of fanfares, while waving their banners amongst which the crowd acclaimed religiously those of Metz and Strasbourg in mourning.

There was another huge rally in 1920, addressed by Barrès himself, to celebrate the return to France of those provinces; and another again in

1946 when General de Lattre de Tassigny, the Gaullist veteran, laid a marble cross in the presence of 80,000 pilgrims. Then, in the centenary year of 1973, a smaller turn-out of 10,000 attended a ceremony of Franco-German reconciliation – and this, happily, is now a major theme at Sion, where the plaques of some French and German twin-towns lie at the foot of a simple monument to peace and friendship. I myself was more favourably impressed by this than by the Lourdes-like pious kitsch that still invests much of the enormous shrine of Sion: it has cheap souvenir stalls, a missionary museum, a hotel, various grottoes of the Virgin, and a gigantic white statue of Her on the church tower, visible from far across the plain. Two miles along the hilltop is a hideous memorial to Barrès, erected soon after his death: I passed by hurriedly, for by now the mystic spirit of his hill was throwing up unmistakable vibrations of hysterical nationalistic religiosity, and so I went instead to inspect the gaunt ruins of the Brunehaut tower in the semi-derelict village of Vaudrémont, which, plays some role in the novel.

Outside Verdun, on the hills above the Meuse north-east of the town, are the grim battlefields of 1916–18, where 800,000 died – and anyone of any faith or no faith is certain to find them genuinely moving. The various memorials and the excellent museum are entirely devoid of nationalistic feeling but seem to embody what is now Verdun's official designation, 'Haut-lieu de l'humanité' – not of France, nor of Germany, but of all mankind. The theme of reconciliation is here much stronger than in Sion: inside the museum, next to the rooms filled with agonising war scenes, are happy photographs of post-1945 Franco-German youth exchanges, while below the towering ossuary of Douaumont lies the plaque laid in 1987 by Chancellor Kohl and President Mitterrand, pledging their two countries to undying reconciliation and friendship. Above the door of the museum is a quotation from Paul Valéry about those who fought in this battle: 'All came to Verdun, as if to receive I do not know what supreme consecration. They seemed to be moving up the Sacred Way to make an offertory without parallel at the most formidable altar that ever man has erected.' And inside is a sentence from Maurice Genevoix' novel, *Sous Verdun*: 'What we did was more than men can be asked to do, and we did it.' Of the other novels written by survivors of that senseless conflict, perhaps the best known are *Prélude à Verdun* and *Verdun* by Jules ROMAINS, two parts of his lengthy sequence, *Les Hommes de bonne volonté*. These two books, both semi-documentary, severely criticise the French High Command for this needless sacrifice of lives; and, though less powerful and poetic than Barbusse's rather similar *Le Feu* (see p. 161), they give a picture of the battle that is lucid and graphic, and generally held to be accurate:

Over the whole front, from the Bois d'Haumont to Herbebois, taking in the Bois des Caures and the Bois de Ville, to a depth of several kilometres, the same dance of dust, smoke and debris went on, to a thunderous accompaniment of noise. Thousands

Pages 190–91: Lamartine, like Wordsworth, heard in nature the still, sad music of humanity – especially around his childhood home at Milly, in Burgundy.

of men, in groups of two, of three, of ten, sometimes of twenty, bent their backs to the storm, clinging together at the bottom of holes, most of which were no better than scratches in the ground, while many scarcely deserved the name of shelter at all. To their ears came the sound of solid earth rent and disembowelled by bursting shells. Through cracks in the walls that protected them they could breathe in the smell of a tormented world, a smell like that of a planet in the process of being reduced to ashes. Most of them had given up all hope of surviving, though a few still clung to a belief in their lucky star. These were the men who, as like as not, would be killed just as they thought it was all over.

Neighbouring Alsace, despite its strong regional personality, has produced remarkably few significant writers of its own: but many others have come to it as visitors – especially to Strasbourg, its distinguished capital. Johannes Gutenberg of Mainz was not himself a writer: but literature owes an immeasurable debt to his invention of the printing press, which he achieved during the years that he lived in Strasbourg, 1434–48. Voltaire spent a year just outside the city in 1753–4 and attacked local society in his *Lettres d'Alsace*. And in 1792 'La Marseillaise' was written and composed in Strasbourg by the poet and musician Claude-Joseph Rouget de Lisle, then a captain in the Engineers. The story goes that the mayor wanted a rousing patriotic anthem which the volunteers of the Army of the Rhine could sing while marching, so he asked the young poet to try his hand, and words and music were composed in a single night. The song was first called the 'Chant de guerre de l'Armée du Rhin', but it acquired its present name – and was then adopted as the national anthem – when soon afterwards revolutionary volunteers from Marseille took it up and sang it in Paris.

Victor H U G O came to Strasbourg in 1839 with his mistress Juliette Drouet. They stayed on the broad place Kléber at the Hôtel Maison-Rouge, which today has been rebuilt a few metres distant. Hugo devotes a chapter to the city in his travel book *Le Rhin*, describing in particular the cathedral ('truly a marvel' but 'shamefully plastered over'), where he is irritated by an ignorant English tourist and then joyously climbs the 328 steps to the top of the belfry:

You know my liking for perpendicular travel... From where I was, the view is admirable. One has Strasbourg at one's feet, an old town with notched gables and huge roofs containing skylights, a town punctuated with towers and churches, as picturesque as any in Flanders. The Ill and the Rhine, two pretty rivers, enliven this sombre mass of buildings with their green and clear waters. All around the walls there stretches to the horizon an immense countryside full of trees and scattered with villages. The Rhine, which comes within a league of the town, loops its way through this land. By walking round the belfry's platform one can see three mountain ranges, the crest of the Black Forest to the north, the Vosges to the west, the Alps to the south. One is so high that the landscape is no longer a landscape... but a map... The bells of a hundred villages were chiming; some red and white insects, which were a herd of cows, were lowing in a meadow to my right; other insects, blue and red, which were artillerymen, were doing firing practice in the polygon to my left; a black beetle, which was a stage-coach, was racing along the road to Metz...

That is still roughly the scene today, give or take a few oil refineries and high-rise blocks, and the European Parliament building. Sixty years after Hugo, René Bazin (see p. 89) stayed in Strasbourg to prepare his novel *Les Oberlé* (1901), about an Alsatian family's conflicting loyalties towards France and Germany during the decades of annexation. Nearer to our own time, Françoise Mallet-Joris, the Belgian writer, has used Strasbourg as the setting for a novel about youthful drug-addicts. The American poet LONGFELLOW visited Alsace in the 1830s and wrote a very bad poem about Strasbourg cathedral (set to music by Liszt), but a better one about a cobbler in Hagenau, to the north:

> . . . A quiet, quaint, and ancient town
> Among the green Alsatian hills,
> A place of valleys, streams and mills,
>
> Where Barbarossa's castle, brown
> With rust of centuries still looks down
> On the broad, drowsy land below. . .

Of all the foreign writers who have stayed in Alsace, Johann Wolfgang von GOETHE holds pride of place. He spent a year at Strasbourg as a university student in 1770–1, living in a *pension* at 36 rue du Vieux-Marché-aux-Poissons, a busy main street: the red-and-black half-timbered building today bears a plaque, and there is a statue of Goethe outside the Palais de l'Université. He admired the cathedral, but had much less of a head for heights than Hugo: however, to test his will-power he would dare himself to climb up the belfry, and he did this often.

Goethe's strongest connections with Alsace are not in fact with Strasbourg but with the pretty village of Sessenheim, 20 miles to the north-east, near the Rhine. Here in October 1770 he was taken by a friend to visit the local Protestant pastor, M. Brion, and his family – and Wolfgang and the younger daughter Friederike fell tenderly in love. He frequently went to see her, often on horseback. But after he had won his doctorate the following summer he returned to Frankfurt, and Friederike grieved so much that she almost died. Eight years later, by now a famous poet, Goethe came again to Sessenheim – but their delicate youthful love never revived. Today the village has a number of souvenirs of this episode. In the church with its grey onion-cupola is the pew where the young couple sat side-by-side, and the stone tombs of her parents are by the south aisle. The presbytery is no more, but next to where it stood is the black-timbered barn where the lovers would meet; and just across the railway-line is the little hill where they used to sit, now disfigured by a gloomy and ill-kept pavilion. A Goethe memorial room stands opposite the church; and the modern auberge Au Boeuf has two rooms devoted to a small museum, containing portraits and letters. In his memoirs, Goethe mentions his love-affair in 'this magnificent land' of Alsace; and he fondly remembers Friederike in one of his best-known poems, *Willkommen und Abschied*:

> Doch ach, schon mit der Morgensonne
> Verengt der Abschied mir das Herz
> In deinen Küssen welche Wonne!
> In deinem Auge welcher Schmerz!

(But, oh, at sunrise already / the pain of parting pressed on my heart. / What ecstasy there was in your kisses! / What sorrow in your eyes!)

Over to the west of Sessenheim, near Saverne, is the ugly little town of Phalsbourg (today just inside Lorraine), where Emile ERCKMANN (1822–99) was born and lived. He and Alexandre Chatrian produced a number of simple tales of Alsatian life that were very popular at the time and still have a certain cult appeal, if only for the charming Schuler illustrations of the original editions. Though they signed their books jointly, Chatrian was merely the sales manager and Erckmann the writer. Their books were mostly published just before the Franco-Prussian war and are not at all anti-German. The best-known of them *L'Ami Fritz* (1864) is a cosy sentimental tale about a confirmed bachelor who finally falls in love and weds. It is set in an imaginary town based on Phalsbourg, where today there is a small Erckmann museum and an annual Erckmann festival; the leading local beer is Fritz Brau, La Bière de l'Ami Fritz. Down a side-street of this dreary little town I was surprised to find a synagogue, now closed, and was told that once there was a flourishing Jewish community here. This explains the big role played by Jews in *L'Ami Fritz* (the hero's best friend is a rabbi):

> He went down the rue des Capucins as far as the courtyard of the synagogue, which one entered by an old carriage-gate. Everyone passed through that gate, to go down the little stairway opposite, in the rue des Juifs. It was as old as Hunebourg itself; all one saw there was great grey shadows, tall decrepit buildings, lined with rusty gutters; and all Judaea was hanging from the attic windows all around, right to the very top – stockings with holes in them, old filthy skirts, patched-up trousers. . .

The descriptions in these books of Alsatian village festivities and folk traditions may today seem naïve and outdated. But subject-matter of this kind is again becoming fashionable, at a time when Alsace like some other French regions is seeking to strengthen its identity through a local cultural revival. Jean Egen and André Weckmann are two of a number of modern Alsatian novelists who write about village life and traditions. Egen's books are more commercial and folksy, set in the past: *Les Tilleuls de Lauterbach*, also a successful television series, describes the Florival valley near Guebwiller, north-west of Mulhouse. Weckmann is a more poetic writer, concerned with regional spirit and the links between past and present, and most of his work is in German or in Alsatian dialect. Lastly, let us not forget Tomi Ungerer, the cartoonist and satirist, who was born in Strasbourg but today lives mainly in Ireland. The provocative and often pornographic tone of his work has made him not universally popular in his native province, of which he has written, '*L'Alsace est comme les toilettes, toujours occupée.*'

Besançon, capital of the Franche-Comté region, is a fine old town with a fortress on a hill. Rousseau lived here for a while, Mallarmé taught English at the lycée, and Arthur Young on July 28, 1789 found himself refused a passport, which made him very angry: 'I do not like the airs and manners of the people here – and I would see Besançon swallowed up by an earthquake before I would live in it.' Above all, this city and its region are connected with STENDHAL's *Le Rouge et le noir* (1830): Julien Sorel attends the seminary there, flirts with a barmaid, and meets his mistress Madame de Rénal in the cathedral. Stendhal, who came from Grenoble (see p. 215), did not share Young's gloomy view of Besançon, but wrote: 'It is not only one of the prettiest towns in France, it's full of people of feeling and wit.' Stendhal gives the name of Verrières to the home town of Sorel and the Rénal, where so much of the book is set, and it is thought that he had Dôle in mind, which is west of Besançon. He often used to visit Dôle, on his way by stage-coach between Paris and Italy, staying at the Hôtel de Lyon which is now the Grand Hôtel Chandioux; and the view from the promenade there is the same as that of Verrières at the start of the novel:

Its white houses with their steep, red tile roofs spread across a hillside, the folds of which are outlined by clumps of thrifty chestnut trees. The Doubs flows a couple of

The citadel at Besançon – 'one of the prettiest towns in France, full of people of feeling and wit', according to Stendhal.

Opposite: *Dole, on the Doubs, was often visited by Stendhal, and was probably the town he had in mind for 'Verrières', of which Monsieur de Rênal was mayor in Le Rouge et le Noir.*

hundred feet below the town's fortifications... How many times, my mind still dwelling on the balls of Paris which I left the night before, have I leaned on these great blocks of bluish-grey granite, gazing deep into the valley of the Doubs! Over yonder, on the left bank, wind five or six valleys...

This great novel, so full of wit and insight, has very few descriptions of places or scenery that can be quoted as extracts. But it may be worth mentioning where its main plot came from. Stendhal used to stay with his sister at Thuellin, north of Grenoble, and one day in 1827 he read in a legal gazette of a drama that had taken place in the adjacent village of Brangues. Antoine Berthet, a highly gifted ex-seminarist of peasant origin, had been sent to the guillotine for shooting his ex-mistress in the local church, in circumstances extraordinarily similar to those which Stendhal then used for his portrayal of a young provincial destroyed by his social ambition.

Burgundy, land of wine, one might expect to be overflowing with vinous comedy. Its greatest native writer, the Romantic poet Alphonse de LAMARTINE (1790–1869), was too high-flown and humourless a figure to be anywhere near the stereotype of a jolly down-to-earth Burgundian: but he did have a warm feeling for his homeland, the hills of the Mâconnais, as is evident from many of his poems. In Mâcon, the house where he was born exists no more, but his home from 1805 to 1820 is still there, at 15 rue Lamartine, and the nearby Hôtel Senecé contains a museum devoted to Lamartine souvenirs. His family were land-owning minor aristocrats who had a number of manor-houses in the villages west of the town; and here the poet spent much of his time, when he was not busy elsewhere as career diplomat and then Paris politician. The import-ance that he attached to the natural surroundings of his youth, and to their secret influence on his character, has a Wordsworthian ring (and, just as Rousseau influenced Wordsworth, so Lamartine in turn took up the message from Grasmere):

> La lune qui décroît ou s'arrondit dans l'ombre
> L'étoile qui gravit sur la colline sombre,
> Les troupeaux des hauts lieux chassés par les frimas,
> Des côteaux aux vallons descendant pas à pas,
> Le vent, l'épine en fleur, l'herbe verte ou flêtrie,
> Le soc dans le sillon, l'onde dans la prairie,
> Tout m'y parle une langue aux intimes accents,
> Dont les mots entendus dans l'âme et dans les sens
> Sont des bruits, des parfums, des foudres, des orages,
> Des rochers, des torrents, et ces douces images,
> Et ces vieux souvenirs dormant au fond de nous,
> Qu'un site nous conserve et qu'il nous rend plus doux.
> Là mon coeur en tout lieu se retrouve lui-même!
> Tout s'y souvient de moi, tout m'y connaît, tout m'aime!
> Mon oeil trouve un ami dans tout cet horizon;
> Chaque arbre a son histoire et chaque pierre un nom.

(The moon waning or waxing in the shade, / the star climbing above the dark hill, / the herds from the highlands driven down by the frost, / descending step by step from the hillsides to the valleys, / the wind, the thornbushes in flower, the grass green or faded, / the ploughshare in the furrow, the billowing grassland, / All these speak to me a most intimate language, / whose words heard in the soul and in the senses / are sounds, perfumes, lightnings, storms in the rocks, / torrents, and these sweet images, / and these old memories that sleep deep within us, / that a landscape preserves for us and makes sweeter for us. / There my heart everywhere finds itself again! / There everything remembers me, knows me, loves me! / My eye finds a friend in all this horizon; / every tree has its history and each stone a name.)

So Lamartine too heard often-times in nature the still, sad music of humanity. Those lines are from a long poem, *Milly ou la terre natale*, about the village where he spent most of his childhood:

> Voilà le banc rustique où s'asseyait mon père,
> La salle où résonnait sa voix mâle et sévère,
> Quand les pasteurs, assis sur leurs socs renversés,
> Lui comptaient les sillons par chaque heure tracés. . .
> Voilà la place vide où ma mère, à toute heure,
> Au plus léger soupir sortait de sa demeure. . .

(Here is the rustic bench where my father sat, / the room where his severe male voice resounded, / when the shepherds, sitting on their upturned ploughshares, / counted up for him the furrows that they had worked each hour. . . / Here is the empty place where my mother, at any moment, / at the slightest sigh would leave her house. . .)

Lamartine's tomb in the chapel at St-Point, Burgundy.

Milly, set on a hill above a pretty valley west of Mâcon, is today one of the main stops on the 'circuit Lamartinien' signposted for tourists. Here is the family's old stone house, where later he wrote *L'Isolement*, the first of the *Méditations*, and where he recalled 'the sweet and melancholy voices of the little frogs that sing on summer evenings'. A bust of the poet stands at the top of the village. Down towards Mâcon, up to the left of the main road, the mellow golden-brown château of Monceau was one of Lamartine's favourite residences in his middle years: here this lover of pomp lived in high style as a country squire, but he was also a spendthrift and had difficulty in coping with importunate creditors. Neither this château nor the house at Milly is open to visitors; nor is the manor at Pierreclos, south of Milly, home of the lady who was his model for Laurence in his epic poem *Jocelyn*.

Much the most interesting Lamartinian site in this area is the château of St-Point, over to the west, and this *is* open to visitors. Lamartine received it from his father as a wedding gift in 1820, and lived there frequently. In the little church are two pictures by the poet's English wife, and in an adjacent chapel are his tomb and hers. The house itself contains his bed, his writing-desk and other mementoes. The stone bench still standing under the lime-trees in the garden is where he wrote many of the *Méditations*, and nearly is the oak-tree under which he wrote *Jocelyn*. All this is authentic. But a notice by the pond in the park states 'Le Lac' – and this seems mischievously misleading (see p. 210).

On the north side of Burgundy, north-west of Dijon, is the country château of a minor writer but most outrageous and flamboyant figure – Roger de Rabutin, Comte de B U S S Y. He was exiled here by Louis XIV for lampooning court life, and then took a lonely revenge by decorating his

The château where Roger de Rabutin, Comte de Bussy, took his lonely satirical revenge on Louis XIV.

walls with bitchy cartoons and epigrams on his ex-mistresses and other fashionable figures of the day. These rooms shed fascinating light on the times of the Sun King. Bussy-Rabutin, a cousin and regular correspondent of Madame de Sévigné, wrote his *Histoire amoureuse des Gaules* in 1660 (the title is a pun, for *gaule* can also mean stick, or phallus in slang): this novella is a wickedly accurate portrayal of certain ladies at court, thinly disguised, and their adulteries. A copy found its way to Paris, and the king was prevailed on to send Bussy to the Bastille, although he had just been elected to the Académie Française. Released a year later, he was exiled for life to his country seat, and then spent years turning it into a sardonic memorial to the follies of his age. Few of the murals he commissioned are of much artistic quality; but they vividly illumine his quirky character.

The imposing château, outside the village of Bussy-Rabutin, has a moat, a lovely Renaissance courtyard, and a terraced garden modelled on Versailles. Inside, the Salles des Devises has some curious allegorical paintings with Latin inscriptions. One is devoted to Madame de Sévigné, who had rejected his bid to become her lover: she is depicted as a jug

*The courtyard of
St-Sauveur-en-Puisaye,
Colette's childhood home
and the source of many
of her poetic memories.*

pouring cold water on hot coals, with the tag, 'She is cold and enflames
me.' In the Salon des Grands Hommes, Bussy's scorn falls most heavily
on his faithless ex-mistress, Madame de Montglas, who is portrayed as
the moon 'with more than one face'. This room has 65 paintings of
military leaders, many caustically captioned, including Cromwell, 'condemned by his great crimes to eternal notoriety'. Bussy's bedroom and
the Tour Dorée in the west tower are decorated with mistresses of French
kings (clearly an obsession) and with other court ladies, such as the
Marquise de Baume ('She would have been the prettiest and most
lovable, had she not been the most unfaithful') and the Duchesse de
Choiseul ('Very well informed, notably about other people's faults'). In
his later writings, Bussy compared three powerful, scheming and easy-
virtued mesdames at court to a trio of ancient Roman rulers: 'Not a
triumvirate but a triumputate'.

Two writers in our own century – one virtually unknown outside France,
the other world-famous – have left evocative portraits of their childhood
in Burgundy. Henri VINCENOT, born at Dijon in 1912, spent part of his

8: Savoy, Grenoble and Lyon

(Rhône-Alpes, Auvergne and Limousin regions)

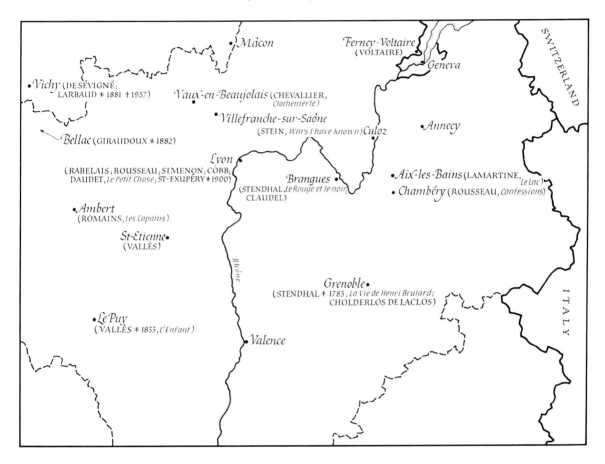

*Scene of Jules Vallès'
unhappy childhood:
Le Puy, with its curious
volcanic pinnacles.*

At this moment began the short happiness of my life, those peaceful and rapid moments which have given me a right to say, *I have lived*. Precious and ever-regretted moments! . . . I rose with the sun, and was happy; I walked, and was happy; I saw Madame de Warens, and was happy! I quitted her, and was still happy! Whether I rambled through the woods, over the hills, or strolled along the valley; read, was idle, worked in the garden, or gathered fruits, happiness continually accompanied me. . .

Thus Jean-Jacques ROUSSEAU, in the *Confessions*, on the periods that he spent with his protectress and mistress in 1736–40, in the trim stone house that she had rented at Les Charmettes, a hamlet just outside Chambéry in Savoy. Rousseau was born in Geneva in 1712; his mother died giving birth to him, his father left home when he was ten, and for a few teenage years he was a vagabond. Then he met Madame de Warens, who was also Swiss, and thirteen years his elder. Despite what some biographers call her 'weak moral character' (she was an adventuress who had to live on her wits), she helped him a great deal, gave him true affection, and was a formative influence on his later development as a philosopher. She became his employer, his mother-figure (he often refers to her as 'Maman'), and more. They were together off-and-on for twelve years, living first in Annecy and Chambéry before they came to Les Charmettes in 1736:

The spot we had concluded on was a valley between two tolerably high hills, which ran north and south; at the bottom, among the trees and pebbles, ran a rivulet, and above the declivity, on either side, were scattered a number of houses, forming altogether a beautiful retreat for those who love a peaceful romantic asylum. . . This house was in good condition, before it a garden, forming a terrace; below that on the declivity, an orchard, and on the ascent, behind the house, a vineyard; a little wood of chestnut trees opposite; a fountain just by, and higher up the hill, meadows for the cattle; in short, all that could be thought necessary for the country retirement we proposed to establish.

Here the idyll was pursued erratically for Rousseau was frequently absent on his travels. At Les Charmettes he would play with the pigeons,

Opposite: 'At this moment began the short happiness of my life' – the house outside Chambéry where Jean-Jacques Rousseau spent his uncertain idyll with Madame de Warens.

The interior of Les Charmettes, still today without electricity or modern heating.

do a little gentle gardening (he had not yet started to write), nurse his fragile health, and wait for his darling to wake up:

The moment the shutter drew back I hastened to embrace her, frequently half asleep; and this salute, pure as it was affectionate, even from its innocence, possessed a charm which the senses can never bestow. We usually breakfasted on milk-coffee; this was the time of day when we had most leisure, and when we chatted with the greatest freedom. These sittings, which were usually pretty long, have given me a fondness for breakfast, and I infinitely prefer those of England, or Switzerland, which are considered as a meal, at which all the family assemble, to those of France, where they breakfast alone in their several apartments, or more frequently have none at all. . .

The château
Brangues: C
where he lie

(O lab
she sl
saw h
far o

9: The South-west

(Poitou-Charente and Aquitaine regions)

Probably the best of all BALZAC's descriptions of a provincial town and its society is provided by the opening chapters of *Les Illusions perdues* (1837), which is set in Angoulême, 'an ancient town built on the summit of a cone-shaped rock towering over the meadows through which the river Charente runs'. Balzac stayed there three times in 1831–3, with his friend Zulma Carraud and her husband who was manager of the local State gunpowder factory. He was collecting material for his book, which forms part of the *Scènes de la vie de province* of the *Comédie Humaine*; and one of its themes is the contrast and conflict between the bourgeois upper town within the ramparts and the newer industrial suburb of L'Houmeau, down below:

About the time when our story begins, the Government was trying to push the town forward into Périgord by building the prefectoral palace, a marine school and military establishments along the hill, and laying plans for roads. But commerce had moved in the opposite direction. Long since, the suburb of L'Houmeau had spread out like a bed of mushrooms at the foot of the rock and along the river banks, parallel to which runs the main road from Paris to Bordeaux. The paper-mills of Angoulême are well-famed: during the last three centuries they had of necessity established themselves along the Charente and its tributaries, where waterfalls were available. At Ruelle the State had set up its most important foundry for naval cannons. Haulage, post-houses, inns, wheelwrights' workshops, public transport services, all the industries which depend on roads and waterways clustered round the base of Angoulême in order to avoid the difficulties presented by access to the town itself. . . And so the suburb of L'Houmeau became a busy and prosperous town, a second Angoulême, arousing resentment in the upper town where the administration, the Bishop's palace, the courts of justice and the aristocracy remained. For this reason L'Houmeau, despite its increasing activity and importance, was a mere appendage of Angoulême. The nobility and the political authority held sway on high, commerce and finance down below: two social zones, everywhere and constantly hostile to each other; as a consequence, it is difficult to guess which of the two towns more cordially hates its rival. This state of things had remained fairly quiescent during the Empire; nine years of Restoration Government had aggravated it. Most of the houses in Upper Angoulême are inhabited either by noble families living on their investments and constituting a sort of autochthonous nation to which strangers are never admitted. It is a rare occurrence if, even after living in the place for a couple of hundred years and contracting a marriage alliance with one of the original families, a family which has migrated from some neighbouring province is received into the fold: the native population still considers it a newcomer. Prefects, Receivers-General and civil service officials who have succeeded one another for forty years have tried to civilise these ancient families perched on their rock like so many watchful ravens: these families have attended their receptions and eaten their dinners, but they have persistently

An old papermill in Angoulême, a town long famous for its paper and printing industries – as Balzac recounts.

Poitiers

St-Maurice (FROMENTIN †1876, *Dominique*)
La Rochelle (FROMENTIN ∗1820;
SIMENON)
•*Rochefort* (LOTI ∗1850)

Cognac
(MORGAN, *The Voyage*) •
Royan
(DURAS, *Moderato cantabile*)

•*Angoulême* (BALZAC,
Les Illusions perdues)

Hautefort
(LE ROY ∗1836; POUND, *Near Perigord*)
Chalais • •*Périgueux* •*Montignac*
(POUND, *Near Perigord*)
Château de l'Herm
(LE ROY, *Jacquou le Croquant*)
Montaigne *Dordogne*
(MONTAIGNE *Bergerac*
∗1533 †1592) (LEROY †1907)

Bordeaux
(MONTAIGNE; MONTES-
QUIEU; MAURIAC ∗1885,
Le Mystère Frontenac,
La Pharisienne, *etc.*)
Verdelais (MAURIAC,
Le Noeud de vipères, etc.)
Labrède
Jouanhaou *Langon*
•*St-Symphorien* *Agen*
(MAURIAC, *Thérèse Desqueyroux*,
Le Mystère Frontenac)

(MONTESQUIEU
∗1689)

Gironde

Biarritz
•*Bayonne*
Hendaye (HEMINGWAY, *Pau* (YATES; JAMMES)
Sare *The Sun also Rises*)
(LOTI †1923) *Cambo-les-Bains*
(ROSTAND)
(LOTI, *Ramuntcho*)

S P A I N

The river Charente at Angoulême.

refused to welcome them to their houses. Disdainful, disparaging, jealous and miserly, these houses intermarry and close their ranks to prevent anyone entering or leaving; they know nothing of the creations of modern luxury; in their view, to send a child to Paris is to seal its doom.

That powerful passage serves to introduce the story: Lucien Chardon, a handsome young man with literary talents, from a poor L'Houmeau family, is taken up by the patrician Madame Naïs de Bargeton who invites him to her smart salons. She encourages him to elope with her to

Paris, but then drops him. (Balzacologues have identified the Chardon home in L'Houmeau as being at 165 rue de Paris; the de Bargeton mansion was in the rue du Minage, within the ramparts: and the printing workshop of Lucien's brother-in-law David is precisely set by Balzac himself at the eastern end of the rue de Beaulieu, also inside the old town, on the site of a present-day post office). Naïs de Bargeton is a kind of higher-class and more intellectual Emma Bovary, bored by her dull elderly husband, stifled by the snobberies of provincial society. She tries her best to introduce a breath of fresh air, through artistic patronage (hence her love for Lucien, the young poet) and through an original style of entertaining:

> She trumpeted throughout the *département* a forthcoming soirée complete with ices, cakes and tea – an impressive innovation in a town where tea was still sold in chemists' shops as a drug for the cure of indigestion.

But tea and sympathy are of little avail. So long as she remained in Angoulême, 'Naïs' brilliant mental qualities and the wealth of sensibility lying dormant in her heart were destined never to fructify, but rather, in course of time, to invite ridicule', because in the provinces,

> for lack of grist, passions dwindle because they exaggerate the importance of insignificant things. That is the reason why avarice and scandal-mongering poison life in the provinces. Very quickly, the most distinguished person adopts the narrow ideas and unprepossessing manners of those around him. Thus perish men born with greatness in them and women who, under the discipline of social education and schooled by superior minds, might have been charming.

The ridiculous guests at the Bargetons' salons are then lampooned in a passage of high comic satire. Later in the book, when the scene shifts to Paris, Balzac is not much less critical of the corrupt and ruthless literary milieu of the capital. As so often, in *Les Illusions perdues* he is playing on his familiar theme of the opposition between Paris and provinces: but, although he was himself a provincial by origin, he was proud of having become accepted in Paris, and in this novel as in some others his cruellest contempt is reserved for provincial life. The Angoulême minor nobility are hammered as much as the Breton peasantry in *Les Chouans* or the money-making Angevins in *Eugénie Grandet*. Only his beloved Touraine escapes his full derision.

From Angoulême the Charente winds down through pretty pastoral landscapes to the brandy-producing district around Cognac, the setting for a rather bad novel, *The Voyage*, by that arch-francophile Charles Morgan, now so out of fashion in Britain but still vaguely admired in France. Further west is the bathing-resort of Royan where Marguerite Duras located her mood-piece *Moderato Cantabile*. The river Charente joins the sea further north, at Rochefort, where the Maison de Pierre Loti conceals some most bizarre delights. LOTI was born in 1850 in this outwardly dull-looking town house, son of an official at the *mairie*. He

Vineyards in the Charente valley near Cognac, where Charles Morgan set The Voyage.

became a naval officer, travelled widely, developed exotic oriental tastes, then indulged them by decking out this residence to suit his extravagant fancies. It is now a municipal museum. Upstairs you can visit the mosque, which he fitted with a minaret and furnished with objects acquired from a mosque in Damascus, including various coffin-like cenotaphs; next door is the Turkish salon with authentic Turkish seats and cushions, and a small oriental *fumoir* where Loti would go to write, read and smoke hashish. He used to dress his servants in Arab or Turkish dress: but, though fascinated by Islam, he never joined that faith, remaining an agnostic. The main room downstairs, the so-called Renaissance banqueting hall, is decorated most strangely in Spanish period style, including a massive chimney-piece, a musicians' gallery, and five Gobelin tapestries: for its inauguration in 1900, Loti threw a costume ball for his friends from Paris with everyone in Chinese dress (the photographs of this are on display). The whole place is absurdly over-the-top, but entertaining, and Loti himself adored living there. But his unhappy wife Blanche was less enamoured of life with this eccentric. And his flamboyant fantasies contrast most intriguingly with the quiet austerity of his own upstairs bedroom, and also with the cosy simplicity of his two best-known novels set in France, *Pêcheur d'Islande* (see p. 25) and *Ramuntcho* (see p. 24).

The former Protestant stronghold of La Rochelle, north of Rochefort, is my own favourite coastal town in France, and has something of the quality of Bruges or Dubrovnik. Jean-Paul Sartre was at school there, and Georges Simenon lived there for a while and described it in *Le Voyageur*

de la Toussaint. But above all it is the home-town of Eugène FROMEN-
TIN (1820–76), art-critic and artist, influenced both by Corot and by
Delacroix, and author of the slight but beautiful romantic novel
Dominique. Partly autobiographical, this follows the familiar French
19th-century theme (c.f. *Le Lys dans la vallée*) of an adulterous mutual
passion that builds up to fever-pitch but is never consummated. It is set in
the flat, melancholy marshlands of the Aunis immediately north-west of
La Rochelle, around the village of St-Maurice where Fromentin himself
had a country property and now lies buried. Today this area has been
overrun by the industrial sprawl of the big port of La Pallice: but, if you
go slightly further north, you can still find the gentle landscapes that
Fromentin described with a painter's sensitivity. He had a feeling for
nature and for wildlife that was not so common in French writing at that
time, as witness the various passages where Dominique de Bray wistfully
recalls his lost love for Madeleine, against the background of his farm and
estate:

When evening put an end to my rambles, I would stand at the top of the terrace
steps and look across the garden to the edge of the park, where the almond trees,
always the first to be tripped by the September wind, held up their fantastic tracery
against the flaring skirts of the sunset. In the park there were many white poplars, ash
trees and laurels, in which flocks of thrushes and blackbirds lived all through the
autumn. . . Wood-pigeons came in May at the same time as the cuckoos. They
murmured softly, with long pauses, especially on damp evenings, or when the air was
filled with an indefinable excitement and a sense of renewed activity in the rising sap
and the youth of the year. All through the night – those long nights when I hardly
slept, when the moon rode high and sometimes rain was falling peaceful, warm and
noiseless like tears of joy – all through the night, deep hidden behind the leaves, at the
far end of the garden, in the white cherry trees and flowering privets, or among the
heavy sweet-smelling clusters of lilacs, to my delight and torment, the nightingales
were singing. . .

This elegiac autumnal tone infuses the whole book with a quiet
lyricism, as the trees, the meadows, the marshes, the shifting patterns
of light, all take on the hues of a canvas by Corot. But Fromentin the
country-lover is less enthusiastic about his home-city, La Rochelle,
which he calls 'Ormesson':

Picture yourself a very small town, pious, gloomy, antiquated, buried in a
provincial dead-end, leading nowhere, serving no purpose, day by day less alive and
more encroached upon by the country: its industry futile, its commerce dead; its
middle class living scantily on their means, its aristocracy sulking in their tents; by
day, no bustle in the streets, at night no lights in the avenues; unfriendly silence,
broken only by church chimes. . .

La Rochelle is today entirely different and very lively – some compen-
sation maybe for La Pallice's destruction of the nightingales' haunts.

South-east of Angoulême lies the ancient *comté* of Périgord, better
known to the English today under the name of the modern *département*
of Dordogne that covers largely the same territory. The English once

invaded the Dordogne bloodily in the Hundred Years War, and today are doing so peacefully with their summer and retirement homes: so it is good that they should now be writing about it too. Among recent works, I can think of Peter Nichols' play *Chez Nous*, about an English family settled there, and Rose Tremain's novel *The Swimming-Pool Season*, chronicling the none-too-happy life of an English expatriate in a village near Périgueux. Cyril Connolly ('Palinurus') has a cryptic reference in *The Unquiet Grave* to his desire to find 'a yellow manor farm inside this magic circle' that he traces a little to the south, between the rivers Dordogne and Tarn. However, the best modern writing that I know about the Dordogne comes from neither a British nor a French hand but from an American, Ezra POUND. Among the nine languages that this embattled genius spoke fluently was Provençal/Occitan, and from early days he made a special study of troubadours including the greatest of them all, Bertrand de Born (c. 1140–1215) who, when he was not away doing battle for or against Henry II of England and Richard the Lion-heart, held sway in the mighty hilltop castle of Hautefort (since much rebuilt, but still surviving), some way east of Périgueux. Pound's exquisite if typically obscure poem, *Near Périgord*, about the troubadour's love for lady Maent in her castle, provides a lovely litany of Périgourdin place-names, easy to identify on any map:

> Think you that Maent lived at Montaignac,
> One at Chalais, another at Malemort
> Hard over Brive – for every lady a castle,
> Each place strong. . .
>
> Chalais is high, a-level with the poplars.
> Its lowest stones just meet the valley tips
> Where the low Dronne is filled with water-lilies.
> And Rouchecouart can match it, stronger yet,
> The very spur's end, built on sheerest cliff,
> And Malemort keeps its close hold on Brive,
> While Born, his own close purse, his rabbit warren,
> His subterranean chamber with a dozen doors,
> A-bristle with antennae to feel roads,
> To sniff the traffic into Périgord.
> And that hard phalanx, that unbroken line,
> The ten good miles from there to Maent's castle,
> All of his flank – how could he do without her?
> And all the road to Cahors, to Toulouse?
> What would he do without her?
>   'Papiol.
> Go forthright singing – Anhès, Cembelins.
> There is a throat; aha, there are two white hands;
> There is a trellis full of early roses,
> And all my heart is bound about with love. . .'
>
> End fact. Try fiction. Let us say we see
> En Bertrans, a tower-room at Hautefort.

Sunset, the ribbon-like road lies, in red cross-light,
Southwards towards Montaignac. . .

. . . Dodging his way past Aubeterre, singing at Chalais
      In the vaulted hall,
Or, by a lichened tree at Rochecouart
Aimlessly watching a hawk above the valleys,
Waiting his turn in the midsummer evening. . .

Bewildering spring, and by the Auvezère
Poppies and day's eyes in the green émail
Rose over us; and we knew all that stream,
And our two horses had traced out the valleys;
Knew the low flooded lands squared out with poplars,
In the young days when the deep sky befriended.
      And great wings beat above us in the twilight. . . .

A rather more down-to-earth picture of Périgord is given in the novels of
the leading French writer of the region, Eugène LE ROY, who was born at
Hautefort in 1836 and died in 1907 at Montignac, close by the caves of
Lascaux. He was a true regional writer who spent all his life in the area,
involving himself closely with local country people; and his books are so
full of *patois* that they require a glossary. He was also a man of the Left:
his best-known novel, *Jacquou le Croquant* ('the revolutionary'), tells of
a peasant uprising against a cruel feudal landlord in the period around
1830. There is not much descriptive lyricism in this book, which gives a
harsh portrait of the rural poverty of the time, when chestnuts, potatoes
and wheat broth were the staple diet and even cabbage soup was a luxury.
The setting is the wild forest of Barade, west of Montignac, where the
crenellated ruins of the 16th-century castle of l'Herm can still be seen
today; Le Roy made this the home of the dreadful Count of Nansac.
Jacquou's father is sent to the galleys at Toulon for killing (in self-
defence) one of the count's servants, his mother dies of grief and
exhaustion, and his fiancée kills herself by jumping off a cliff, after he
himself has been captured by the count and shut up in the castle's
oubliette. But Jacquou escapes, and takes a glorious revenge by setting
the castle in flames. This is all a far cry from the life of today's well-fed
farmers in this smiling touristy area which in those days seemed so
desolate, especially in winter:

A sharp wind had arisen, whirling the snow which was still falling heavily. The
empty countryside was all white; the hillsides seemed covered with a vast white
shroud, like those placed on the coffins of dead paupers. The chestnut trees with their
bizarre shapes held lines of white on their tortured branches. The snow-powdered
bracken leaned earthwards, while the drifts piled up in places on the solider gorse and
heather. A deathly silence hovered over the desolate land, where I could not hear even
the sound of my mother's footsteps, muffled by the thick snow. And yet, as we
entered the heath of Grand-Castang, a nightjar cast into the darkness its hideous cry,
making me shudder.

Pages 232–3: Ezra Pound's Périgord:
'where the low Dronne is filled with water-lilies'.

Aquitaine's capital, the stately city of Bordeaux, has often impressed literary travellers. Arthur Young wrote: 'Much as I had read and heard of the commerce, wealth and magnificence of this city, they greatly surpassed my expectations.' The quay itself, though he admired its busy activity, he found 'dirty, sloping, muddy', but the newly-built theatre he considered 'by far the most magnificent in France', and the life-style of the local merchants he thought 'highly luxurious'. A century later, the quay had been much improved, and Henry James admired its wide sweep and architectural air: 'The appearance of such a port as this makes the Anglo-Saxon tourist blush for the sordid waterfronts of Liverpool and New York.'

Bordeaux is associated with three great French writers who were educated there and had country estates in the area – the three 'Ms', Montaigne, Montesquieu and Mauriac. Michel de MONTAIGNE (1533–92), free-thinking moralist, creator of the essay as an art form, was born in the family château of Montaigne which is 36 miles due east of the city and two miles north of the main road to Bergerac. The son of a prosperous Bordeaux merchant, Montaigne travelled widely in Germany and Italy, worked as magistrate in the *parlement* of Bordeaux, and for a while was mayor of the city. The last twenty years of his life he spent quietly in his château, writing his masterwork, the *Essais*:

> Michel de Montaigne, already long weary of the slavery of the Court and of public duties, has taken refuge in the bosom of the muses while he still feels himself intact, in order there to find calm and complete security and to spend there the days that remain to him. Hoping that destiny will permit him to perfect this habitation, he has consecrated to his freedom, his tranquillity and his leisure this gentle family retreat.

Montaigne wrote little more than this about the château and his daily life there, in a 1,100-page philosophical work that ranges freely over all human affairs and views life in a typically Gascon spirit of shrewdness, frankness and individualism. But he loved his home, and in his mind it was closely linked with his belief that man should live in harmony with nature and his environment. The main building was badly burned in a fire in 1885; since rebuilt, it is now in other private hands. But the old stone tower across the courtyard, where Montaigne would spend much of his time, fortunately survived the fire intact and is now a small museum. Here one can visit the little chapel, and his bedroom, and his 'library' where he did most of his writing, a circular room whose rafters are decorated with Latin and Greek inscriptions dating from this time. It is all very simple and monastic (he was on poor terms with his wife, much preferring the company of his close friend La Boétie). From the terrace outside the castle walls, one can look out over the gentle Dordogne landscape that he loved, with its vineyards and wooded hills.

Charles de Secondat, Baron de La Brède et de MONTESQUIEU (1689–1755), had much in common with Montaigne. Like him, he spent some years in law and politics in Bordeaux but preferred living quietly on his

country domain; like him, he was of a cheerful, optimistic temperament and devoted his skills to writing major works of philosophical reflection – in this case *L'Esprit des Lois*, a treatise on law, society and government. Montesquieu was one of the great luminary figures of the 18th century in France. His château outside the village of La Brède, 12 miles south of Bordeaux, is an imposing mediaeval Gothic pile surrounded by a lake and park; it is still owned by his descendants, and visitors are permitted to inspect his salon, his bedroom and his fine library with its 7,000 volumes. Again like Montaigne, he wrote little about his country home save to explain how much he depended on its peace and beauty; undoubtedly his deep roots in his native soil helped to form his views on the influence of climate and of nature on individuals and societies. He was a devoted landowner and vine-grower, very proud of his white Graves which he sold copiously in England. 'The success that my book *Les Lettres*

Eugène Le Roy's Périgord: near Hautefort.

Montesqieu's Gothic château at La Brède, near Bordeaux.

Persanes has had in England,' he wrote, 'seems to have contributed to the success there of my wine.' There speaks the true Bordelais.

François MAURIAC (1885–1970) was also a true Bordelais, though of a different stamp. He was deeply marked by a pious Jansenist upbringing which was not untypical of the city's bourgeois milieu of that time; and, though later he rebelled against the stifling strictness of his background, its concomitant of true Catholic faith never ceased to glow within him. 'I do not know if I hate you or cherish you, but I know that I owe everything to you,' he wrote of his native town, where he was born at 11 rue du Pas-St-Georges, in the elegant heart of Vieux Bordeaux. His father died when he was a year old and the family then moved to a succession of other houses, notably at 15 rue Rolland just off the broad Cours Clemenceau, where he spent much of his early youth. Today the clanging trams that

echo through *La Pharisienne* and *Un adolescent d'autrefois* have disappeared, and the ancient narrow streets round the rue Ste-Catherine have been beautifully restored and closed to traffic; Mauriac's Bordeaux has grown even more rich and graceful than when he knew it.

Most of his life after the age of 20 was spent in Paris: but he would return for country holidays in the Gironde, where his family owned three houses. Here, south of the city, there are two distinct and contrasting 'Mauriac' areas, in his books as in his life: the broad and prosperous vine-growing valley of the Garonne, around Langon; and, to its west, the vast flat pine-forest of the Landes, largest in western Europe. Until not long before Mauriac's childhood, the Landes (the word means 'heath' or 'moor') was little more than a marshy wasteland, interspersed with oakwoods. Then the ocean of sea-pines was planted out under Napoleon III, and the area began to take on a new life, but in Mauriac's view at least a somewhat sinister one.

Opposite: *The Greek and Latin inscriptions on the ceiling of Montaigne's library, where he 'took refuge in the bosom of the muses'.*

The old stone tower across the courtyard is all that now remains of Montaigne's original château, east of Bordeaux.

He was a very sensual (as well as spiritual) writer, highly sensitive to those forests; few other French novelists have stressed so sharply the influence of landscape upon character, as can be seen especially in his masterwork, *Thérèse Desqueyroux* (1927). And yet, most curiously, the Landes forest in Mauriac's work wears two entirely different faces: oppressive and claustrophobic in *Thérèse*, idyllically sensuous and liberating in his semi-autobiographical *Le Mystère Frontenac*. The explanation for this dichotomy is clear: he had himself adored his childhood holidays in the wild garden at St-Symphorien (the 'Bourideys' of *Frontenac*) and his rambles there in the woods, but he also saw that life in the deeper parts of the forest could be gloomy and imprisoning for those condemned to live there continuously, either the peasant woodcutters or a bourgeois city exile such as his sad Thérèse. Conditions today are much easier: but, in those earlier decades of the forest, the brooding isolation was intense in many areas, and roads were still few. When

Thérèse marries her loutish landowning husband, she goes to live in his
family farmhouse in a hamlet deep amid the pines:

Argelouse is, quite literally, a 'land's end', a place beyond which it is impossible to
go, the sort of settlement which, in this part of the world, is called a 'holding' – just a
few farmsteads, without church, administrative centre or graveyard, scattered loosely
around an acre or so of rye, and joined by a single ill-kept road to the market-town of
Saint-Clair [St-Symphorien], six miles away. This road, with its ruts and potholes,
peters out beyond Argelouse into a number of sandy tracks. From there, right on to
the coast, is nothing but marshland – fifty miles of it – brackish ponds, sickly pines,
and stretches of heath where the sheep, at winter's end, are the colour of dead ash.
The best families of Saint-Clair derived originally from this remote and arid corner.
Towards the middle of the last century, when the grandfathers of men now living
started to draw a certain amount of revenue from timber and resin as well as from
livestock, the families began to establish themselves in Saint-Clair, leaving their
mansion-houses at Argelouse to deteriorate into working farms. Carved beam-ends
and an occasional marble chimney-piece bear witness to an ancient splendour. Each
year the buildings sag more and more beneath their weight, and here and there can be
seen one of the great roofs drooping like the huge wing of an exhausted bird until it
looks almost as though it were resting on the ground.

After she has been caught trying to poison her dreadful husband,
Thérèse for a while is banished alone to this house, where her hold on
sanity wavers further. Throughout the book there recur the images of
suffocating summer heat, of forest fires that would damage the
Desqueyroux' prized prosperity based on timber. Another *motif* is the
wild moaning of the pines, which at night Thérèse does at least prefer to
the lonely silence of her exile:

The effect of the silence of Argelouse was to keep her awake. She liked best the
nights when there was a high and gusty wind, for she seemed to find a hint of human
tenderness in the monotonous soughing of the treetops.

As in her desperation she turns to evil, so this woman craving for
affection comes to identify herself with the landscape ('I was created in
the image of this barren land, where nothing lives but passing birds and
the roaming wild boar'). Even from the start, on her wedding day, she
had been aware of her mistake in marrying Bernard Desqueyroux; and
her premonition of the harm she would thereby do to him and his family
is tinged with the book's central imagery:

She had entered this cage like a sleep-walker, to awake with a feeling of miserable
and defenceless youth at the sound of the heavy gate clanging behind her. . She was
fated to smoulder there, deep in the very substance of this family, like a damped-
down fire worming its way beneath the heather, getting a hold first on one pine-tree,
then on another, till finally the whole forest would blaze like a wilderness of torches.

Mauriac suggests: 'The women of that part of France are markedly
superior to the men, who . . . never cultivate their minds. The heathland
has their hearts, and their imaginations never range beyond it.' This is
certainly true of Bernard, stubbornly obsessed with questions of property and of family reputation. But it was a daring remark on the author's

A timber forest in the Landes, where Mauriac in Thérèse Desqueyroux
traced the desolating influence of landscape upon character.

family since 1843, and he acquired it by inheritance in 1918. During all his long years in Paris, and right up until his death, Mauriac would spend part of each spring and autumn at Malagar, and he regarded it more than anywhere as his spiritual home – 'Here, with the Garonne plain at my feet, I could know myself at last.' Part of the property is still used for holidays by the family of Mauriac's son Claude, also a well-known writer. On my own visit in 1988, the main building was soon to be opened as a museum, and I found it still rather cluttered. I was shown the book-lined library where François Mauriac did his writing, and a suite of salons full of rather ugly pre-war furniture and photographs of that solemn ferret-like sharp-nosed face and its little toothbrush moustache. Upstairs, his simple bedroom still bore a portrait of Christ above the bed and a crucifix by the mirror. Little had been changed since his death. The inside of the house is rather depressing, but the outside is lovely – a fine line of cypresses beside the vineyards, and wide views down across the Garonne to the Château d'Yquem preparing its sweet magical nectar on the far hillside. Claude Mauriac himself produces a wine, Château Malagar, which is a perfectly respectable Côtes de Bordeaux. And Malagar provided the setting for a number of his father's novels – most notably, *Le Noeud de Vipères*, where in one memorable scene an August storm wrecks the ripening grapes, thus intensifying family discord. This is another telling example of the close links between man and nature, in so much of Mauriac's work.

From Jouanhau I drove down through the never-ending Landes to Bayonne and Biarritz on the Basque coast. Both these towns have been much admired and visited by English and American as well as French writers. Bernard Shaw and Kipling, among many others, stayed at Biarritz. Arthur YOUNG thought Bayonne 'much the prettiest town I have seen in France', and its women 'the handsomest I have seen in France'. HEMINGWAY, too, registered approval, in his usual laconic way. The narrator of *The Sun also Rises* (now sold as *Fiesta*) clearly had the makings of a great architectural critic: 'Bayonne is a nice town. . . It seemed like a nice cathedral, nice and dim, like Spanish churches.'

A number of other English-speaking writers have been drawn to the beautiful Pyrenean south-west corner of France. Hilaire Belloc, Anglo-French by birth, wrote about his walks in the Gavarnie sector of the Pyrenees (but the inn that he asked Miranda if she remembered was more probably on the Spanish side). Dornford Yates had a house near Pau, at a time when the English resident community in that town was one of the largest on the Continent, and he describes their doings in some of his 'Berry' novels. Curiously, the Béarn and Basque regions have themselves produced few writers at all well known in France, though one exception is the poet Francis JAMMES (1886–1938): he was born near Pau and then lived in the Basque village of Hasparren where his home is now a small museum. His work includes a large number of scarcely

The high Pyrenees,
beloved of Francis Jammes.

distinguished topographical poems about south-western towns and places, such as this fragment, *La Ville de Pau*:

> Elle ouvre l'éventail d'azur des Pyrénées
> Sur les côteaux du gave aux villas fortunées.
> Son boulevard, balcon où s'attarde l'été,
> Où l'hiver ne connait que la sérénité,
> Ne cesse de fleurir d'Anglaises élégantes
> Que suivent de grands chiens et des lords qui se gantent.

(It opens out the blue range of the Pyrenees / Onto the slopes of the mountain torrent with their wealthy villas. / Its boulevard, a balcony where summer lingers, / where winter knows only serenity, / Flowers perpetually with elegant English ladies / Who are followed by large dogs and by lords wearing gloves.)

The Béarn, of which Pau is the capital, was historically the homeland of the 'three musketeers' in Alexandre Dumas' famous tale. But Dumas himself was from the Paris area, and that is where he sets most of the action. His fourth musketeer, d'Artagnan, is from neighbouring Gascony and the author endows him with typical Gascon qualities of shrewdness, bravery and hot-headedness. Another romantic Gascon

equally celebrated in literature is of course Cyrano de Bergerac: Edmond
ROSTAND based his play (1897) on a 17th-century Parisian writer of
that name, but transforms him into a chivalrous Gascon knight.

The play was written before Rostand, himself a Provençal, had settled
in the Basque country. He visited Cambo-les-Bains for his health in
1900, fell in love with the area, and then built for himself the sumptuous
Villa Arnaga, using the money he had amassed from the vast success of
Cyrano and *L'Aiglon*. This enormous chalet in local Basque style, with
its formal terraced garden facing the Pyrenees, is now a beautifully-kept
museum, well worth a visit. Its interiors are not at all Basque, being a
mixture of Empire and Art Nouveau styles, all lavishly ornate; and they
are full of vivid souvenirs of the Belle Epoque life of this most stylish
individual. Among these are photographs of the celebrities who came to
visit him at Arnaga (including his mistress, Countess Anna de Noailles)
and of his son Jean who as a boy had long flowing curls and looked
incredibly pretty and girlish (much later, a famous biologist, he was bald

*At Cambo-les-Bains,
Edmond Rostand's Villa
Arnaga and its formal
garden.*

The country around Ascain, 'green, green, magnificently green', where Pierre Loti sought out the soul of the Basques.

and ugly). Although he adored the Basque country, Rostand never wrote about it – save that his third well-known play *Chantecler*, a satire on human foibles set anthropomorphically in a farmyard, is said to have been vaguely inspired by a farm that he used to visit on the edge of Cambo, down the St-Jean-de-Luz road (it is now the touristy Auberge du Vrai Chantecler, eagerly flaunting its Rostand credentials). The playwright loved animals, but they had to be white ones: he surrounded himself with white dogs and cats and a flock of white doves.

The Basque people themselves have produced a number of works of literature in their own ancient and mysterious language. In the French Basque provinces, the foremost writer is Pedro de Axular who was curé of the village of Sare in the early 17th century and whose *Gero* is a collection of religious folk-tales; it is still read today, by devotees of the current Basque cultural revival. Of modern Basque writers, however, most live on the Spanish side of the frontier and few have been translated into

French. As for French literature, the best descriptions of the Pays Basque and its people are in Pierre LOTI's *Ramuntcho* (1897), to my mind a more interesting book than his better-known *Pêcheur d'Islande* (see p. 25). Loti, like Rostand, was an adoring immigrant to the Basque country, but unlike Rostand he did write about his love. He came to the area first as captain of a naval vessel stationed at Hendaye, where later he built a holiday villa down by the port, and there he died in 1923. Closed today to visitors, it is a tall green-timbered Basque house in a garden full of palms and tropical shrubs, facing across the Bidassoa estuary to the hideous suburbs of Irun, in Spain.

Before the villa was built, Loti in order to research and write his novel stayed up in the hinterland in the very pretty village of Ascain, at the still-extant Hôtel de la Rhune (named after the conical rain-attracting Pyrenean peak that dominates this landscape). The simple story is of Ramuntcho, a young shepherd and smuggler (nearly everyone smuggled, in those parts in those days), and his tender romance with a local girl: but her mother opposes the match, and when the lad is away on military service she has Gracieuse put in a nearby nunnery. Ramuntcho makes a bid to abduct her, but she by now has chosen God and will not leave. The book may not suit all sophisticated tastes, for the lyrical tone is over-insistent and the ingenuous true-love saga sometimes seems too syrupy. But there are other qualities. Loti's folksy portrayal of Basque life may be a little too studied, even a shade patronising: but he was writing at a time when the unique Basque customs and traditions were still little known in the rest of France, and his descriptions are certainly vivid and sympathetic – the neat flowery villas, the *pelote* and the high-bounding dances, the church services where men and women sit separately, the piercing cries of the shepherds 'like the call of some redskin tribes in the American forests'. And the incessant smuggling forays into Spain, for phosphates, absinthe and much else (smuggling was then an essential means of livelihood, but today it has largely disappeared on this frontier, as the peasants have grown more prosperous and Spanish prices for most goods have crept up to French levels). There are also numerous lyrical passages about nature, landscape and the changing seasons which set the mood of the whole story, as the peasants await the dread winter storms or joyously greet the return of spring. The book is set in the village of Sare, which Loti calls Etchezar, right below the Rhune which he calls the Gizune; today with its red and green shutters and cross-timbers it is one of the best-preserved of Basque show-villages, where all new building must be in the local style, and apart from the inevitable inrush of cars and tourists it probably looks much the same as it did in Ramuntcho's day:

All that he saw around his house was green, green, magnificently green, as in springtime is every corner of this land of rain and shadow. The ferns, which in autumn take on so warm a colour of rust, were now, on this April day, in their most brilliant green freshness, and they covered the mountainsides like a vast carpet of

The lavish interior of Rostand's villa: souvenirs of the Belle Epoque.

curly long wool, specked by red patches of digitalis flowers. Below, in a ravine, the torrent murmured under the branches. On high, the clusters of oaks and beeches clung to the slopes, alternating with the meadows; then, above this tranquil Eden, towards the sky, there rose the great bare summit of the Gizune, lord here of the region of clouds. And a little further back one could see also the church and the houses – this village of Etchezar, alone and high-perched on one of the Pyrenean foothills, far from everything, far from the lines of communication which had convulsed and ruined the lowlands by the beaches: sheltered from curiosity and from alien profanations, and living still its Basque life of times gone by.

And the winter nights:

It was the season when the Pyrenean villages, disencumbered of the walkers that the summer brings, enclosed by the storm-clouds, the mists or the snows, return to what they were in olden times. In the cider-houses – the only little spots that are bright and alive, amid the vast empty darkness of the countryside – a little of the spirit of bygone days revives again, during the winter evening get-togethers. In front of the great casks of cider ranged in the dark recesses, the lamp, suspended from the rafters, casts its light on the images of saints that decorate the walls, and on the groups of mountain folk talking and smoking. Sometimes someone sings a ballad from far-off days; the striking of a tambourine revives old forgotten rhythms; a guitar-chord re-awakens some sadness from the time of the Moors. . .

This nostalgia gives way at the book's end to a tense dénouement. Ramuntcho, increasingly agnostic, is confident that true love will prevail over the religious vows that have been foisted on his darling Gracieuse: but, when he arrives in her Basque convent to woo her away, he finds her serenely happy in her new life as a novice – and the reader is left uncertain whether the author is suggesting that she has found her true spiritual destiny, or has been wickedly brainwashed by the older nuns. This passage lies at the heart of Loti's own equivocal attitude to religion, something that he yearned for yet also rejected. He came as an outsider to the Basque country as he had to Brittany, deeply attracted by mysterious religious lands that he felt he never really understood. At the end of *Ramuntcho*, just before the convent scene, he expresses his fear of 'these ancient granite crosses, like a signal of alarm, crying beware', and his awe before an atavistic Basque spirituality that proves too strong for Ramuntcho's mere earthly romance:

In the shadows of the branches, under the banks of these roadways, there are digitalis roses, catch-flies and ferns, almost the same flora as in Brittany; moreover, these two lands, Basque and Breton, have so much resemblance in their omnipresent granite and habitual rain; also in their immobility, and the continuity of the same religious dream. . . Immobility across several centuries, immobility in beings and in things – one becomes more and more aware of this as one penetrates deeper into this country of forests and silence. Under this dark veil of sky, enveloping the peaks of the high Pyrenees, isolated dwellings emerge and then vanish, ancient farms and occasional hamlets, always shaded by the same canopy of oaks and ageless chestnuts, whose twisted roots border the pathways like mossy serpents. They are all the same, these hamlets separated by so much woodland, such a jumble of branches, and inhabited by an ancient race, contemptuous of all disturbance and change. . .

The river Bidassoa along the Spanish frontier, where Loti's Ramuntcho went smuggling.

Montségur citadel:
was Wagner inspired here for Parsifal?

10: Languedoc and the Pyrenées

(Midi-Pyrénées and Languedoc-Roussillon regions)

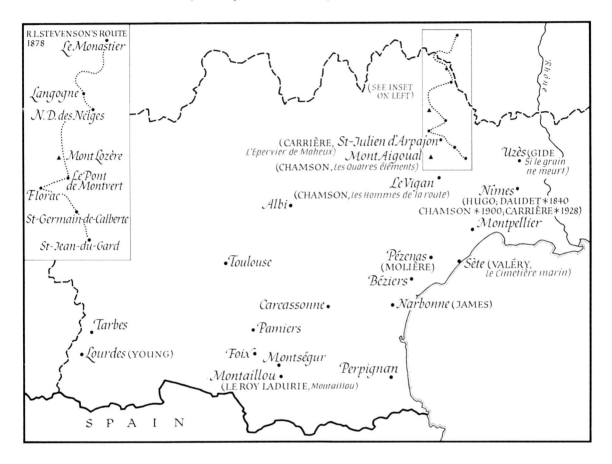

The foothills of the central Pyrenees, like the Béarn and the Basque country to their west, have long attracted writers. Arthur YOUNG came to Lourdes in 1787, before the visions of Bernadette Soubirous had made it into a place of pilgrimage, and he was upset by what he saw:

Take the road to Lourde [*sic*], where is a castle on a rock, garrisoned for the mere purpose of keeping state prisoners, sent hither by *lettres de cachet*. Seven or eight are *known* to be here at present; thirty have been here at a time; and many for life – torn by the relentless hand of jealous tyranny from the bosom of a domestic comfort; from wives, children, friends, and hurried for crimes unknown to themselves – more probably for virtues – to languish in this detested abode of misery – and die of despair. Oh, liberty! liberty! – and yet this is the mildest government of any considerable country in Europe, our own excepted.

South of Lourdes, the big thermal resort of Cauterets has springs that since Roman times have been thought to benefit sterile women – is it a coincidence that the town spa has also been fertile in 19th-century romance? Victor Hugo womanised there, and it was at Cauterets that Georges Sand discovered the thrills of adultery, with the first of her lovers, the young Aurélien de Sèze. Chateaubriand, on a visit to soothe his rheumatism in 1829, there met the mysterious young Occitan girl who wrote him letters and pursued him, yet remained tantalisingly inaccessible. Baudelaire and Heinrich Heine were also visitors to Cauterets and both have mentioned it in their poems; but they do not appear to have had any romantic involvements.

Further to the east, between Toulouse and the Mediterranean, is the country of the Cathars (also known as Albigensians), whose heresy flourished so widely in the 13th century and was then so brutally suppressed. It was at the lonely citadel of Montségur, on a hilltop south-east of Foix, that in 1244 some 200 Cathar *parfaits* or 'perfect ones' made their final stand against the armies sent from Paris, and were burned alive. According to one legend, a mysterious Cathar treasure was smuggled out of Montségur before it fell, and was then buried in the area; and one theory has it that this was none other than the Holy Grail. German writers in particular have been fascinated by this story; Richard Wagner visited Montségur when he was preparing *Parsifal* and, although this opera is much less about Catharism than about the Grail itself, it is thought that Wagner may have had Montségur vaguely in mind for the Castle of Montsalvat where his Knights guard their holy treasure. Much later, the Nazis tried to appropriate Catharism as an element in their Aryan creed; one Nazi philosopher and SS officer spent some time at Montségur during the war and wrote a book on this theme. Then in the 1970s a few young neo-Nazis took to visiting the castle and trying to steal stones from its ruins as souvenirs, so the French police became obliged to restrict access.

All this however is no more than a minor gloss on the true historical story of the Cathars, which has frequently been written about, more often in fact than fiction, and never more brilliantly than by the French social historian Emmanuel Le Roy Ladurie, in his best-selling book *Montaillou* (1978). As he relates, after Simon de Montfort's crusades against it and the defeat at Montségur, the Manichean heresy of Catharism had mostly died out from the region: but it lingered on in some upland villages of the Foix area, and even had a modest revival after about 1300. This greatly troubled the zealous Bishop of Pamiers, Jacques Fournier, and with the Pope's blessing he staged an Inquisition. Hundreds of people were arrested, in Montaillou and nearby villages, and by the end of a mass trial lasting seven years, 1318–25, five of those found

*Minerve, scene of
a Cathar massacre.*

guilty had been burned at the stake. The voluminous transcript of the trial has survived, and has always been known to scholars; but it was Le Roy Ladurie who had the idea of re-arranging and interpreting this material, so as to draw from it a vivid picture of mediaeval village life that reads almost like a novel. Here is a gallery of beguiling characters – Béatrice de Planissoles the generous and promiscuous *châtelaine*, Pierre Clergue the priest and double agent, the villainous Bélibaste, the saintly Authie brothers, and many others, all involved in cooking, loving, stealing, intriguing, holding supper-parties, and a great many other activities not so alien from our own today, together with regular mutual de-lousing (a mark of friendship and intimacy) and more than a dash of superstition ('Béatrice de Planissoles kept the first menstrual blood of her daughter to use as a love potion to bewitch some future son-in-law. She preserved the umbilical cords of her grandsons as talismans to help her win her lawsuit').

The small village of Montaillou stands amid pastures and woodlands on a broad empty plateau about 35 miles south-east of Foix. It seems remote, for even today access is not easy up the steep mountain road from Ax-les-Thermes, down in the Ariège valley; but eastwards the country rolls more gently towards Quillan and the coast. The village still contains some traces of its 14th-century past: on a hilltop dominating the plateau are the crumbling ruins of the old feudal château, while just below it, 'partly at least, both church and chapel are in the Romanesque style and date from before 1300', says Le Roy Ladurie. In this sleepy and half-deserted village, all the other houses are of more recent construction: but

there is still a Clergue living there, certainly a descendant of the family that features so prominently in the book. In the 1300s, the houses clustered close below the castle, while the 'perfect ones' had their hiding-places out in the woods.

In Montaillou as elsewhere, these *parfaits* formed the ascetic élite of Catharism, which was never a formal church but a loose network of sects. It preached a doctrine of purity, in reaction against the Church of Rome which at that time was undeniably corrupt, and widely despised. The Cathars were Manicheans, holding that the universe was made up of two contending forces of good and evil; all that was spiritual was good, but the world and the human race, including the Church, were in the hands of the powers of evil. One might have expected this doctrine to have produced a puritanical and unworldly society amongst its believers in Languedoc, but far from it. There was in fact a two-tier morality. For the majority, no restrictions and total liberty of life and manners; for the *parfaits*, a highly chaste and ascetic code, plus the responsibility of reconciling ordinary believers (sinners), on their deathbeds, with the principle of purity and good. To a modern reader, this may all seem magnificently hypocritical – and terribly convenient – as when Béatrice recounts to the court what her lover the priest has said:

Pierre Clergue told me, that both man and woman can freely commit any sin they like during their life. And do whatever they please in this world. Provided only that at

The approach to the Cévennes.

the end they are received into the sect or into the faith of the good Christians. Then they are saved and absolved of all the sins they have committed in their life. . . thanks to the laying on of hands of these good Christians, as it is received on the brink of death.

Perhaps it is thus not surprising that one of the more interesting aspects of the book is the light it sheds on mediaeval sex life. Pederasty was rife in the towns, concubinage was tolerated in the villages, strange herbs were used for contraception, and a respected woman such as Béatrice could have many lovers, including priests (these were *not* the same as the *parfaits*). Another girl says of her happy liaison with Clergue:

In those days it pleased me, as it pleased the priest, that he should know me carnally and be known by me; and so I did not think I was sinning, and neither did he. But now, with him, it does not please me any more. And so now, if he knew me carnally, I should think it a sin!

What a strangely contemporary note that strikes – the notion that sex is not wrong so long as it is combined with true feeling. In the Montaillou area, priests were held to make the best lovers. Pierre, the village priest and 'the womaniser par excellence of the Clergue family', had at least a dozen mistresses according to the Fournier records and would make love with Béatrice in his church:

Pierre was a swashbuckler. Cathar, spy and rake – he was everywhere. . . He scattered his desires among his flock as impartially as he gave his benediction, and in return won the favours of many of his female parishioners. He was helped by the general tolerance with which concubinage among ecclesiastics was regarded in the Pyrenees. At an altitude of 1,300 metres the rules of priestly celibacy ceased to apply. . . He coveted all women. . . He said so straight out to Raymonde Guilhou, wife of the shoemaker Arnaud Vital, one day when she was delousing him on the bench in Arnaud's workshop. He took the opportunity of ogling the girls as they went along the village street. Hunting was his vocation. He adored his mother and burned with incestuous passions, sometimes carried into practice, for his sisters and sisters-in-law.

All this would surely have horrified the prim and prissy Henry JAMES, who was shocked even by the cuisine and social informality of the Midi when he passed this way in 1882. In *A Little Tour of France* he describes a visit to a hotel in Narbonne:

I was obliged to cultivate relations with the cuisine of this establishment. Nothing could have been more *méridional*; indeed, both the dirty little inn and Narbonne at large seemed to me to have the informalities of the south, without its usual graces. Narrow, noisy, shabby, belittered and encumbered, filled with clatter and chatter, the Hôtel de France would have been described in perfection by Alphonse Daudet. For what struck me above all in it was the note of the Midi, as he has represented it – the sound of universal talk. The landlord sat at supper with sundry friends, in a kind of glass cage, with a genial indifference to arriving guests; the waiters tumbled over the loose luggage in the hall. . . At ten o'clock in the morning there was a table d'hôte for breakfast – a wonderful repast, which overflowed into every room and pervaded the whole establishment. I sat down with a hundred hungry marketers, fat, brown, greasy men, with a good deal of the rich soil of Languedoc adhering to their hands and boots. I mention the latter articles because they almost put them on the table. It was very hot, and there were swarms of flies; the viands had the strongest odour; there was in particular a horrible mixture known as *gras-double*, a light grey, glutinous, nauseating mess, which my companions devoured in large quantities. A man opposite to me had the dirtiest fingers I ever saw. . .

So much for one of the most delicious French recipes for tripe. Later in the book, in another gastronomic town, Bourg-en-Bresse, James had 'an excellent repast – the best repast possible – which consisted simply of boiled eggs and bread and butter'. Throughout his tour, he shows distaste for many of those aspects of French life which other Anglo-Saxon francophiles most adore; and the only consolation that one can offer to his stiff shade is that the Hôtel de France, still there at 6 rue Rossini, no longer has a restaurant.

Just four years before James glided through Languedoc in a train, another and hardier English-speaking traveller hiked into it from the north over the Cévennes – with a donkey. Robert Louis STEVENSON began his celebrated journey at Le Monastier, up in the Haute-Loire department near Le Puy. Here for 65 francs he acquired Modestine, who was to carry his baggage, and together they set off south along a zig-zag route that any tourist can follow today with the aid of a good map. (If you are prepared to cheat, then most of the trip can easily be done by car, even over the heights of Mont Lozère. But, if you want to trace Stevenson's path exactly, then you will have to walk along parts of it). Once on his way, he sets out the raison d'être of the enterprise:

> I travel for travel's sake. The great affair is to move; to feel the needs and hitches of our life more nearly; to come down off this feather-bed of civilisation, and find the globe granite underfoot and strewn with cutting flints. . . To hold a pack upon a pack-saddle against a gale out of the freezing north is no high industry, but it is one that serves to occupy and compose the mind.

Thus disposed, he trekked first to the village of Goulet, then made a westward detour to Le Bouchet, where at the inn he found himself sharing the only bedroom with a young married couple ('I kept my eyes to myself, and know nothing of the woman except that she had beautiful arms'). Next his route lay south again, through the Gevaudan country where in the 1760s a notorious wolf had roamed the land, devouring women and children. He crossed the old stone bridge over the Allier at Langogne, now destroyed, and came up through the pines to the Trappist monastery of Nôtre-Dame-des-Neiges, east of La Bastide; 'I have rarely approached anything with more unaffected terror than the monastery of our *Lady of the Snows*. Thus it is to have a Protestant education.' But this Presbyterian Scot soon found that these silence-bound Catholic monks were not ravening wolves: they greeted him at first a little suspiciously, but then with warmth, and they fed and lodged him. Of those not bound to vows of silence, a few made efforts to convert the alien Protestant intruder to their Catholic faith, but Stevenson retorted amicably and

The high Cévennes, where Stevenson walked with Modestine.

The Camargue and its white horses: part of Mistral's Provençal heartland.

11: *Provence*

(Provence/Côte d'Azur region)

The best-loved and most visited of all French regions has inspired a vast miscellany of writers. Some have come from elsewhere, attracted by its sensuous Mediterranean qualities, the wild beauty of its hinterland or the sophisticated pleasures of the Riviera. But in the past 150 years Provence has also produced an important number of its own regional writers, closely involved with its landscape and traditions. Amongst them, one should maybe draw a distinction between the lighter and more popular authors, such as Daudet and Pagnol, essentially story-tellers and satirists of the quirky Provençal character, and those with a more poetical and philosophical bent, notably Jean Giono, concerned with man in communion with elemental nature and with the cosmic or primitive mysteries of this land.

All of them were influenced, to some extent, by the movement that developed in the mid-19th century for promoting the Provençal language as the vehicle for a widespread regional revival. This movement, the

Félibrige, was without parallel in the France of that time. It succeeded only very partially in its linguistic aims, for since then French has remained the language of almost all the region's writers and Provençal has continued to die out from daily use. But the Félibrige did in a wider sense stimulate the region's culture and its sense of identity. And along with a few goodish minor writers it did throw up one poet of genius who not only provided a charismatic leadership at the time, but who still today seems to personify Provençal folk-culture and to provide it with a focus and point of reference – the larger-than-life figure of Frédéric MISTRAL.

He came from a well-to-do farming family, and was born and spent all his life (1830–1914) in the village of Maillane, south of Avignon. He was at a *lycée* in Avignon and at university in Aix, and then aged 24 he founded the Félibrige, along with Joseph Roumanille, who had been one of his professors, and six others. Their aim was to revive an interest in the customs, history and spirit of Provence, as well as in its language. At the age of 29 Mistral then wrote his first major work, *Mirèio* (in French *Mireille*), which he never later surpassed. This long epic poem is a swirling fresco of rural life in the Crau and Camargue areas, to the east and south of Arles, and Mistral's purpose behind it was in part didactic, even political: he wanted to fix in his readers' minds, and to set down for posterity, a record of the folklore, customs and landscapes of his *pays*, which he felt to be menaced by industrial and economic change. Written in Provençal in a musical free-flowing style, *Mirèio* is also a hymn of love to Provence as well as a tragic love-story (Mistral later collaborated with Gounod on the opera, *Mireille*, which was based on it). He wanted also to revive the classical epic form – and the poem opens in true Virgilian style ('*Arma virumque cano. . .*'):

> Cante uno chato de Prouvènço.
> Dins lis amour de sa jouvènço,
> A través de la Crau, vers la mar, dins li bla,
> Umble escoulan dóu grand Oumèro,
> Iéu la vole segui. . .

(Of a young girl of Provence I sing. / In the loves of her youth, / across the Crau, towards the sea, amid the cornfields, / humble pupil of the great Homer, I want to follow her. . .)

The story Mistral sings is of Vincent, young and humble basket-maker from Vallabrègues (on the Rhône, north of Tarascon), who goes to woo Mireille, daughter of a wealthy farmer on the plain of La Crau. He arrives at the time of gathering in the mulberry-leaves for the silkworms:

> Cantas, cantas, magnanarello,
> Que la culido es cantarello!
> Galant soun li magnan e s'endormon di tres;
> Lis amourié soun plen de filho
> Que lou bèu tèms escarrabiho,
> Coume un vòu de blóundis abiho
> Que raubon sa melico i roumanin dóu gres.

(Sing, sing, you silkworm breeders, / for the harvest loves your singing. / Beautiful are the silkworms, and they are sleeping their third sleep; / the mulberry-trees are full of girls / that the fine weather makes alert and gay, / like a swarm of blonde bees / that steal their honey from the rosemary-shrubs in the stony fields.)

Silkworm breeding (*magnanage*) was then a staple activity in Provence, and today a number of the old silkworm farms have been converted into hotels, calling themselves *La Magnaneraie*. Mistral paints a joyful picture of the harvesters at work, in a serene land of sunlight, wine and beauty. But Mireille's parents sternly oppose her love for this penniless suitor: so the fifteen-year-old girl decides to make a pilgrimage to the shrine of Les Saintes-Maries-de-la-Mer, in the Camargue, to seek advice and protection. As she crosses the Rhône, this gives Mistral the pretext for one of his many lyrical digressions:

The high church at
Les Saintes-Maries
where Mireille comes to die.

*At Maillane, the old house
where Mistral
lived with his mother.*

Muséon Arlaten, the large and magnificent museum of Provençal traditional life that Mistral created in 1896 and later enlarged with the help of
the money from his 1904 Nobel prize for Literature. This museum is an
intensely personal creation, and many of its exhibits still bear the labels
and explanations that he wrote in his own hand (printed French ones are
now added). Some rooms are filled with Provençal costumes and Arlesian
coifs, or have big tableaux vivants depicting traditional peasant scenes.

Among the many portraits of Mistral on display, one large and
remarkable painting depicts him in the crowded Roman arena at Arles,
acknowledging the acclaim of the crowd – a tall handsome figure with a
neat pointed beard, clad in a black cape. Never one for false modesty,
Mistral saw himself as the Messiah of a Provence reborn, and his
followers saw him that way too. But his movement remained cultural in
the broader sense, never becoming autonomist in a political sense, and so
Paris did not interfere with it. However the Félibrige's demand for
Provençal to be taught in schools soon ran up against the Third Republic's

campaign against regional languages, and so made little headway. Today, as in the case of Brittany (see p. 18), it seems ironic that Paris has ended its ban just at a time when younger Provençaux are neglecting their ancient tongue and would rather learn 'useful' modern languages such as English. It would seem that the future of Provençal will be restricted to a few intellectuals and fervent regionalists. But, even if it dies out as a living language, it remains enshrined in Mistral's work – and one can easily buy a Provençal/French bilingual edition of *Mireio*, and thus enjoy the songfully sonorous original without missing its meaning. In short, Provence owes a huge debt to Mistral. He gave a new force and focus to its traditions, and has thus helped them to survive into a modern age.

Alphonse DAUDET (1840–97), though he wrote in French and lived in Paris, was among the many writers influenced by Mistral. They met in 1860, when the poet helped to awaken the budding storyteller's enthusiasm for the life of the Midi. Daudet the creator of burlesques and simple country tales was of course a slighter figure than Mistral, but his feeling for Provence was real. Born in Nîmes and schooled in Lyon (see p. 219), he soon moved to Paris but from there would go often to stay with friends in the village of Fontvieille, north-east of Arles. He is known, amongst much else, for the romantic drama *L'Arlésienne*, later set to music by Bizet, and for the *Tartarin de Tarascon* trilogy which genially caricatures the exuberant and boastful Provençal character. The people of Tarascon at first felt insulted by this satire: but today Tartarin has passed harmlessly into local folklore and even plays a role in the annual festival of the Tarasque, the town's legendary monster. A small Tartarin museum contains some amusing tableaux vivants.

Daudet is known above all for the *Lettres de mon moulin* (1866), the quaint tales that every French schoolchild is given to read. He wrote them

Ruined by floods in the 17th century, the famous 'Pont d'Avignon' (Pont St-Bénézet), described by Mistral and Daudet.

The Vieux Port at Marseille, scene of Pagnol's Marius *trilogy.*

Trees in the Camargue, where Mireille was warned by butterflies.

Of all French novelists of all epochs, Jean GIONO (1895–1970) is the one most intimately and passionately involved with landscape and the natural world – or at least this is true of the Giono of the pre-1939 period when he was in his prime (in his later years he changed, as we shall see). His ideas about the influence of nature upon man may derive somewhat from Rousseau: but Giono's world of nature is more wild, less gently pastoral than Rousseau's and his vision is more cosmic and mysterious. He was not a Christian, and declared himself to be 'not gifted for God': instead his books are informed by a radiant pantheism that certainly has its mystical side but is also intensely sensual, and he developed a philosophy of joy in the physical world, its sounds, smells and tastes. He believed that man is truest to himself when close to wild nature, and often in his books he talks of people as if they were natural objects: in *Que ma joie demeure* (a truly Gionesque title), the peasant Bobi has nobility because 'his shoulders and his back were like walking mountains and his head was a tree', and in that other seminal book, *Les Vraies richesses* (i.e. those of the earth), Giono says of himself, 'Like God I felt my head, my hair and my eyes to be filled with birds... my chest inflated with goats, horses and bulls.' According to Giono, it is not educated people or townsfolk but the simple peasants of the uplands who are closest to the 'true riches', and it is the lonely heights that 'reconcile man with the universe'. Landscape and the elements – the wind especially – thus become characters in the novels. It is not surprising that Giono has often been compared with an even greater writer, Thomas Hardy: there are certainly some similarities, but Giono does not share Hardy's view of a malign destiny shaping all human affairs; nor does Hardy, although also a great countryman, have Giono's particular vision of the union between man and nature.

Giono's *pays* is the upper part of central Provence, between Digne and Apt: he was born in the little town of Manosque in the Durance valley and lived there most of his life. He came from a simple background (his father was a cobbler) and had little formal education. After his war service, he worked for some years with a local bank that would send him on trips to small branch offices in the villages, and from this and from holidays spent with a shepherd family he came to know intimately the wild hilly country north and north-west of Manosque. Here he set his early *Pan* trilogy (1929–30), *Colline*, *Un de Baumugnes* and *Regain*, which lyrically describe the life of peasants battling with the elements in beautiful but lonely settings.

Regain, one of the best and most characteristic of his large output of novels, is set in an abandoned hamlet 'fixed against the side of the plateau like a little wasps' nest', somewhere between Vachères and Banon, to the west of Forcalquier. Here the young bachelor Panturle stays on alone after all his neighbours have departed for the gentler climate of the lower slopes; and after a hard winter of struggle his life finds a radiant renewal when he is joined by a loving and sensuous woman, and together they

A hamlet in the Giono country, near Manosque.

make the upland flourish with fruit and corn, and exult in their triumphant liberty. Certainly there is an element of utopian allegory. And Giono's animism makes natural objects behave like people, sometimes with a touch of whimsy:

They left by the Saint-Martin road, which was shorter. First there was a tall poplar that began to talk to them. Then it was the Sauneries stream that accompanied them very politely, rubbing itself against their road, whistling like a tamed grass-snake; then the wind of evening joined them, went along with them a little way, then left them for the lavender, then came back, then went off again with three big bees. Just like that. And that amused them. Panturle carried the bag, with all their shopping. Arsule, beside him, went with a man's stride to keep pace. And she laughed. Then came the night, at the moment when, leaving the wood, they were about to slip into the vale of Aubignane; so the night came, the old night which they knew and loved, the night with its arms all damp like a washer-woman, the night all shining with dust, the night that brings the moon.

The wind, ever howling or making the trees sing, plays a big role in the book:

It came full in their faces and placed its great tepid hand on their mouths; as if to prevent them from breathing. . . Then the wind began to scrape their eyes with its nails. Then it tried to undress them. . . Arsule drew the harness-strap and so leaned forward. The wind entered into her corsage as if going home. It flowed between her breasts, it descended to her belly like a hand; it flowed between her thighs, bathing all her thighs, refreshing her like a bath. Her kidneys and hips were drenched in wind. . .

Finally the great springtime arrives:

The south has opened like a mouth. It has blown a long breath, damp and luke-warm, and the flowers have quivered in the corn, and the whole round earth has begun to ripen like a fruit. The flotilla of clouds has cast its moorings. This has made a great long convoy of high clouds, moving to the north. This has continued; and with it, one has felt the earth swelling up with all the rain and the reawakened life of the grass and herbs. Then at last, for one lovely moment, the free sky has bubbled up beneath the prow of the last cloud. But there remained one wisp in the sky and it floated there, stuck to the church-tower of Aubignane like a piece of linen around a stone in a stream.

Just as some critics have accused Giono of 'utopianism' and of over-idealising his peasants, so he can perhaps also be criticised for excessive lyricism and for using metaphors or similes that are sometimes too quaintly fanciful (one is reminded of the transposed epithets and poetic phrasing of Dylan Thomas): 'the spring fastened on his shoulders like a fat cat', 'the sky is open like an oven door', 'little villages all closed like surprised tortoises', or the stream whose tail is pulled like a snake. This can become irritating. But the style is certainly original, and there is much true poetry in Giono's exaltation of natural innocence – as in the description of the horses' wedding in *Que ma joie demeure*:

The horses' wedding lasted all the day beneath a horse sky full of gallopades, of running clouds mixed with sun and shade. The stallion bit the neck of the black mare. She hollowed her loins as if to open herself below, and she leapt away towards the greenery of Randoulet. They galloped side by side, their manes steaming. The stallion kept trying to bite her ears. The mare sensed on her neck the saliva of the stallion, cooling in the wind of their gallop. She wanted shade, grass and peace. She galloped towards the shade, grass and peace. . . The two beasts . . . sniffed the odour of the pool. Their eyes were dazzled by the reflecting waer. They heard the sudden smack of the fins of the big awakened fish. They began to dance there, and the water splashed up in long white streaks that sparkled in the sun as they rose above the grass. The freshness touched their bellies, their loins, their thighs, and it was already like a beginning of love-making. They felt a calming within them of the wildness of that passion which was drawing them together. Crushing the grass, they rolled in the water and the mud, on the edge of the pool. As the water bathed them, they felt the wild passion changing to tenderness, and when they stood up, a little dazed, shivering, and covered with mud, they licked each other's muzzles gently, first around the mouth then around the eyes.

The summer of 1935, the year of the publication of *Que ma joie demeure*, saw the beginning of the 'Contadour' venture that made Giono

The tumbledown farmhouse of Giono's Contadour venture.

into a kind of prophetic Socrates figure, somewhat against his better judgement. Together with a group of some forty friends and admirers, many of them from Paris, he went hiking in the hills, and one night they bivouacked outside the remote village of Contadour, up on a broad glorious plateau below the Montagne de Lure. They liked this spot so much that they decided to settle awhile, even buying a tumbledown farmhouse – and so for the next five summers Contadour became the centre for a series of non-religious retreats, or seminars, on the themes of nature, ecology and pacifism. Giono expounded his views on the abuses of urban and technical civilisation, on the need to move closer to the 'vraies richesses' of nature and the human heart, and on the evils of war – an increasingly urgent topic in the later 1930s. He had fought in the trenches in 1914–18, and had already expressed his pacifism in a powerful novel, *Le Grand troupeau* (1931), which recounted not only the horrors of battle but the dreadful impact of war on civilian life in the countryside.

The modest Giono was not happy at being treated as a Socrates by his disciples, some of them pale Paris intellectuals who came eager to imbibe the divine truth of his rural pantheism amid these lonely hills. But he felt so strongly about war that he allowed himself to be pushed forward as a spokesman of the pacifist movement – and for this he was imprisoned in Marseille when hostilities broke out, but later released thanks to the intervention of André Gide. During the Occupation, although not the slightest bit pro-Nazi, he fell into an acutely invidious position. Not only did his stance against violence lead him to refuse to help the local Resistance, but the Vichyists realised gleefully that his back-to-nature credo had something in common with Pétain's crypto-Nazi philosophy of a return to the land, of 'wearing green and working in the woods' – and so they tried to make use of him for propaganda purposes (just as they did with Mistral's heritage). Therefore at the Liberation he was again put in prison, this time as a collaborator, but was later freed without trial.

These experiences, and the tragedy of the war itself, marked him in a way that left him bitter and disillusioned. He ceased to evangelise, he never repeated the Contadour experience, and his writing changed, too, for the joyous philosophy of nature gave place to a more sombre and misanthropic tone; he became the detached observer, rather than the seer. However, he continued to write about the villagers of his native region, and this later period did produce some novels which in their own manner are graphic and compelling. Probably the best is *Le Hussard sur le toit* (1951), about the cholera epidemic of 1848 in Upper Provence, containing a remarkable description of Manosque in high summer:

> The town's skin of tiles began already to exhale a syrupy air. The sticky layers of heat that were stuck to all the surfaces drenched their shapes in iridescent gossamer-like shrouds. The incessant screeching of thousands of swallows whipped up the torrid stillness like a biting hailstorm. Thick columns of flies hovered like coal-dust over the cracks in the streets. Their perpetual droning created a kind of sonorous desert. . . The town [was] both burnt and rotten, it smelt foul like a piece of putrid meat grilled on a coal fire, this town of dung and typhoid. . .

Giono lived in this town for 39 years, on a pleasant hill in the outskirts called Le Mont d'Or, reached by a road that today is suitably named the Chemin des Vraies Richesses. His house remains the home of his widow, now in her nineties, and there are plans for it to become a museum after her death. Meanwhile, a Giono enthusiast can always join one of the local groups that organise hiking or biking tours through his *pays*. These will take you up to Contadour, where the old rough stone farmhouse is now the property of the last survivor of the pre-war seminars, an elderly Parisian. Just to the south, down a steep gully, is the ruined village of Redortiers which was in part the model for the 'Aubignane' of *Regain* (but this book is set further south, and Aubignane is probably an amalgam of Redortiers and Carniol, south of Banon). This gorgeous region of wide rolling panoramas is today more thinly populated than ever, but good new roads have been built for the tourist trade, and in summer at least it seems far less remote than it may have done in the 1930s. And, by the most savage of ironies, the French Army's principal nuclear missile base is today a bare six miles from Contadour, on the Plateau d'Albion to the west.

Giono's novels are set in three or four different areas of Upper Provence and the Dauphiné Alps. While the hills north-west of Manosque are the scene of *Regain* and *Colline*, some of the later books such as *Les Récits de la demi-brigade* are located on the plateaux to the east of the Durance, around Valensole and Gréoux-les-Bains where Giono spent some holidays. Another group of novels, including *Les Âmes forts*, are situated much further north, towards Grenoble, in the Trièves mountains which he also knew well. Here just off the N75 is the tiny hamlet of Baumugnes which gave its name to one of his best-loved early novels. Its hero, Albin, comes from this far-off upland paradise ('*j'ai dans moi Baumugnes tout entier*'), and moves south to the Durance where the main action is set, near the village of Lurs. Incidentally, it was here soon after the war that the English family Drummond were massacred while camping, and suspicion fell on the old patriarch Gaston Dominici who lived by the main road just opposite Lurs station. Giono attended his trial and then wrote a book, *Notes sur l'affaire Dominici* (1954), suggesting that probably the old man was innocent and had been framed by his own family.

From the sinister Dominici peasant clan to the pure and noble characters of *Regain* or *Un de Baumugnes* seems a very long way indeed. Was Giono idealising the Provençal peasantry out of proportion, as some critics believe? Certainly it is true that, rather like Georges Sand before him, or Rousseau in *La Nouvelle Héloïse*, he had some ideological motive in trying to show that man alone with nature is innocent and good, and only the city and money corrupt. So there is some degree of allegory in the earlier books. Even in his later novels, the simple country people are still shown in a good light, but Giono by then had become more pessimistic about man's ability to withstand the darker side of his nature. He had come to recognise that the utopian idyll of the uplands was possible for only a very few.

Henri B O S C O (1888–1978), born in Avignon, is a novelist who has some affinities with Giono. Nearly all his books are set in the Provençal countryside, either in the lower Rhône or to the east in the Durance valley: they describe man in relation to the landscape, his struggles and exaltations, sometimes with a hint of primitive mysteries or darker forces. The best of these novels is probably *Le Mas Théotime*, which won the Prix Renaudot in 1945; Bosco locates it in the hills east of Aix, though in fact he was describing his own *mas* at Lourmarin in the Lubéron hills. There are lyrical evocations of summer heat and winter storms, the life of the farm, and of animals – for example, this picture of a stampeding herd of wild boar:

In the bed of the stream a dark mass emerged. It was panting, growling, blowing, even trumpeting, with a kind of furious haste and brutal greed. They moved forward in a black column. In front the biggest: powerful backs and heavy jowls. Hemmed in by the steep banks of the stream, they tore up the brushwood as they passed. From their sweating hides there rose a savage smell of horsehair, of dried mud and acid dung. They passed without seeing me and went down towards Théotime with an irresistible force and bestial intoxication, bent on devastation... The further they went into the field, the more excitement became apparent. A mysterious animal frenzy had seized them bit by bit, and they gambolled in the heart of the devastation. I saw them running, jumping, charging, snorting with an inexplicable passion, as their ravages spread wider. But the breach that they had made in the maize led direct towards the Aliberte hill. Between the noble vineyard and this maize, we had just put down a thousand young plants, still tender. I knew that they would be lost.

But then the heroine, a mysterious child of nature, uses her powers to tame and quieten the herd. In the semi-autobiographical *L'Enfant et la rivière*, Bosco describes his boyhood adventures on the Durance, the trips down the river in a stolen dinghy and the dreamy days spent watching the birds, fishes and butterflies and the changing colours of the water.

René CHAR (1907–88), one of the most highly regarded of 20th-century French poets, was born in the water-girt town of l'Isle-sur-la-Sorgue east of Avignon, and spent most of his life there apart from periods in Paris. He began as a Surrealist but then broke with the movement and settled into his own style of terse, elliptical verse and prose-poems, sometimes obscure. Some of them touch elusively on his native Provence, as this fragment about a country girl, *Congé au vent*:

A flanc de coteau du village bivouaquent des champs fournis de mimosas. A l'époque de la cueillette, il arrive que, loin de leur endroit, on fasse la rencontre extrêmement odorante d'une fille dont les bras se sont occupés durant la journée aux fragiles branches. Pareille à une lampe dont l'auréole de clarté serait de parfum, elle s'en va, le dos tourné au soleil chouchant. Il serait sacrilège de lui adresser la parole...

(On the hillside of the village, there bivouac fields full of mimosa. In the season of their gathering, it happens that, far from the scene, one has an extremely fragrant meeting with a girl whose arms have been occupied with these fragile branches all day. Like a lamp whose bright aureole might be of perfume, she departs, her back turned to the setting sun. It would be sacrilegious to speak to her...)

Or this extract about the river Sorgue that flows through the poet's native town:

Rivière trop tôt partie, d'une traite, sans compagnon,
Donne aux enfants de mon pays le visage de ta passion.
Rivière où l'éclair finit et où commence ma maison,
Qui roule aux marches d'oubli la rocaille de ma raison.
Rivière, en toi terre est frisson, soleil anxiété.
Que chaque pauvre dans sa nuit fasse son pain de ta moisson.

(River too soon departed, straight off, without companion, / give to the children of my land the visage of your passion. // River where the lightning ends and my house begins, river that rolls the rocks of my reason to the steps of oblivion. // River, in you the earth is shivering and the sun is anxious. / May every poor man in his night make his bread from your harvest.)

Several other well-known French writers have been connected with the towns of western Provence or with the hinterland. The astrologist Michel de Nostradamus, who wrote his prophecies in verse quatrains, was born at St-Rémy in 1503 and spent the last 19 years of his life at Salon-de-Provence; his house there is now a small museum. At Grignan, north of Orange, is the château where Madame de Sévigné came several times to stay with the daughter she adored, Madame de Grignan: her letters tell of her love for Provence (apart from the mistral), and of her enjoyment of the fat quails and partridges, the melons and figs, and the view from the terrace: this today can be admired by tourists, who can also visit her bedroom, decorated in the style of the period. Over to the east the small cathedral town of Digne is the setting for some of the early scenes of Hugo's *Les Misérables* (here Valjean steals the silver candlesticks of the generous and saintly bishop who, according to Hugo, is so poor that he goes on foot or by donkey to visit the parishes of his diocese). Emile Zola spent all his boyhood in Aix where his father, an engineer, was constructing a canal: under the name of Plassans, the town is the setting for *La Fortune des Rougons*, the first volume of the Rougon-Macquart series of novels. Lastly, Albert Camus spent the final years of his life at Lourmarin, north of Aix; he died in 1960 in a car accident south of Paris and now lies buried in the village cemetery.

Avignon and its region have been written about by quite a number of non-French authors – from PETRARCH the Tuscan to Judith Krantz the New Yorker (*Mistral's Daughter*, 1982 – no kin of Frédéric). The great Italian poet and scholar was born in Arezzo in 1304, but his lawyer father moved in 1312 to Avignon where the Papal court had by then settled. After studies at Montpellier and Bologna, Petrarch spent some years at Avignon in the service of a cardinal. At first he relished the sophisticated life of the city under the Popes, and even went through a period of happy dissipation: but later he grew increasingly shocked by the corrupt life of the papacy, then largely concerned with secular matters, and he wrote of Avignon:

. . . an abode of sorrows, the shame of mankind, a sink of vice . . . a sewer where all the filth of the universe has gathered. There God is held in contempt, money is worshipped, and the laws of God and man are trampled underfoot. Everything there breathes a lie; the air, the earth, the houses and above all the bedrooms.

Into Laura's bedroom Petrarch never penetrated, so it appears, for he was a religious man and she was married and virtuous. He first met his great love in the church of Ste-Claire on April 6, 1327, and though her true identity has always remained a mystery, we know that Petrarch's chaste adoration of her coloured all his life and inspired his best work, the Italian poems (*Rime*). At the age of 33 he retired from worldly Avignon to a rural retreat at Fontaine de Vaucluse, to the east, where waters surge

up from a cave in a limestone cliff – 'Vaucluse means everything to me,' he wrote; 'this solitude. . . has become my second home.' Here he spent sixteen years before moving back to Italy, and during this time Laura died of the plague. Today there is a small Petrarch museum on the spot where he is believed to have lived: but the serenity that he sought and knew has been brushed aside by a steady inrush of tourists. Mostly they come to goggle at the gushing natural fountain, rather than to honour the noble harbinger of the Italian Renaissance.

In our own time, six centuries later, Lawrence DURRELL has described Avignon in words that seem to carry just a few echoes of Petrarch:

Avignon! Its shabby lights and sneaking cats were the same as ever; over-turned dustbins, the glitter of fish scales, olive oil, broken glass, a dead scorpion. All the time we had been away on our travels round the world it had stayed pegged here at the confluence of its two green rivers. . . It had always waited for us, floating among its tenebrous monuments, the corpulence of its ragged bells, the putrescence of its squares. . . Here it lay summer after summer, baking away in the sun, until its closely knitted roofs of weathered tile gave it the appearance of a piecrust fresh from the

Opposite: Near the Fontaine de Vaucluse: 'This solitude. . . has become my second home', wrote Petrarch.

The 'putrescent' Avignon that Lawrence Durrell adores.

oven. It haunted one although it was rotten, fly-blown with expired dignities, almost deliquescent among its autumn river damps. There was not a corner of it that we did not love. Often in summer as we sat down round a fire of olive-trimings in some field near Remoulins or Aramon a moon like a blood-orange would wander into the sky and hang above the river, waiting for our return. Avignon, so small, stuffy and parochial, was in my blood.

That choice morsel comes from *Monsieur or the Prince of Darkness* (1974), a novel set in 20th-century Provence, Venice and Egypt, and written after Durrell had settled at Sommières, where he still lives, a village between Nîmes and Montpellier. His joy in this sensuous Mediterranean world shines clearly through the pages of this book:

Far away, on the stony *garrigues* by the fading light of the harvest moon one could hear the musical calling of the wolves. Provence slumbered in the moist plenitude of harvest weather, the deep contented mists and damps of fruition. The dusty roads were furrowed by the wobbling wains and carts and tractors bearing their mountains of grapes to the vats. Blue grapes dusted with the pollen of ages. In the fields lines of harvesters moved with their pruning hooks and sickles; followed by clouds of birds.

One of the best books written by a foreigner about this part of Provence is not a work of fiction. In 1950 the American sociologist Laurence WYLIE made a detailed study of the hill-village of Roussillon 30 miles east of Avignon, well-known for its ochre quarries. The result was *Village in the Vaucluse*, the portrait of a tight-knit rural community, full of personality and tradition but economically backward and despondent about its future. Wylie revisited Roussillon many times, updating the book for successive editions so as to show how it had changed across the years. He analysed the impact of modern prosperity and mobility on ancient static values, as the old-style peasant farming died away, artisans became skilled factory workers, and intellecual summer residents arrived from Paris with new ideas. Along with Edgar Morin's book on Plozévet in Brittany (see p. 24), this is about the best sociological study of post-war change in rural France, and Wylie's conclusions are on balance optimistic. According to him, the sharpest changes in attitudes occurred during the earlier post-war period of the 1950s, and this he has assessed most succinctly in the chapter that he contributed in 1963 to another excellent book, *France: Change and Tradition*:

The most remarkable change between the Roussillon that I first knew in 1950 and the village as it is today is psychological. In 1951 the Roussillonnais seemed haunted by despair. They had a dream of what life should be and were frustrated because it seemed less and less possible to realise. They spent a great deal of energy trying to conserve the remnants of the days before the First World War when they believed their dream had been fulfilled. In 1961 I found that the despair they had felt in 1950 had at length killed the dream. The nostalgic yearning for an outdated ideal had all but disappeared, and the energy formerly devoted to preserving it was being used for other purposes... By 1950 the feelings of helplessness and despair were strong in France. The people of Roussillon, traditionally inclined to accept the worst with a fatalistic shrug and words 'C'est comme ca!' found little to hope for in the gloomy future. 'Pauvre France!' they said. 'On est foutu!' (We're done for!). . . 'Why should I plant fruit trees?' said Jacques Baudot. 'So the Russians and the Americans can use my orchard for a battleground? No, thanks. . .' In 1960, however, Baudot took me to see the apple and apricot trees he had planted. . . There was no more talk about being 'done for'.

Another American's post-war insight into Provence, and a great deal more sombre than Wylie's, has come from Mavis GALLANT in *The Affair of Gabrielle Russier* (1971). This is the true documentary story of a 30-year-old woman teacher in Marseille in 1969 who had a love-affair with a 16-year-old boy pupil. Amid a deluge of public controversy, Gabrielle was then cruelly hounded by society, the judiciary, and the boy's Communist intellectual parents, until finally she killed herself. As Ms Gallant points out in her long introductory essay, the affair cast a grim light, not only on the level of social tolerance at the time, but on the inhuman harshness of the French legal system. As far as French writing is concerned, the nation's largest seaport and second city (equal with Lyon) has featured only spasmodically in literature. Edmond Rostand was born there; Arthur Rimbaud died there, of an illness contracted in Africa; Alexandre Dumas set the opening scenes of *Le Comte de Monte Cristo* in the notorious offshore fortress prison of the Chateau d'If. But one of the best quotations about the city comes from Jean ANOUILH's play *Eurydice*, when the enigmatic Monsieur Henri looks out of his hotel bedroom window and remarks to Orphée:

> A fine town, Marseille. This human ant-heap, this smutty vulgarity, this squalor. They don't kill each other as much as it's said, in the alleys of the Vieux-Port – but it's a fine town all the same.

The stretch of coast from Marseille to the Italian frontier, and especially the eastern part that the French call the Côte d'Azur and other nations used to call the Riviera, has attracted scores of writers, most of them foreign. In the Riviera's great days, practically everyone who was anyone stayed there at one time or another. Several books have vividly related the gilded social life of the visitors and expatriates – for example, Michael Arlen's *The Green Hat* – but few have had much to say about the scenery or the local inhabitants, who were simply a backdrop to the non-stop party.

The French, often a little resentful of the English appropriation of the Riviera, are quick to point out that Prosper Mérimée arrived in Cannes in exactly the same year (1834) as Lord Brougham, who was the first to turn this unknown fishing-village into a resort. From 1858, Mérimée spent every winter in Cannes. Guy de Maupassant came there too, a little later, and anchored his yacht *Bel Ami* in the harbour of Antibes. Gide, Camus and others used often to stay in the hill-village of Cabris, near Grasse, and Cocteau had a summer home at Cap Ferrat; but he wrote little about the Côte d'Azur, although he loved it dearly and some of his most attractive frescoes today adorn the *mairie* in Menton and a chapel in

Villefranche. Colette spent some time at St-Tropez and describes it in *La Treille muscate*. Of living French authors, Max Gallo the historian and Socialist politician has written a trilogy of novels, *La Baie des Anges*, about the life of his native Nice from the 1880s to the present day; J.-M.-G. Le Clézio also lives in Nice, and his somewhat abstruse novels contain some elusive passages about it. Françoise SAGAN's first novel *Bonjour tristesse*, which brought her fame when she was only eighteen, is about a teenage girl on holiday in a 'large white villa' on the Esterel coast near St-Raphaël:

Parasols against the noonday Riviera sun – but tender is the night.

> It was remote and beautiful, and stood on a promontory dominating the sea, hidden from the road by a pine wood; a mule path led down to a tiny creek where the sea lapped against rust-coloured rocks.

The first English writer to visit the Riviera was Tobias SMOLLETT, who spent several months in Nice for his health's sake during 1763–5 and then wrote about it in his *Travels through France and Italy* (see p. 153).

Eze hill-village,
between Nice and Monaco.

He found the town 'remarkable' and confessed himself 'inchanted' [*sic*] when standing upon the ramparts – 'The small extent of country which I see, is all cultivated like a garden. Indeed the plain presents nothing but gardens, full of green trees, loaded with oranges, lemons, citrons and bergamots.' But on other occasions Smollett was his more familiar cantankerous self, for he disliked the cooking, especially the garlic, and found the people of Nice uncultured and inhospitable – 'Our consul, who is a very honest man, told me, he had lived four and thirty years in the country, without having once eaten or drank in any of their houses.' Some other Smollettian *aperçus*: 'Most of the females are pot-bellied; a circumstance owing, I believe, to the great quantity of vegetable trash which they eat'; and, 'The great poverty of the people here is owing to their religion. Half of their time is lost in observing the great number of festivals; and half of their substance is given to mendicant friars and parish priests.' Smollett also sheds a curious light on the habits of the local nobility:

their children and to punish her for leaving him – and it was clear that this paranoid monster belonged to a powerful underground network, against which the police and the local judiciary did not dare to act. Certain police officers were protecting the criminal. Greene, furious, decided to use his prestige in France to try to help the family. First, in protest against the failures of the authorities, he returned the Légion d'Honneur which he had been awarded under the Pompidou Presidency. Then he wrote a sharp pamphlet, *J'Accuse*, setting out the facts as he knew them. It begins:

> Let me issue a warning to anyone who is tempted to settle for a peaceful life on what is called the Côte d'Azur. Avoid the region of Nice, which is the reserve of some of the most criminal organisations in the south of France; they deal in drugs; they have attempted with the connivance of high authorities to take over the casinos in the famous 'war' which left one victim, Agnès Le Roux, daughter of the main owner of the Palais de la Méditerranée, 'missing believed murdered'; they are involved in the building industry which helps to launder their illicit gains; they have close connections with the Italian Mafia.

The book was published in London in a bilingual edition, but in France it was banned. The powerful Right-wing mayor of Nice, Jacques Méde-cin, even claimed that Greene had been put up to writing it by his friend

Left and opposite: Monte Carlo's casino, where Fitzgerald, Greene, Maugham and so many others have chronicled 'the lost caviare days'.

Max Gallo (see above), then a Socialist deputy for Nice and Médecin's chief local rival. Gallo told me later that the mayor saw the whole thing as a political plot to discredit his own administration. Anyway, the affair ended happily, for the woman was able to keep custody of her children, and the attacks against her gradually ceased.

In the 1930s, another Englishman had written luridly about the Côte d'Azur and its atmosphere of pagan decadence, to which the expatriates were handsomely contributing, so he felt. *The Rock Pool*, the only novel of critic and essayist Cyril CONNOLLY, was based on visits that he made to Haut-de-Cagnes; it was published in Paris in 1936, after being rejected by London publishers on grounds of obscenity. His hero, a prim young snob from Oxford, called Naylor, goes first to Juan-les-Pins, which he hates:

> The beach, where the fetid waves of sunburnoil lapped tidelessly on the sand; the boardwalk where the hairy ugliness of the men was so much more noticeable than the beauty of the women; the hotels and modern shops; the scream of buses; the casino with its false smartness; the big cabaret with its curiously plump and vicious Soho band-leader, all disgusted him.

Later Naylor gets involved with a louche expatriate community of artists, homosexuals, lesbians and others, including an unfrocked clergy-man and an American girl who drinks Pernod for breakfast. He plans to observe them like the creatures in a rock pool, but gradually they drag him down – and towards the end, at Antibes, he ponders upon the ancient corrupting influence of the Mediterranean:

> The taxi took them along by the sea margin; a belated cicada chirred in a dusty pine; scattered uncomfortable villas gave way to broken rocks; the woods of the cape, spotted with hoardings, came down to the inhospitable beaches, filling the air with the scent of resin, and a shameless chocolate-box sunset disfigured the west. The intolerable melancholy, the dinginess, the corruption of that tainted island sea overcame him. He felt the breath of centuries of wickedness and disillusion; how many civilisations had staled on that bright promontory!

Did this same coast not also help to destroy Dick Diver, who found the night there too tender? I began this literary tour of France on the Breton shore, where Per-Jakez Hélias, watching a Bigouden girl swimming with a *coiffe*, reflected on the changes in his old peasant culture as it drifted into the modern age. So perhaps it is fitting that I should now end on the 'bright tan prayer rug' of a Mediterranean beach where the dazzling *poète maudit* of the Lost Generation pondered upon the decline of a very different society, to produce what is certainly the best novel ever written about the French Riviera.

Possibly Scott and Zelda would never have come to this coast, were it not for their friends Gerald and Sara Murphy, art-lovers from Boston. Until the 1920s the Riviera had been purely a winter resort, for the August sun was considered too hot for visitors: it was the Murphys who then first set the fashion for passing the summer there. They stayed

The hill-village of Haut-de-Cagnes: Connolly stayed here, and set The Rock Pool *here.*

initially in the palatial Hôtel du Cap, at Cap d'Antibes, and in 1923 they persuaded its owner to keep it open in summer for the first time. Then the Murphys bought a house just below Cap d'Antibes lighthouse which they called the Villa America (it is still there today, but has changed its name), and here they entertained Picasso, Gertrude Stein, Dorothy Parker and others equally illustrious. The FITZGERALDS first came to visit them in 1924, later returning to the Riviera several times. Often they and the Murphys would go to bathe at the Plage de la Garoupe, on the eastern side of the lovely peninsula. In those days it was almost empty, for summer bathing was still quite a novelty: but today it is almost unrecognisable, a fenced-in private beach where you pay to enter. When Scott wrote *Tender is the Night* (1934), he took that beach as his model, and also the Hôtel du Cap:

. . . a large, proud, rose-coloured hotel. Deferential palms cooled its flushed façade, and before it stretched a short dazzling beach. Now it has become a summer resort of notable and fashionable people; in 1925 it was almost deserted after its English clientèle went north in April; only the cupolas of a dozen old villas rotted like water-lilies among the massed pines between Gausse's Hôtel des Etrangers and Cannes, five miles away.

The hotel and its bright tan prayer rug of a beach were one. In the early morning the distant image of Cannes, the pink and cream of old fortifications, the purple Alp that bounded Italy, were cast across the water and lay quavering in the ripples and rings sent up by the sea-plants through the clear shallows.

Rather like so many French novelists, Fitzgerald jumbles up the geography, for in reality the Hôtel du Cap has no sandy beach, and the Divers' (i.e. Murphys') house seems to be over to the west of Cannes, while at one point La Turbie is visible from Cannes, which is impossible. But no matter. Today the Hôtel du Cap is still very much there, the most expensive and exclusive on the entire Côte d'Azur, much frequented by senior German tycoons and flashy American showbiz characters. Its clientèle is no longer so grand as in the days when regular visitors ranged from Haile Selassie to Betty Grable. But you can walk down through its stately park to the hotel's Eden Roc restaurant with its swimming-pool by the sea, where Scott champagne-glass in hand would watch poor mad Zelda diving from the rocks. By the end of their time on the Riviera, the Fitzgeralds' social behaviour was growing more and more wild and shocking. In the first part of the novel, Dick and Nicole Diver are undeniably based on the Murphys, but as Nicole's mental illness worsens, and Dick too begins to disintegrate, so they turn into characters closer to the Fitzgeralds themselves. Scott, with some anguish, was portraying a smart expatriate society which he knew to be corrupt and destructive, but also found as romantically attractive as the coast itself:

. . . The diffused magic of the hot sweet south had withdrawn into them – the soft-pawed night and the ghostly wash of the Mediterranean far below – the magic left these things and melted into the two Divers and became part of them. . .

It was pleasant to drive back to the hotel in the late afternoon, above a sea as mysteriously coloured as agates and cornelians of childhood, green as green milk, blue as laundry water, wine dark. It was pleasant to pass people eating outside their doors, and to hear the fierce mechanical pianos behind the vines of country estaminets. When they turned off the Corniche d'Or and down to Gausse's hotel through the darkening banks of trees, set one behind another in many greens, the moon already hovered over the ruins of the aqueducts.

Fled is that music – but who else has captured so well the magic of that place and that time?

The chauffeur, a Russian tsar of the period of Ivan the Terrible, was a self-appointed guide, and the resplendent names – Cannes, Nice, Monte Carlo – began to glow through their torpid camouflage, whispering of old kings come here to dine or to die, of rajahs tossing Buddhas's eyes to English ballerinas, of Russian princes turning the weeks into Baltic twilights in the lost caviare days. . .

The Eden Roc restaurant at Cap d'Antibes, 'where Scott champagne-glass in hand would watch poor mad Zelda diving from the rocks.'

Bibliography

This list of the books described or quoted from in the text is intended mainly to let my non-French-speaking readers know which of the books exist also in English translation. In these cases, there is an (E) after the book, and I have given the title too when it differs greatly from that of the French original. An asterisk (*) indicates that the English translation was out of print, as of January 1989: but it will usually be possible to track these books down via a good library, and all are in the British Library.

I can especially recommend the excellent translations in the Penguin Classics series.   J.A.

2: BRITTANY
Per-Jakez Hélias, *Le Cheval d'Orgueil* (E)
Henri Queffélec, *Le Recteur de l'Ile de Sein* (E: *Isle of Sinners*) (*)
Pierre Loti, *Pêcheur d'Islande* (E)
Jean Genet, *Querelle de Brest* (E)
Colette, *Le Blé en herbe* (E: *Ripening Seed*)
Pierre Abelard, *Historia calamitatum* (E: in *The Letters of Abelard and Héloise*)
Madame de Sévigné, *Selected Letters* (E)
François-René de Chateaubriand, *Mémoires d'outre-tombe* (E: *Memoirs*)
Arthur Young, *Travels in France* (in English) (*)
Honoré de Balzac, *Les Chouans* (E)

3: THE LOIRE
François Rabelais, *Gargantua* and *Pantagruel* (E)
Pierre de Ronsard, *Poems* (some E)
Joachim du Bellay, *Poems* (some E)
Honoré de Balzac, *Eugénie Grandet* (E)
        Le Lys dans la vallée
Georges Sand, *La Mare au diable* (E) (*)
Alain-Fournier, *Le Grand Meaulnes* (E)
Maurice Genevoix, *Raboliot*
        Remi des rauches
Emile Zola, *La Terre* (E)
René Bazin, *La Terre qui meurt* (E: *Autumn Glory*) (*)
Charles Péguy, *Poèmes choisis*
Marcel Proust, *A la recherche du temps perdu* (E: *Remembrance of Things Past*)

4: NORMANDY
Victor Hugo, *Contemplations* (some E) (*)
Gustave Flaubert, *Madame Bovary* (E)
        Un coeur simple (E: in *Three Tales*)

Guy de Maupassant, *Selected Short Stories* (E)
    Une vie (E: *A Woman's Life*)
    Pierre et Jean (E)
Jean-Paul Sartre, *La Nausée* (E)
Raymond Queneau, *Un rude hiver* (E) (*)
André Gide, *La Porte étroite* (E: *Strait is the Gate*)
    Si le grain meurt (E: *If it Die*)
Jules-Amédée Barbey d'Aurévilly, *Une vieille maîtresse*
    L'Ensorcelée (E: *Bewitched*) (*)

5: ILE-DE-FRANCE
Jean-Jacques Rousseau, *Confessions* (E)
    Julie ou la Nouvelle Héloïse (E)
Gérard de Nérval, *Sylvie* (E) (*)
Victor Hugo, *Les Misérables* (E)
Christiane Rochefort, *Les Petits enfants du siècle* (E: *Josyane and the Welfare* (*)
Henry James, *The Ambassadors* (in English)

6: THE NORTH
Tobias Smollett, *Travels through France and Italy* (in English)
Edith Sitwell, *Collected Poems* (in English)
John Ruskin, *The Bible of Amiens* (in English) (*)
Siegfried Sassoon, *Collected Poems* (in English)
Edmund Blunden, *Selected Poems* (in English)
F. Scott Fitzgerald, *Tender is the Night* (in English)
Henri Barbusse, *Le Feu* (E: *Under Fire*)
Emile Verhaeren, *Les Flamandes*
Maxence Van der Meersch, *La Maison de la dune*
Germaine Acremant, *Le Carnaval d'été*
Marguerite Yourcenar, *Souvenirs pieux*
    Archives du Nord
Georges Bernanos, *Sous le soleil de Satan* (E: *Star of Satan*)
    Journal d'un curé de campagne (E)
Victor Hugo, *Lettres à Adèle*
Emile Zola, *Germinal* (E)
    La Débâcle (E)
Julien Gracq, *Un balcon en forêt* (E) (*)
Arthur Rimbaud, *Oeuvres complètes* (E)
Paul Verlaine, *Oeuvres poétiques complètes* (some E)
Charles de Gaulle, *Mémoires d'espoir* (E)

7: EASTERN FRANCE
George Bernard Shaw, *Saint Joan* (in English)
Maurice Barrès, *La Colline inspirée*
Jules Romains, *Prélude à Verdun* and *Verdun* (E) (*)
Victor Hugo, *Le Rhin*
Henry Wadsworth Longfellow, *Collected Poems* (in English)
Johann Wolfgang von Goethe, *Gedichte* (E)
Emile Erckmann and Alexandre Chatrian, *L'Ami Fritz* (E) (*)
Stendhal, *Le Rouge et le noir* (E)
Alphonse de Lamartine, *Oeuvres Complètes* (some E) (*)
Roger de Rabutin, *Historie amoureuse des Gaules*
Colette, *La maison de Claudine* (E: *My Mother's House*)

8: SAVOY, GRENOBLE AND LYON
Voltaire, *Epitre à Horace*
Gertrude Stein, *Wars I Have Seen* (in English)
Stendhal, *La Vie de Henri Brulard* (E) (*)
Jules Vallès, *L'Enfant*
Alphonse Daudet, *Le Petit Chose* (E: *My Brother Jack; The Little Weakling*) (*)
Gabriel Chevallier, *Clochemerle* (E)

9: THE SOUTH-WEST
Honoré de Balzac, *Les Illusions perdues* (E)
Eugène Fromentin, *Dominique* (E)
Ezra Pound, *Selected Poems* (in English)
Eugène Le Roy, *Jacquou le Croquant*
Michel de Montaigne, *Essais* (E)
Charles de Montesquieu, *L'Esprit des Lois* (E)
François Mauriac, *Thérèse Desqueyroux* (E: *Thérèse*)
    Le Mystère Frontenac (E)
Francis Jammes, *Poèmes*
Pierre Loti, *Ramuntcho* (E: *A Tale of the Pyrenees*) (*)

10: LANGUEDOC AND THE PYRÉNÉES
Emmanuel Le Roy Ladurie, *Montaillou* (E)
Henry James, *A Little Tour of France* (in English)
Robert Louis Stevenson, *Travels with a Donkey* (in English)
André Chamson, *Les Quatre éléments* (E: *A Mountain Boyhood*) (*)
Jean Carrière, *L'Epervier de Maheux*
Paul Valéry, *Le Cimitière Marin* (E)

11: PROVENCE
Frédéric Mistral, *Mirèio* (E: *Mireille*) (*) (also tr. into French)
    Lou Pouemo dou Rose (tr. into French)
Alphonse Daudet, *Lettres de mon Moulin* (E)
    Tartarin de Tarascon (E)
Marcel Pagnol, *La Gloire de mon père* (E: *The Days were too Short*) (*)
    Jean de Florette, Manon des Sources (E)
Jean Giono, *Regain* (E: *Harvest*) (*)
    Que ma joie demeure (E: *Joy of Man's Desiring*) (*)
    Le Hussard sur le toit (E) (*)
Henri Bosco, *Le Mas Théotime* (E) (*)
René Char, *Poems*
Lawrence Durrell, *Monsieur or the Prince of Darkness* (in English)
Laurence Wylie, *Village in the Vaucluse* (in English)
Mavis Gallant, *The Affair of Gabrielle Russier* (in English)
Jean Anouilh, *Eurydice* (E: *Point of Departure*)
Françoise Sagan, *Bonjour tristesse* (E)
Katherine Mansfield, *Collected Short Stories* (in English)
Graham Greene, *Loser Takes All* (in English)
    J'Accuse (in English)
Cyril Connolly, *The Rock Pool* (in English)

Acknowledgements

Some of the translations in this book are my own work. For the others, I am indebted to the following translators (and I am grateful especially to those among the translators and their publishers who have allowed me to quote extracts free of charge):

W. P. Baines for Loti's *Pêcheur d'Islande*; Gregory Streatham for Genet's *Querelle de Brest*; Roger Senhouse for Colette's *Le Blé en herbe* and *La Maison de Claudine*; Betty Radice for Peter Abelard's letters; Leonard Tancock for Madame de Sévigné's selected letters, de Maupassant's *Pierre et Jean*, Zola's *Germinal* and *La Débâcle*; Marion Ayton Crawford for Balzac's *Les Chouans*; J. M. Cohen for Rabelais' *Gargantua*; Douglas Parmée for Zola's *La Terre*; C. K. Scott Moncrieff and Terence Kilmartin for Proust's *A la recherche du temps perdu*; Alan Russell for Flaubert's *Madame Bovary*; Roger Coley for de Maupassant's selected short stories; Robert Baldick for Sartre's *La Nausée*; Dorothy Bussy for Gide's *La Porte etroite* and *Si le grain ne meurt*; Norman Denny for Hugo's *Les Misérables*; W. Fitzwater Wray for Barbusse's *Le Feu*; Jean Stewart and B. C. J. G. Knight for Stendhal's *Le Rouge et le noir*; Robert M. Adam for Stendhal's *La Vie de Henri Brulard*; Jocelyn Godefroie for Chevallier's *Clochemerle*; Herbert J. Hunt for Balzac's *Les Illusions perdues*; Edward Marsh for Fromentin's *Dominique*; Gerard Hopkins for Mauriac's *Thérèse Desqueyroux and Le Mystère Frontenac*, and Romains' *Verdun*; Barbara Bray for Le Roy Ladurie's *Montaillou*; Irene Ash for Sagan's *Bonjour tristesse*.

Lastly, I should like to thank P. & O. Ferries, Vacances Franco-Britanniques, and a number of the people in London, Paris and the French provinces who gave up their time to help me, and were often generous too with their hospitality. Among them: in Brittany, Per-Jakes Hélias, the Stourm family, the Bousquet family; in the Loire area, Bernard and Cathérine Desjeux, Henri Lullier, René Compère; in Normandy, Joël Dupont, Patrick Le Roc'h, Marie-Françoise Rose; in the Nord, M. Imbert; in eastern France, the Harmel family, Cathérine Vassilieff; in the Lyon area, Jean-Paul Gasquet, Roger Bellet; in the South-West, the Levieux family, Bernard Cocula, Elena Touyarou Phagaburu, Henri Lauqué; in Toulouse and Languedoc, the Péchoux family, Jean Carrière; in Provence, Georges Berni, Louis Michel, Max Gallo; in Paris, Suzanne Genevoix, Emmanuel Le Roy Ladurie, and Jean Gattegno, Directeur du Livre at the Ministry of Culture who kindly put me in touch with many of his regional officers. In London, my thanks go especially to Claire Fons, Librarian of the Institut Français in Kensington, as well as to Michel Monory, Director of the Institut, to Gilles Chouraqui, Patrick Vittet-Philippe and Eric Charnay, all of the cultural section of the French Embassy, and to Terry and Joanna Kilmartin,

Richard Mayne and Yvette Wiener. Above all, I owe an immense debt of gratitude to Francine Walsh, whose erudite knowledge and understanding of French literature was of great help. And my thanks go, as always, to my publishers, Hamish Hamilton, who were unfailingly kind, and to my wife Katinka whose literary and practical help was invaluable.   J.A.

Photographer's Note

I would like to thank the librarians of the Institut Français, in particular Claire Fons, for their enlightened advice and obliging search for specific books, some of them out of print for many years.

Although I had my share of bad weather in the freak spring of 1988, I enjoyed every moment of this solitary quest in the footsteps of great French writers and poets. The landscapes and places which had inspired them made their presence tangible to an intense degree and I am richer for the experience.

I would like to thank my dear husband Jorge Lewinski for his comforting words coming through from distant England to the usually rain-spattered telephone booths of little French villages, during our daily evening chat.

For readers interested in photographic technique, may I say that I mainly used 35mm Nikons and Pentax 6×7. Apart from the usual range of fixed-focus lenses, I used Angenieux zooms, whose extremely fine and sharp definition and comparative lightness I found invaluable when climbing rocks and walking miles with minimum equipment. For colour I used exclusively Fuji 50 ASA and 100 ASA films, and for monochrome Kodak's T-max 125 ASA and 400 ASA. M.M.

Index

Books are indexed under each author, but only if they are quoted from. Regions are not indexed if their place in the book is obvious from the Contents list, and small places have been indexed only if their association with a writer is an important one.